ASSAULT TROOP

Spring 1945 – Hitler's Thousand Year Reich was crumbling, dissolving in a welter of blood, panic and death. Refugees and deserters fled from the terrible advance of the Russian armies. In the vanguard of that merciless army stormed Colonel Piotr's Guards Punishment Battalion – the desperate, expendable scrapings of the Siberian prison camps. These men had no future but a blood-lusting, reckless present and would advance, slaughtering and destroying, ever westwards. Only Captain Corrigan's battle-hardened Assault Troop could match them in ruthless, lethal determination. Only they could stop their advance, halt their drive across Europe.

Please note: **This book contains material which may not be suitable to all our readers.**

ASSAULT TROOP

ASSAULT TROOP

by

Ian Harding

Magna Large Print Books
Long Preston, North Yorkshire,
BD23 4ND, England.

British Library Cataloguing in Publication Data.

Harding, Ian
    Assault troop.

    A catalogue record of this book is
    available from the British Library

    ISBN   0-7505-1909-6

First published in Great Britain 1984 by New English Library

Copyright © 1984 by Ian Harding

The moral right of the author has been asserted

Published in Large Print 2002 by arrangement with
Eskdale Publishing

Magna Large Print is an imprint of Library Magna Books Ltd.

Printed and bound in Great Britain by
T.J. (International) Ltd., Cornwall, PL28 8RW

PRELUDE

THE WOLF PACK

The moon was ice-cold. It hung at a slant in the black velvet of the winter sky. Like silver the frost glittered on the skeletal branches of the trees, quivering slightly in the icy wind. All was tense brooding expectation. There was no sound save the muted rumble of the permanent barrage on another front.

Hidden in their foxholes, the assault troops waited. Two hours ago they had been issued with a hundred grams of vodka. But that was long gone. Now they were sober and cold – and afraid. The Fritzes would undoubtedly be waiting for them on the other side of the river. They would be mown down like cattle. But there was no alternative. Behind them the green-capped swine of the NKVD* were dug in; they would not hesitate to open fire on anyone who attempted to desert the line. As always they were between the devil and the deep blue sea.

A sudden crack! They jumped. A hush... To their right the first flare hissed into the dark night. It burst in a shower of red. Instantly all their upturned faces were coloured a blood-red, eerie hue. Another flare whooshed into the sky – and another.

*NKVD: the wartime Russian secret police.

It was the signal.

Colonel Pavlov Piotr, Commander of the First Punishment Battalion, sprang to his feet, sabre already drawn, glittering silver in that glowing unnatural light. 'Come on, you rats, do you wish to live for ever? *Davai!*'

'*Davai!... Davai!*' His officers and NCOs took up the command all along the line, urging their men forward, kicking and striking the more reluctant ones, drawing their pistols to make their meaning quite clear.

The men stumbled towards the river in a ragged line, following their giant of a colonel, fur hat set at a rakish angle at the side of his shaven skull, waving his sword and laughing uproariously like a crazy man.

The German machine-gunners opened up at once. Tracer, white, glowing and lethal, started to hiss across the surface of the river. With a roar the Russian artillery joined in. Shells started to explode on the far bank, the near-misses plunging into the water, sending up great spouts of writhing, wild white water. In an instant, all was ear-splitting noise and confusion, as the soldiers of the Guards' Punishment Battalion went down everywhere in the slippery mud, to be trampled ever deeper by the boots of their frenzied comrades.

Colonel Piotr strode into the water, still waving his sword and laughing. Bullets cut the surface all around him as the Germans intensified their fire, but Piotr did not seem to notice. He waded steadily towards the other side, sword flashing in the flames of the fires that had broken out on the bank.

Now, carried away by a fevered blood lust, more and more of his men were wading in after the big colonel, scrambling and slipping through the mud and jellied, bloody gore of their dead and dying comrades. Screaming inhumanly, their teeth bared wolfishly, their eyes wide and wild, they splashed into the water to meet the slaughter on the other side.

Colonel Piotr, still laughing madly, swung his sabre. The blade cleaved through the German's arm. It fell to the mud at his feet. He stared at it as if bewildered. But only for an instant. Next moment Piotr swung his terrible, blood-red weapon again. The Fritz went down, screaming horribly, his face almost split in two.

'*Davai!... Davai!*' Piotr cried at his men still struggling through the water, now running a bright crimson and littered with the floating bodies of the dead.

'The Colonel's got a hole in his arse!... Follow the Colonel!... The Colonel's got a hole in his arse!' they bellowed. '*Follow the Colonel!*'

Already the terrified Germans were beginning to surrender. Dropping their weapons and raising their hands, eyes bulging with

11

fear, they begged for mercy: *'Kamerad…
Kamerad… Nicht schiessen, bitte… NICHT
SCHIESSEN!'*

But Piotr's crazed ex-convicts had no
mercy. Carried away by the frenzied blood-
lust of battle, they stabbed, slashed, sliced,
chopped, cutting the Germans down where
they stood. Teeth gleaming white against
their blackened faces, eyes glittering like
those of the demented, they flung themselves at the hated enemy and massacred
them.

Now there was no stopping Colonel Piotr's
men. They ran straight at the remaining
enemy machine guns. Men fell screaming
and howling in their lonely misery, writhing
and tearing at the earth with their clawed
hands. But the rest kept going, springing
into the enemy weapon pits, the brass butts
of their rifles slamming into upturned
German faces, their razor-sharp shovels
cleaving German skulls. And all the while
Colonel Pavlov Piotr laughed and laughed
and laughed like a man possessed…

'Here they come now, Comrade Marshal,'
reported General Dmitrov, commander of
the First Guards Rifle Division, a look of
awe on his face as he pointed, his voice
subdued.

Like slow grey ghosts, the survivors of the
First Punishment Battalion were beginning

to filter through the shell-shattered trees, backs bent like infinitely weary old men. Most of them had been wounded, to judge by the bloodstained bandages wrapped around heads and limbs. Some of them were limping badly, supported by their comrades. A few lay bundled up in groundsheets, being dragged through the ankle-deep mud by men whose skinny shoulders heaved with the effort, as if they were sobbing broken-heartedly.

Even Marshal Rokossovsky, handsome and cynical, as he sat there in his looted German Mercedes next to the plump woman in Red Army uniform who was his current mistress, was a little awed. In his long fighting career he had seen enough decimated infantry battalions returning from battle, but never one like this. He watched the first group of survivors stumble by his car, their eyes glassy and unseeing, like men escaping from some terrifying nightmare, not saying a word, save for those who had gone mad and were mumbling the insane gibberish of the demented.

'*Boshe moi!*' he muttered aloud, throwing away the long cigarette he had been smoking. 'What kind of men are these?'

'I shall tell you, Comrade Marshal!' Colonel Piotr's booming bass voice cut into the heavy silence. 'We are the rats from the camps!' Piotr threw the Marshal and his mistress a tremendous salute with his sabre, its blade still bright with German blood. 'Traitors, reactionaries, murderers, pimps, perverts – the scum of the Soviet Fatherland! We murder, we burn, we rape!' The giant paused for breath, winking broadly at the Marshal's mistress whose face had gone ashen with fear at the sight of this blood-stained monster. 'And we die! *Boshe moi,* how we die for our beloved Fatherland!' And he threw back his shaven head and laughed dementedly.

The sound of Piotr's mad laughter made the small hairs at the back of Marshal Rokossovsky's head stand erect with fear. General Dmitrov, standing beside the Mercedes, took out a bottle of cheap eau-de-cologne, dabbed some on his handkerchief and mopped his brow with a hand that trembled visibly.

Colonel Piotr did not seem to notice the effect he was having on the two senior officers. He turned to one of his men, a one-eyed rogue with a hangman's face. *'You,'* he bellowed, gesturing with his sword. 'Up that tree! See if the dead Fritz apes have got any of that good schnapps of theirs tucked away in their pockets.' He indicated a shattered Tiger tank lying on its side of the ditch a few yards away, one of its crew hanging from the tree above it like some monstrous human fruit, a chunk of bright silver shrapnel, half a metre long, protruding from his dead body. He beamed at Marshal Rokossovsky and said, as if in explanation, 'Killing Fritzes is thirsty work, Comrade Marshal.'

The elegant commander of the First White Russian Front* looked away hurriedly as the one-eyed officer began to shake the tree to dislodge the corpse. 'Here, Colonel,' he said, proffering his own bottle of vodka. 'Drink ... drink your fill.'

Piotr grabbed the bottle in one huge fist, the knuckles gnarled with old sabre scars, and, tilting back his head, took a tremendous swig. '*Nastrovyapan ... spasivo!*' he gasped, winking at Rokossovsky. He seemed utterly unimpressed by the fact that he was facing a man who had the power of life or death over two million soldiers. Then he asked, almost slyly, 'And what brings the Comrade Marshal this far forward? You know Fritz shells make no distinction between marshals and common hairy-assed soldiers?'

The Guards General frowned warningly.

Piotr ignored the warning; he knew he was going to die before this was over anyway. 'And why does the Comrade Marshal tender his precious vodka to a humble colonel commanding the scum of the Gulag too, eh?'**

*Front: Russian usage for an army.
**The Soviet concentration camp system was known as the Gulag.

15

Marshal Rokossovsky pretended to be amused by the man's insolence. He knew instinctively that threats would have no effect on this man. He had death written all over him – and how could one frighten a dead man? So he humoured the 'humble colonel'. 'Because, my dear Colonel, I need your help. Your battalion–'

'What's left of it,' Piotr interjected, taking another mighty swig at the precious vodka.

Rokossovsky ignored the remark. 'You see, I have an important mission for the First Guards Rifle Division, a most important mission, and your battalion leads the Guards.'

Piotr looked at the elegant Marshal shrewdly. 'Berlin?' he rapped.

Rokossovsky shook his head. 'No,' he said. 'Berlin is now virtually surrounded by our armies. It is no longer of importance. Comrade Stalin has ordered–'

Even Piotr was impressed. He whistled softly. 'You mean Old Leather Face has his hand in this?'

Rokossovsky nodded. 'Yes – Old Leather Face, as you call our political master.' His expression had hardened at the mention of the dictator; a few years ago, in the late thirties, he had found himself in disgrace as a result of which Stalin had sent him – him, Rokossovsky! – to the Gulag too. 'In his infinite wisdom Stalin thinks there is still one more important political goal to be achieved before the Fritzes surrender.'

At his side, the Guards General cleared his throat nervously. 'Comrade Marshal, don't you think we ought to discuss this matter elsewhere?' he said. 'The men might hear…'

Piotr held up his hand for silence. 'What is our objective, Comrade Marshal?' he demanded harshly.

Rokossovsky hesitated for a moment as the Russian multiple mortars known as 'Stalin Organs' erupted into frenetic life. *'The Baltic,'* he bellowed over the roar of mortar-fire. *'That is to be your last objective of the war, Colonel Piotr – the German Baltic.'*

With the practised ease of a veteran tactician, Marshal Rokossovsky swept his manicured hand over the rash of blue and red crayon marks on the big map spread out on the table. 'Here are our own positions, well advanced into Mecklenburg. Here are the Fritzes, remnants of von Manteuffel's Third Panzer Army and von Tippelskirch's Twenty-first Army. Both are beaten, but being Fritzes they don't realise it.' He smiled faintly.

Piotr nodded, his gaze fixed on the plump pigeon's shapely knees clad in black silk. Only the day before he had raped three German women, one the usual granny he took not on account of her withered charms, but because he was still a superstitious Cossack at heart, who believed that sexual intercourse with an old woman meant luck. Inwardly he chuckled at the memory: it had been the German granny who had been lucky. *Boshe moi,* how the old bag had thrashed about as he danced the mattress polka on top of her on the kitchen floor, while his men cheered him on! Still looking at those shapely legs, Piotr felt he could use a woman right now.

Rokossovsky frowned. He knew what was going on in the damned Cossack's mind, and he didn't like it. He raised his voice. 'Now, Comrade Colonel, with the Fritzes virtually finished, we must look to other tasks. In the Kremlin, Old Leather Face, as you call him, has decided we must gain as much territory in the west as possible before the Fritzes finally collapse.'

Piotr took his eyes off the Marshal's mistress. 'For instance?'

'Denmark, possibly Norway.'

Piotr looked at the elegant Marshal, with the usual long cigarette jutting from the corner of his mouth. 'I am just a simple soldier, Comrade Marshal,' he said slowly. 'I know nothing of grand strategy, but I would have thought that Denmark and Norway would come under the area of operations of the Anglo-Saxons, our allies in the west.'

Rokossovsky sneered. 'Our allies in the

North-West Germany, April 1945

west? How naïve you are, Piotr! Our beloved leader in the Kremlin knows no allies. Now that the war is virtually over he has no need of the Anglo-Americans any more. Don't you realise that they are now the new enemies?'

Uneasily Piotr fingered the little bag of his native earth that always hung around his neck. When he died, it would be buried with him, so that he could fulfil the Don Cossack tradition of being buried in his native soil. 'I don't like it, Comrade Marshal,' he muttered. 'Even my pimps and cut-throats would not betray comrades who had fought along side of them in battle. No, I don't like it.'

Rokossovsky dismissed his doubts with a wave of his manicured hand. 'Loyalty among thieves, eh? Well, in the Kremlin there exists another kind of morality, that of dog eat dog. So, with effect from now, General Dmitrov's Guards Division, and naturally our own battalion, will be withdrawn from the line. You will be re-equipped with the best available Russian and American equipment and brought up to full strength with reinforcements. You will then be returned to the line – here at Prenzlau. From there you will advance at speed through Neubrandenburg, Güstrow and Wismar to the Baltic at Lübeck.' He paused, looking out of the window of the little German farmhouse kitchen. Outside some of Piotr's rats were amusing themselves with a woman. Four of them, obviously drunk, had pinned her down in the mud, where she threshed and turned, her skirts thrown up to reveal the soft white belly and hairy black triangle, while a fifth man was eagerly unbuttoning his flies, saliva dribbling down his bearded chin from his slack lecher's mouth. Rokossovsky looked away quickly. The Red Army was leaving behind it a trail of rape and destruction that the Germans would not forget for many years.

'You will hold Lübeck,' he continued, 'until the ships of the Red Fleet arrive. They will land the force of infantry and armour that will make the main thrust through Schleswig-Holstein into Denmark.'

'And if the Anglo-Americans object?'

Rokossovsky shrugged carelessly. 'As the peasants say – he who arrives first, eats first.' He stared at the big Colonel as if he were trying to imprint his every feature on his mind's eye. 'It is your task, Piotr, to ensure that *you* arrive first at Lübeck.'

'And if I don't?'

Rokossovsky crooked his finger as if he were pulling the trigger of a pistol. 'Old Leather Face will have no mercy. Clear?'

'Clear,' Piotr echoed. He raised his bottle of vodka as if in a toast and cried, 'We who are about to die, O Caesar, salute thee!'

In the farmyard outside the German woman was screaming hysterically. The Marshal shivered in distaste.

Piotr abruptly drained the last of the vodka and with a wild gesture, a mixture of contempt and rage, flung the empty bottle against the wall. He left Rokossovsky staring at the broken glass while he strode out of the kitchen.

A moment later Rokossovsky glanced out of the window. Piotr was swaggering across the farmyard, unbuckling his belt and kicking apart the group of rapists crouched over their victim. And the Marshal shivered again as Piotr roared his battle cry: *'Come on, you rats, do you want to live for ever?... Davai, davai!'*

BOOK ONE

THE BREAK-OUT

The Rhine and all its fortress lines lie behind the 21st Group of Armies. Once again they have been the hinge upon which massive gates revolved. Once again they have proved that physical barriers are vain without the means and spirit to hold them.

A beaten army not long ago Master of Europe retreats before its pursuers. The goal is not long to be denied to those who have come so far and fought so well under proud and faithful leadership.

Forward all on wings of flame to final Victory.

Winston Churchill's Message to his Troops, The Rhine, Germany. March 1945.

ONE

One by one the heavily camouflaged vehicles of the Assault Troop clattered down the muddy embankment of the Rhine, scattering mud and pebbles behind them in their wake, to form up on the cobbled German road beyond. To their front the horizon was on fire, as the heavy guns pounded the Red Devils' position. Somewhere close by, an enemy machine gun hissed hysterically, sending white tracer zipping across the littered fields.

Standing boldly upright in the turret of the Crocodile, Captain Corrigan, commander of the Assault Troop, frowned, his harshly handsome face set and worried. Crouching next to him, Troop Sergeant Hawkins knew why. If the Assault Troop didn't link up with the paras, who had landed twenty-four hours before, they would be overrun. The Jerries would put in one of their usual counter-attacks, and lightly armed as they were, the Red Devils would not be able to stand up to the German armour. They'd be sunk.

Corrigan seemed to read what was going on in the little Sergeant's mind. Taking his eyes off the dead bodies of the paras sprawled about a shattered glider, he rasped, 'All right, Hawkins, let's move it. Those poor buggers up there' – he indicated the burning horizon – 'have taken enough stick as it is.'

'Sir!' Hawkins barked, his breath fogging on the dank morning air. He poked his head down inside the tank, which they had 'borrowed' for the link-up – if anything could get them through the German line it would be the Crocodile – and said, 'Trooper Wolfers! Stop feeding yer frigging face and advance!'

The giant soldier bolted the rest of his corned beef sandwich and thrust home the gear. The Crocodile – stolen from the laager of a tank regiment waiting to cross the Rhine just before dawn – lurched forward. Up in the turret Corrigan pumped his hand up and down three times rapidly, the infantry signal for 'advance', and unslung his rifle ready for trouble. The Assault Troop was going in!

The troopers crouched in tense expectation on the decks of the rumbling vehicles, hands holding their weapons damp with sweat. On both sides of the road, the ditches were overflowing with the corpses of British and German soldiers, and in the fields beyond lay the shattered gliders, the trees around them festooned with red, yellow and white parachutes, some with dead Red Devils still attached, their bodies swaying slightly in the branches. The troopers rattled past a group of dead paras, caught by an 88mm shell as they attempted to cross the road: an officer burst apart like an overripe marrow; a youth, his clenched fists buried in the obscene grey snake of his own guts, as if at the moment of death he had been attempting to stuff his entrails back in again; a sergeant, his upper body flayed by shrapnel to expose his rib cage, which glittered against the caked dark red blood like sticks of polished ivory.

Sergeant Hawkins shook his head sadly. 'Poor sods,' he muttered. 'Kids, half of 'em – and dying *now,* when it's about all over.'

'It's always the best who die young,' Corrigan said bitterly, 'while the scum survive.'

'Thank bloody Christ Mrs Sanders' handsome son belongs to the bleeding scum,' commented Slim Sanders, the Australian member of the Assault Troop, crouching behind the Crocodile's frightening weapon. 'There's gonna be some right good old looting soon, once we get off the frigging Rhine–'

'Target, fifteen hundred yards, three o'clock!' Corrigan's urgent voice cut into the little Australian's remarks. 'Prepare to fire!'

Sanders' hands moved like lightning. The

turret and its deadly weapon began to swing around even as Corrigan focused his glasses.

The little farmhouse swept into the twin circles of calibrated glass. He had been right. There was no mistaking the squat shape of the German self-propelled gun parked next to the barn, a little group of infantry dug in beside it. 'An SP and infantry, Sanders. Got 'em?'

'Got 'em, the poor buggers!' Sanders bellowed above the roar of the engine as Wolfers accelerated. 'But we ain't in range yet, sir. We're gonna have to sweat this one out.'

'Sweat it out then!' Corrigan cried harshly, as the machine-gunner in the half-track behind them, sensing that the German SP outranged the Crocodile, sent a burst of tracer hissing across the fields towards the farmhouse, trying to put the German off his aim. The other gunners immediately followed suit. Now tracer hissed like a swarm of angry hornets towards the farmhouse.

Abruptly the German SP shuddered. A faint wisp of smoke drifted from the muzzle of its long cannon. Through his glasses, Corrigan caught a glimpse of a hurrying white burning blob.

'*AP!*' he screamed over the head-set.*

*AP: armour-piercing shell.

Wolfers reacted instinctively. He hit the massive brake and pulled back the tiller bars. The tank shuddered to a stop in the same instant that the shell struck the road just in front of them, sliding in a flurry of red sparks across the tarmac and burying itself harmlessly in the field on their left.

Wolfers jerked at the right bar. The Crocodile careened round. 'Hold on to yer hats!' he yelled over the intercom. 'We're going cross-country!' Suddenly they were bumping down the slope onto the fields, the two men in the turret holding on frantically as the Crocodile swayed and trembled alarmingly, as if it might overturn at any moment.

Somehow Wolfers got the thirty-ton monster down safely. They were rolling across the field now, with the half-tracks spreading out behind them to the left and right, enemy tracer bullets already howling off their steel plating.

The SP trembled again. Another thin spurt of blue flame burst from its muzzle, followed by drifting smoke. This time the German gunner didn't miss. One of the half-tracks came to an abrupt stop, a huge silver hole suddenly skewered in its side. Screaming mutilated men tumbled crazily over its sides, leaving their dead comrades buried in its mangled remains.

Corrigan cursed. 'Sanders, fire as soon as

you're in range! The bastard's gonna slaughter us if we're not careful!'

'Don't worry, sir,' Sanders' voice crackled tinnily over the intercom, 'I'm lining the sonovabitch up right now…'

The SP belched fire once more. There was a great ringing blow on the side of their turret. Corrigan and Hawkins ducked as one. To their right, the steel hissed and sizzled and glowed a bright white. Corrigan caught his breath. If the damned AP shell penetrated the turret and went whizzing round it in its mad lethal fury, it would rip them all to shreds.

But abruptly it was gone, leaving behind it only the acrid stink of molten metal as that frightening white glow faded and disappeared.

'Christ Almighty!' Hawkins gasped. 'That was frigging close! I nearly shat myself, honest!' He wiped his brow with a shaking hand. 'I swear I'm getting frigging well too old for this kind of a lark.'

'Go on, Sarge,' Wolfers jeered from below. 'You wouldn't miss this for all the tea in fuckin' China. You thrive on the–'

He was interrupted by a vicious hiss as Sanders fired his terrible weapon. It was as if some primeval monster had drawn its first fiery breath. A thick yellow rod of flame spurted out from the ugly nozzle of the Crocodile's flame-throwing gun. Out and out. Up and up. It made the noise of someone wielding a thick leather strap.

Suddenly the flaming rod curved. Burning particles of oil splattered everywhere, incinerating the grass on all sides. *Smack!* The rod of flame hit the German SP. A dozen fiery fingers leapt from the point of impact, probing greedily for cracks, holes, apertures – anywhere they could insert themselves to reach the quaking human flesh inside.

Standing together in their turret, Hawkins and Corrigan saw how the very paint of the SP's outer armour bubbled and popped, as if the steel had suddenly erupted into some kind of loathsome skin disease. Next moment, the armoured vehicle was engulfed in a roaring ball of flame. Then, as abruptly as they had been born, the flames died back in a cloud of strange-smelling smoke. As the smoke drifted away it revealed the blackened hull of the SP. Something was hanging from its turret: a charred shape that had once been a man.

It was too much for the infantry. Screaming wildly, fighting and clawing at each other in their frantic attempts to get away from the Crocodile's awesome weapon, they were fleeing back towards the village of Haminkeln, where the paras were trapped.

'Shall I flame the buggers?' Slim Sanders yelled triumphantly. 'I could roast the flaming lot of them, if you want, sir.'

'No,' Corrigan cried, 'save your juice. We're gonna need it, if we're to winkle out this lot. Can you see? They're dug in all around the houses to our front.'

Down in the green-glowing bowels of the tank, the little Australian cursed.

Corrigan gave the order to advance again, and the little link-up force rolled towards the village. As they approached they were met with red stabs of flame erupting from virtually every red-brick house. Glancing up at the church steeple Corrigan caught the glint of glass: someone up there was probably directing the enemy fire.

'Let's hope the buggers haven't got *panzerfausts*, sir,'* Hawkins said urgently, as the morning sky was torn apart by a German multiple mortar. Six trails of blinding white smoke rushed straight towards the heavens and then, just when it seemed they would disappear into space, hurtled back down towards the advancing column. 'I don't mind yon moaning minnies, but then bleeding *panzerfausts* are–'

The rest of Hawkins's words were drowned by the tremendous impact of six rockets slamming into the earth at a thousand miles per hour. Instantly the front was blacked out by a tornado of mud and stones. The blast wave swept over them.

Panzerfaust: a German rocket launcher.

Five-ton half-tracks swayed and rocked, as if they had been struck by a tremendous hurricane. Corrigan hastily opened his mouth to prevent his eardrums from bursting. The fierce wind seemed to snatch the very breath from his lungs. It struck his face like a blow from a hot flabby hand. For a moment he gasped for air, choking like an asthmatic in the throes of a fatal attack. Then they were through the crazy maelstrom and the little brick houses loomed up once more, vicious spurts of scarlet flame still cutting the morning from every window.

Corrigan shook his head to clear the ringing from his ears. 'Prepare to flame, Sanders!' he rapped. The defenders were pretty well protected, especially if they were below ground in one of those damned German cellars which gave splendid cover and turned every civvie house into a miniature fortress. Still, the psychological effect of the Crocodile's terrible weapon might force the defenders into surrendering.

'Ready to fire, sir!' Sander's voice came over the headset, and Corrigan could visualise the little Australian crouching over his cannon, gaze fixed on the little red indicator lamp, eager for action.

'Right then. Schoolhouse at ten o'clock, Sanders. *Flame 'em!*'

Sanders fired. There was a great hiss, an

urgent sucking in of air, and that terrifying rod of flame shot forward, scorching and searing everything in its path. A grove of trees was engulfed by the flame; they ignited at once, falling like burning matchsticks. The grass blackened and withered. Then, like a vicious yellow wild-cat, the rod of flame curled itself around the schoolhouse. Windowpanes cracked. Paint on the walls bubbled and spat. A black oily mushroom of smoke rose into the grey morning sky.

Corrigan wiped the sweat from his face, blinking his eyes to prevent himself from being blinded by the sweatdrops congregating in his eyebrows. 'Excellent, Sanders!' he cried, his parched voice cracking. 'Give 'em another burst. That should do the trick!'

'Ay, ay, sir… Wolfers, get me to within a hundred yards!'

'Watch out for the *panzerfausts!*' Hawkins yelled.

Wolfers did not seem to hear. He thrust home the massive gears and urged the thirty-ton monster ever closer to the smoking schoolhouse, ignoring the howl and whine of enemy slugs skidding off the armour plating.

Sanders fired again. Another burst of flame. The heat was terrific. Corrigan and Hawkins, crouching down behind the protection of the turret, could feel the breath being dragged from their lungs. They

36

gasped frantically for air, mouths gaping like stranded fish.

Suddenly their nostrils were assailed by the sweet ghastly stench of burning flesh. Sanders flamed again. Once more the flame-thrower roared. Corrigan wanted to scream. His whole body was drenched in sweat. He clutched the turret with white-knuckled claws to steady himself. How could men stand such horror? How could men torture their fellow men like this? Where was God and His mercy this day?

A moment later it was all over. A group of burning human torches stumbled out of the schoolhouse, their screams echoed eerily by shrieks from those still inside. Aghast, but unable to avert his eyes, Corrigan saw how the pearly white bones gleamed in the charred flesh of the men's raised hands. Then the crocodile was crunching over their writhing bodies, turning them into a blackened, scarlet, pulpy paste...

It was dark now but still the street-fighting continued in the little Rhenish town. Scarlet flame stabbed the gloom in chaotic pro-fusion. Machine guns rattled. Tracer zipped back and forth between the ruined houses. Voices, angry, confused, fearful, called out in English and German. Somewhere a voice was crying in a thick Geordie accent: *'Where are ye, hinnies?... Where are ye, mates?... I canna frigging see…'*

The Assault Troop squatted in the lee of a wall while Corrigan assessed the situation, squinting round the burning wreck of a jeep that had once belonged to the Red Devils. The flames cast lurid red shadows down the street – the street along which they must advance if they were ever going to link up with the trapped airborne men.

'What do you think, sir?' Trooper Wolfers asked, sucking at huge dripping pawfuls of bottled peaches that he had looted in one of the cellars.

'Not much, Wolfers,' Corrigan answered dourly, as he rested there, crouched over his old Mark IV infantry rifle. 'But the Jerries are there all right, waiting for us.'

'We could flame 'em, sir,' Wolfers suggested, cramming another peach into his mouth, the syrup trickling down his massive unshaven jaw.

'Be yer age,' Sanders snarled. His own forays among the houses abandoned by German troops had been unsuccessful. Even the German corpses he had examined had proved a dead loss: not one single gold tooth among them. 'The fuckers'll be waiting for us with them *panzer*-frigging-*fausts* of theirs. We wouldn't stand a frigging chance, cobber.'

'Would you kindly hold your frigging mouth,' Corrigan interjected with excessive politeness, *'because I can't frigging well hear myself frigging think.'*

'Well – if you put it like that, sir...'

Hawkins glared at the skinny little Australian threateningly, then cast a sideways glance at Corrigan. 'We could mouse-hole through to them, sir,' he suggested. 'Burrow our way from house to house.'

Corrigan shook his head. 'That would be the best way, Hawkins, but we simply haven't got the time. Listen to that barrage further up front. You know what that means. The Germans are softening up the airborne for the counter-attack – and soon.'

Hawkins pulled a face. He knew what Corrigan's next order would be and he didn't like it. There would be casualties. His beloved Assault Troop would take losses and by now most of the replacements were mere kids; they could have been his own children. Eighteen-year-olds, still wet behind the lugs, he thought sadly. 'Down the street, sir?'

'Down the street, Sergeant,' Corrigan echoed wearily. 'But don't go broody on me, Hawkins, you silly old fart. We're not going to incur casualties if we do it properly. After all, those lads of yours have been trained to do this sort of thing.'

'Training!' snorted Hawkins, then muttered something about 'battle know-how' and 'no substitute'.

But Captain Corrigan was no longer listening to the little sergeant, with his yellow false teeth and dyed hair, who was really far too old for combat. He had made up his mind.

'All right – Sanders and Wolfers, you take the right side of the street. I'm taking the left. Hawkins, you give us twenty yards and come up with the rest. Take no chances. Shoot first and ask questions afterwards. And for God's sake, watch your backs! Are you ready?'

There was a murmur of agreement.

Corrigan wasted no more time. 'Right, then, here we go!'

'On your feet!' Hawkins snapped, all doubts dismissed from his mind. There was no alternative.

Hastily the men rose to their feet, weapons at the ready. Fearful anticipation was clearly reflected in the faces of some of the latest reinforcements as they gazed down that blazing street along which they must now pass. The houses on both sides were deceptively silent, but they were occupied all right. Behind those doors waited desperate young men like themselves, waiting to sacrifice their lives for a cause that was already lost.

But Corrigan did not give his young soldiers time to get too nervous. He sprang right into the centre of the battle-littered street, his tall lean body clearly outlined in the writhing flames of the burning jeep. *'Bash on Recce!'** he bellowed at the top of his voice. Next instant a white phosphorous grenade exploded against the wall of the nearest house on the right hand side of the street. It burst in a brilliant flurry of incandescent white pellets. A familiar coal-scuttle helmet popped out of an upper window of the same house. Corrigan fired from the hip. There was a shrill scream of agony as the sniper toppled from the window and smacked onto the pavement below.

Like an American football player going to make a touchdown, head tucked low between his shoulders, Corrigan pelted for the shadows on the left side of the street, angry slugs kicking up vicious spurts of blue flame at his racing feet. Sanders and Wolfers seized the chance that Corrigan had offered them. They rushed for the opposite side, Sten guns belching flame, their bullets cutting brick and timber splinters from the walls of the enemy-held houses.

Now with Hawkins and his men bringing up the rear, snapping off shots to both sides as the Germans opened up, the three men at point began to work their way up the street.

*Recce: the Reconnaissance Corps, to which the Assault Troop belonged.

It was nerve-racking work, demanding boldness, split-second timing and a great deal of luck, with always the possibility that some German sniper might pop out of the rubble to their rear and slap them down with a treacherous shot in the back. A boot against the door. *Duck!* A grenade lobbed inside and the door pulled closed once more. A great deafening, trembling roar. The door flung open. Crouched like a western gun-slinger – *in!* Finding your way through the blinding acrid fumes of the grenade, flinging open each door and firing. Up the stairs, body pressed to the wall in case they rolled down grenades. Smash in the door. Another grenade. A burst of fire and then on to the next house. Every second was electric, nerve-tingling tension: one slip, one false move and you were *dead.*

Wolfers' big boot lashed out. The door splintered and went flying back on shattered hinges. He crouched, chest heaving painfully. All was silent in the house. But he knew they were there somewhere in the dark interior, the lurid flames outside casting huge moving eerie shadows on the walls.

Then Wolfers heard it. The stamp of boots on broken glass. He ripped off a burst from the hip. The noise was ear-splitting. A big German fell, reeling blindly along the wall, rifle tumbling from nerveless fingers.

Another dropped his weapon and came stumbling from the shadows, hands raised. '*Kamerad!*' he cried frantically. '*Kamerad!*'

Instinctively Wolfers lowered his Sten. Sanders, behind him, was not fooled. 'Silly cunt!' he screamed in an ecstasy of fear. '*DUCK!*' And he ripped off a blast that deafened the big Yorkshireman.

There was a shrill scream as a third German staggered forwards, past the crouching figure of the one who had surrendered. Sanders' shot had hit him full in the face. Already his features were sliding down onto his chest like a mask of red molten wax.

Wolfers lashed out. The German who had surrendered now reeled back with a moan as the Sten butt slammed into his face. He went down without another sound, toppling forwards onto the rough wooden floorboards. As he fell, his false teeth escaped from his slack mouth and landed on the floor beside him.

Sanders savagely crunched his boots onto the teeth. '*Starve to frigging death, Kraut!*' he snarled, then turned to follow Wolfers out of the house.

Now they were almost there. Up front, Corrigan could hear the cries of the trapped paras. '*Airborne here... We're over here, chaps... Bash on the British... The Airborne for fucking ever!*'

He slumped against a wall and slotted in another magazine. He was gasping for breath and sweat was dripping down his face in great opaque pearls. At his feet a German lay. Once he must have been a handsome young man in the stern Prussian fashion. Now he was a horror. One eye had been shot away, leaving a scarlet suppurating pit, and two dark holes full of pink-tinged mucus were all that remained to show where his nose had been.

Corrigan felt the hot vomit welling up into his throat and threatening to choke him. He took his gaze away swiftly.

'Rally on me, lads!' he cried. 'One last effort! *Bash on Recce!*'

'*Bash on Recce!*' echoed the hoarse cries from all sides.

'*Oh why are we waiting ... waiting ... waiting...*' the weary paras sang from their hiding places in the rubble less than fifty yards away. '*Up came a spider, sat down beside her, wiped his old bazooka out and this is what he said,*' some wag sang in a cracked, crazy voice. '*Get hold of this bash, bash! Get hold of that, bash, ba–*' His voice broke off in a last piteous howl as a sniper's slug found its target.

Corrigan drew a deep breath and bellowed with the last of his strength: '*Fix bayonets!*'

'*Fix bayonets!*' Hawkins echoed further down the street.

Corrigan waited for the metallic clicking of bayonets being attached to finish, then he cried, *'CHARGE!'*

Next instant they were all rushing forward, clattering over the debris in their heavy hob-nailed boots, screaming frenzied obscenities, bayonets flashing in the gloom.

All fears now thrown to the wind, the men of the Assault Troop charged forward, slashing and thrusting with their bayonets, here and there skidding to a sudden stop and their knees going under them like newly born foals, or screaming in sudden horror as a slug slammed into their flesh. But there was no stopping them. On and on, forward, forward...

And then they were through. Weary unshaven paras were slapping them on the back, shaking their hands, even kissing them, as the German barrage increased in fury like some wild beast foiled of its prey. They had made the link-up between the ground forces and the airborne. The first phase of Field Marshal Montgomery's great set-piece crossing of the Rhine, Germany's last natural barrier, was over.

TWO

On that chill March day, the Supreme Commander of the Allied Forces in Europe, General Eisenhower, had been working on the problem ever since he had arrived at his office in Rheims' former boys' technical school at precisely 7.45 a.m.

Ancient French locomotives, most of them bullet-pocked, clattered back and forth in the shunting yards opposite. Further up the sloping, cobbled back street in which Supreme Headquarters were located, the two-and-a-half ton trucks of the 'Red Ball' Express roared in a steady stream to the front in faraway Germany. But the broad-faced, balding American heard neither the persistent rumble of trucks nor the clatter of locomotives, as he sat in his bare office of what his GI clerks called the 'little red schoolhouse'.

His mind was concentrated solely on the two cables that lay before him on his desk and the decision they demanded from him: a decision which he realised might be the most important he would ever take in Europe.

One of the cables was from the man who

had 'discovered' him and transformed him from an obscure 'bird' colonel, ready for retirement, into the most powerful soldier in the Western Hemisphere: General Marshall, the US Chief-of-Staff. From Washington Marshall had cabled asking about Eisenhower's present intentions. The German front, Marshall believed, was about to fall apart at any moment. Did he, Eisenhower, now think of perhaps advancing southwards in Germany to the Bavarian Alps, to prevent the surviving die-hard Nazis from organising a national redoubt there where they might hold out for years?

The other cable was from that birdlike little Britisher, Field Marshal Montgomery. Eisenhower had not spoken to him these last six weeks, he had been so angry with him. Montgomery's cable was not a query; it was a *demand*. He wanted the Supreme Commander's approval to drive with his own armies and the attached US Ninth Army straight up the *autobahn* from the Rhine right into Berlin.

The five-star general sat at his raised desk, which had once belonged to some obscure French technical teacher, chain-smoking his favourite Lucky Strikes, wondering what he should do. Over the last three years – in North Africa, Sicily, Italy, London, Normandy, Versailles (his previous headquarters) – he had made decisions, day after day, week after week, month after month: decisions that had hardened and matured him and steeled him against the carping criticism of the envious, the inferior, the impotent. But the decision he would have to make this chill March day would bring down on him more violent criticism than anything he had ever done before.

There were, as all senior commanders knew, only sufficient supplies and men for one major push. Therefore it had to be *either* Berlin *or* Bavaria. If he gave Montgomery his head, the damned little Britisher would gain the kudos of final victory in Germany. And that, naturally, would infuriate his senior American Army commanders, especially 'Old Blood and Guts' Patton, who dearly loved the headlines. But if he gave the go-ahead for the drive into Bavaria and stopped Monty, all hell would break loose in London. Then, in all probability, he would have the British Prime Minister 'Winnie' Churchill breathing down his neck again.

It was a damnable situation. They'd sure got him by the short and curlies this time, Eisenhower groaned to himself. *What in Sam Hill's name was he going to do?*

Just after eleven that morning, the office door swung open and Kay Summersby came in bearing a tray with a steaming cup of coffee on it. Officially his secretary-cum-chauffeuse, the Irish girl with green eyes

48

and a mass of red hair meant much more to Ike than that. Moving across the room with the grace befitting a former model, she placed it next to Eisenhower's overflowing ashtray and announced: 'Coffee break, sir.'

Eisenhower's frown disappeared and he gave her the benefit of that ear-to-ear smile of his, familiar by now to movie audiences all over the western world. 'Swell!' he exclaimed and reached for the cup. 'But cut out the "sir" when we're alone, huh?'

'Okay, Ike,' she smiled, then waved a hand at his paper-littered desk. 'Tough morning?'

He paused, the cup touching his lips, his broad face wreathed in steam. 'You can say that again, Kay. In fact, if you'll pardon my French, it's a sonovabitch.'

She patted his arm soothingly. 'Anything you can tell me about?'

'Hell, Kay, I have no secrets from you – you know that. You know more secrets than most of my top brass!' He rapped his knuckles on Montgomery's top-secret signal, marked in Montgomery's own hand *For Ike's Eyes Only*, and told her about his dilemma. 'I've got to make a decision that's gonna hurt somebody whatever I do,' he concluded. 'So you see, Kay – it's one helluva mess.'

She nodded her head in understanding, her pretty face creased in a worried frown.

For a few moments there was silence – broken by a snatch of conversation from out in the corridor. 'I don't want to be bitchy, Randy,' a peevish voice was saying, 'but I do think those GI clerks are taking damned liberties. I mean, what does an ordinary GI clerk-typist need a French maid for? Gee, it's bad enough for us officers.'

A hearty voice boomed back: 'Well, they sure don't need them to clean out their billet, Elmer!'

Eisenhower scowled. The little conversation had reminded him yet again of his exposed position at this massive headquarters with its 5,000 staff spread out over their luxurious billets in the *châteaux* of the local champagne barons. If the press back home ever found out about the way he and the rest of them lived with their mistresses, dogs, fancy French dinners and all the rest of it, while the GIs slogged it out on C-rations at the front, there would be all hell to pay. Marshall would see that heads rolled – and one of them might well be his own.

'Look...' Kay broke the heavy silence as she sat down on the edge of his desk, next to the little stand bearing the Allied flags, and crossed her long shapely nylon-clad legs. 'You're an American, yes?'

Eisenhower nodded absently.

'Not only that, Ike, you know as well as I do that you have a political career in front of you after this war is over. Everyone is saying that.'

He pursed his lips. 'It's a possibility,' he agreed. 'After every successful war that the United States has fought, our leading generals have always been candidates for office—'

'The *highest* office,' she interrupted him firmly, *'the very highest!'*

He shrugged. 'Well, I don't know so much about that...'

Kay seized his hand and pressed it hard. 'One day, Ike, you are going to be President of the United States – and you know it.' He opened his mouth to protest but she silenced him with a swift kiss. 'Listen, all I'm trying to say is this. Your personal priority number one is to make yourself as popular as you can back home in the States. At this stage of your career, with political office looming up ahead, you can't afford to lose a single trick.'

'How do you mean, Kay?' He was staring at her curiously now.

'I mean, the war doesn't count any more. It's all done with. The Jerries are beaten and soon all of you Yanks will be returning home. What counts now is that the press and radio boys back home know that it was the American Army that won the final victory over the Jerries! Montgomery and Churchill and all the rest of those snooty Limeys are no longer important. They've had their day. So why give Montgomery –

you hate his guts anyway and so do most of your generals – an opportunity to blow his trumpet again?' The Irish girl's green eyes were flashing now and her jaw set hard in that a tough determined manner of hers. 'The only decision you can make today is to let Monty play soldier somewhere up there on the Rhine.'

'But Berlin–' he began to object.

Again she smothered his protest with a swift peck to the lips. 'Forget Berlin,' she said. 'It's only a place-name on the map now. Let the Russians have it if they want. What you have to do now is order Patton to advance into Bavaria. That's the way he and the US Army – *and* you – will get the headlines you need.'

'Do you think so, Kay?' he asked hesitantly.

'I damn well *know* so, Ike!' She thrust the writing block at the man who commanded the destinies of five million young men. 'Now, start drafting that cable to Monty telling him he's out.' She grinned suddenly and hissed into his ear, 'And bad cess to the bastard! *He bloody well deserves all that's coming to him today!*'

The little Field Marshal was walking back to his caravan in the darkness, carrying his usual bedtime glass of warm milk, when the signals officer came running up, waving the message from the Supreme Commander.

'Sir... Sir... Top priority from General Eisenhower's HQ. Your eyes only, sir!'

Montgomery frowned. He hated his routine to be disturbed. It was nearly quarter to ten, and by ten promptly he was normally in his bunk and fast asleep. Even during the tense, nerve-racking ten days of the Battle of El Alamein back in '42, he had never changed his personal timetable by as much as a minute.

'All right, all right, give it to me,' he snapped, having difficulty as always in pronouncing his r's, and took the message from the excited signals officer in his free hand. 'Stand by outside my caravan. I might need you.'

'Sir.' The signals officer saluted smartly and then relaxed as the Field Marshal disappeared into his caravan. 'The Master', as he was called at his small tactical headquarters, had been in a strange mood of late and he didn't wish to incur Montgomery's anger. At this late stage of the war, he didn't relish the prospect of being posted to the front and having his head blown off by some stupid Boche.

Montgomery took a sip of warm milk and sat down at the table, army-issue glasses on the tip of his beaky nose as he opened the message from Eisenhower. Swiftly his keen gaze ran over the opening paragraphs, knowing that Eisenhower was a great one for 'waffle' as he called it, only coming to the heart of the matter towards the end of his long-winded messages.

'As soon as you have joined hands with Bradley* ... the Ninth US Army will revert to Bradley's command... Bradley will be responsible for mopping up ... and with the minimum delay will deliver his main thrust on the axis Erfurt-Leipzig-Dresden to join hands with the Russians.' Montgomery sniffed – and then he spotted it: *'The place – Berlin, – has become, so far as I am concerned, nothing but a geographical location and I have never been interested in these. My purpose is to destroy the enemy's forces and his powers to resist...'*

Montgomery almost dropped the bit of paper in disgust. So that was it! His enemies at Ike's headquarters had triumphed at last and turned Eisenhower against him. He was not going to be allowed to attack Berlin. Instead he was being given what was essentially a flank-guard operation, a drive north towards Hamburg with no strategic purpose.

Montgomery sat there sunk in thought. Outside, his little tented camp settled down for the night. Even the noise from the officers' mess, which housed his 'eyes and ears'

---

*General Bradley, Montgomery's opposite number and rival, commanding the US 18th Army Group.

– those young officers he sent out daily to report to him directly from the front – was muted, as if the youthful captains and majors sensed his trouble and had no heart for drinking this night. From a long, long way off he could just hear the rumble of his artillery on the Rhine, where his troops were still desperately trying to break out.

'For what?' he asked himself bitterly under his breath, staring unseeingly at a large photograph of Field Marshal Model – for the walls of his caravan were covered with photographs of his principal German opponents. Was this what he had been fighting for, these five long years: relegation to a minor side-role? Had all that effort, that sweat and toil, that great sacrifice of young men's lives been for *this?* He sucked his teeth in despair.

But there was more to it than that. For the sake of US army prestige and public opinion back home, Eisenhower was throwing away the great political prize. As a result of his foolishness, the Russians, the new scourge of the West, would gain not only the politically important capitals of Vienna and Prague, but also Berlin.

His face twisted as if he were in physical pain, Montgomery slammed his puny fist on the table. What fools the Americans were! What absolute bloody simple fools! Once they had withdrawn their great armies from Europe, the Soviet dictator would be free to do as he wished with the Continent. What could a war-weary Britain, a weak France and a beaten, disarmed Germany do to stop him? The further the Americans allowed Stalin to penetrate westwards, the sooner the Russians would reach the Channel coast. Then it would be summer 1940 all over again.

From London and his own intelligence sources, Montgomery already knew the Russians were landing para-agents far behind German lines in north-west Germany. There had been some unconfirmed reports that they had landed agents on the Danish island of Rügen, in Schleswig-Holstein, and even in Denmark itself, where they were attempting to co-ordinate members of the very strong and active Danish communist party. What that signified was easy to guess: he didn't need a crystal ball for that. The Russians were not going to stop on the Elbe. They were going to push as far west as possible. Once they had reached the Baltic coast, there would be no stopping them. The Germans would be able to put up only a token resistance. Then the Red Army would be pushing up through the Schleswig-Hostein peninsula into Denmark, and the mouth of the Baltic would be theirs. Thereafter it would be the devil's own job to make them withdraw before they had set up a 'popular fraternal government' in Copenhagen as they had done in Poland, Bulgaria, Rumania and all the other countries the Red Army had occupied over these last months. The Baltic would become a Russian lake.

Outside the caravan, all was silent. The headquarters slept. The only sounds were the slow crunch of the sentry's boots, as he paced up and down the gravel path leading to the caravan, and the occasional muffled cough from the signals officer, still waiting in case there was a message to be sent.

But what message – and to whom? Montgomery slumped there gloomily, the milk in his mug already cold and scummed over. On the wall Model stared at him through his monocle quizzically, almost as if he could feel for his opponent at this moment. By sheer effort of will, Montgomery forced himself to think. Not only were there political factors to be taken into consideration, now that Eisenhower had made his damnfool decision, but there was the personal factor too.

Montgomery had come a long way since that celebrated Battle of El Alamein, which had catapulted him into the limelight and made his name a household word. 'Monty': everyone knew him now. Everyone recognised his floppy black beret, with its assortment of regimental badges; his sloppy civilian corduroy trousers; the green 'gamp' he sometimes affected, like the Duke of Wellington. Everyone knew the stories about him: how he made elderly generals, who for years had done nothing more strenuous than lift a whisky-and-soda, go out for morning runs; how he ordered his own King not to cough or smoke during a briefing; how he had even ticked off Churchill himself for interfering in military matters. After years of defeat, he had produced Britain's first victory of the war. He was the country's major hero. Was he now, at this moment of triumph, to sink back into the obscurity from which he had come?

By God no! Sudden resolution flushed his skinny cheeks. He felt fresh energy coursing through his blood. There was still a chance to gain something for himself out of the mess that Eisenhower was going to make of things. He sprang to his feet, almost over-turning the mug of cold milk, and padded across the caravan to a big wall map of the front.

For a moment he peered at it, glasses perched at the end of his long beaky nose, his bright blue eyes abruptly wild and sparkling with barely restrained excitement. He made up his mind.

'It'll have to be the Sixth Airborne,' he muttered to himself, in the fashion of all lonely men. 'They've lost about a third of their effectives in the drop, according to the latest casualty figures, and they've no transport to speak of – but they're the best I've got for this kind of op. If anyone can do it, it will be the Red Devils.'

He pressed his glasses back firmly on the bridge of his nose and stepped to the door. He flung it open.

The signals officer was leaning against the nearest tree, a cigarette cupped in one hand, smoking lazily. He started as he saw the figure framed there in the sudden shaft of yellow light from the caravan and dropped the cigarette hastily. 'Sorry, sir, about the smok–'

'Never mind, my boy.' Montgomery was in high good humour now that the decision was made. 'When you've taken this signal I'm personally going to give you one of Churchill's own cigars! Now then, in you come and let's get cracking. There's no time to lose...'

THREE

Somewhere up the shell-cratered road, littered with the debris of battle, the trees on either side stripped of their branches like gigantic match-sticks, an 88mm cannon was banging away like a hammer in hell. At regular intervals, its shells slammed into the line of houses held by the Red Devils, making them shake and shimmy like stage backdrops.

But Colonel Jones, the paras' commander, a lean, highly strung officer with a jaw like the prow of a destroyer, did not seem to notice. As he briefed the officers grouped round him in the hissing white glare of a pressure lantern, he appeared completely oblivious to the pounding, though Corrigan watching could see the para commander was taut and wound-up.

'So this is the set-up,' Colonel Jones was saying. 'The Boche are dug in on both sides of that road up there as far as the bridge. That's held by their paras, the German elite.' He glanced round the ring of white faces, approving of their air of tense concentration. 'Now, according to prisoners, the chaps defending the road are second-line troops, all from a "stomach battalion" – invalids, grouped into a unit so it's easier for their cooks to feed them the special diet they need for their rotten guts.' He forced a weary smile, but Corrigan noticed the two worry lines form down the sides of his thin lips.

'But the pricks are well armed, sir – and they say bad guts make for mean men,' someone said, and everyone laughed; Jones's officers all knew their colonel suffered from ulcers and was decidedly 'mean' at times.

'Probably, probably, Andrews,' Jones conceded, standing erect to ease his aching back. 'Anyway, we're going to have to rush them and hope for the best. There's no other way. It'll pin them down at least, and the paras on the bridge won't blow it as long as they hear firing from the road.' Jones turned to Corrigan and stared at him, red-rimmed eyes seemingly angry. 'That's where you come in, Corrigan.'

'Sir?'

'Well, so far nothing much has followed you up the road from the Rhine. I was hoping for tanks.' He shrugged, like a man sorely tried. 'No matter, we'll have to try to take that bridge with your vehicles.'

'A *coup de main*, sir?'

'Exactly. Take 'em from the left flank with your vehicles, including that flame-throwing monster. Don't give them a chance. Hit 'em fast and hit 'em hard – and no stopping for casualties. Understood?'

'Understood, sir,' Corrigan snapped. Whatever else Jones was, he was a fighter, a man who commanded from the front; he was exactly right for this kind of op.

'Anything else, Corrigan?'

'No sir.'

'All right.' Jones raised his arm, his camouflaged smock falling back to reveal his wrist-watch. 'Good... Gentlemen, the time is now zero six hundred hours. Shall we circumcise our watches?'

Nobody laughed.

'I don't want to fraternise with 'em,' Sanders was saying, idly cleaning his toenails with the tip of his bayonet as he sat crosslegged on the straw in the barn, *'I just want to fuck 'em!'*

'But it's forbidden, Slim,' Wolfers objected. 'We're supposed to have nowt to do with the Jerries. It's forbidden, even with the kids, never mind the womenfolk. You can get into trouble for fraternising with a Jerry. They'd probably put yer in Dartmoor if they caught yer going with a Jerry bint!'

Slim Sanders, who had been recruited into Corrigan's squadron way back in '42 after having deserted from the 9th Australian Infantry Division in the Middle East, looked at his big pimply running-mate in undisguised contempt. 'Christ Almighty, Wolfers,

I sometimes think you've got yer arse where yer head should be.'

'Yer mean his *guts*, Sanders,' another of the assault troopers lying in the straw quipped, 'the way he knocks back the grub.'

Sanders ignored the interruption. 'Do you *frigging* well think that *frigging* Field Marshal *frigging* Montgomery will come up here to check whether Mrs Sanders' handsome son gets a piece of Jerry nookie or not?' He spat, narrowly missing the boots of the man who had joked abut Wolfers' fabled appetite. 'Course he won't. Nor that Yank general Eisenhower either. They're all right back there behind the line, sticking it up some frog countess or Belgie princess or the like. They're getting the old pearly gates all the frigging time. But what about yer poor old PBI? What are *we* getting, eh?'

'The toe of my ammunition boot up yer lazy arse, if you don't shut up.' It was Sergeant Hawkins' voice. The men all turned as one and saw the little NCO standing at the open barn door. Pipe stuck in his mouth, dew-drop hanging from the end of his red nose, and wearing a sleeveless leather jerkin, he looked more like a caricature of 'Old Bill' from the Great War than a non-commissioned officer in the British Army's newest corps. 'By Christ, Sanders, I thought all you Aussies were supposed to be tall and lean and silent. You're just a short-arse, running to fat, and you rabbit on all the bleeding time.'

Sanders was not in the least put out. He scraped another piece of dirt from his big toenail with a delicate twist of his bayonet, surveyed it as if it were important to do so, slung it away, and said: 'I'm just a kind of superior Aussie that's all, Sergeant Hawkins.'

The old NCO, who mothered the Assault Troop as if it were composed of his own sons, gave up. 'All right, that's enough; we're wasting time. Captain Corrigan wants a word with you lot. On yer bleeding feet!'

They rose with groans and the usual loud farts, even the replacements attempting to look bored. 'Frig it,' someone complained. 'I was just gonna slip Hedi Lamarr a link, too, in me dreams! Ain't there any justice in this frigging world?'

'Atten-*shut!*' Hawkins barked, as Corrigan came in, rifle slung over his shoulder, spare bandolier of ammunition hanging from his chest and pouches bulging with grenades.

As they stiffened to attention, Wolfers muttered out of the side of his mouth, 'Trouble, Slim. The old Man's a walking arsenal. We're in for trouble–'

'Stop talking, that man, or I'll have your name,' Hawkins roared; then, swinging round, he flung Corrigan a tremendous salute.

64

Corrigan's cynical mouth twisted into a grin. 'What's this, Sergeant Hawkins? Since when has the Assault Troop been so regimental?'

'Just getting 'em ready for peacetime, sir,' Hawkins replied. 'Now the war's nearly over, I'm starting to get 'em ready for some *real* soldiering, sir!'

Corrigan's grin vanished as he thought of what lay ahead for the Assault Troop. 'Well, it's not over yet, Hawkins… All right, the lot of you, stand at ease.'

There was another outburst of coughs and farts as the men relaxed and stared at the big Captain expectantly. Corrigan took his time, staring back at them, pleased with what he saw. Even the greenhorns in their rough jerkins and battered khaki, their faces red and weathered by constant outdoor living in all kinds of conditions, looked tough and unstoppable. Only months ago they had been skinny pale-faced schoolkids, or factory hands whose main interest in life had been visiting the local flea-pit and the pub. Now they had filled out on the plain diet of 'armoured pig' and 'armoured cow', as they called their rations of corned beef and spam; and they had been hardened by their tough training and the way they were forced to live at the front, with no cover at night save a groundsheet or a gas cape thrown over the top of their foxhole. If any

Allied troops could capture the bridge from the best soldiers the enemy still possessed, the paras, it would be these men.

'All right,' he broke the tense silence, 'I'm not going to attempt to pull any wool over your eyes. We've been given a beaut. While the Red Devils take on the infantry to our front, we are going to outflank the German positions, rush and capture that bridge up there. Its capture is vital if the Sixth Airborne Division is to move out of the bridgehead.'

'Well, why don't they have a crack at it themselves, sir?' Sanders asked. 'Them Red Devils get an extra bob a day for being paras. Let 'em bleeding well earn it.' He stared around at the others, as if he expected his eminently sensible statement to be greeted with a round of applause – but none was forthcoming.

'Why?' Corrigan repeated. 'Because the paras are bushed and have no armour. And because I tell you, you little Aussie rogue.'

Sanders shrugged eloquently, but he said no more.

'All right,' Corrigan continued, 'I'll make it short and sweet. I've decided we should go in from the left flank. We have a bit of cover from that fir wood up there. Of course, the German paras on the bridge will hear the sound of our motors, but I'm hoping they won't suspect we're making a rush for the bridge. I'm reasoning that they'll think we're too scared of their anti-tank guns and *panzerfausts* for that, without the cover of infantry.'

Wolfers looked at Slim and the latter said out of the corner of his mouth: 'Well, I'm frigging scared for one, mate!'

'Now, this is how we're going to do it.' Corrigan picked up an old straw besom, dropped by the German farmworkers when they had fled, and drew a line in the dust of the floor. 'The Crocodile – here – will be in the lead. I've already had its floor packed out with sandbags and put extra bogies and track on the glacis plate as more protection against their anti-tank weapons. It's going to be our battering ram – I hope. To left and right, in two columns, the half-tracks and bren-gun carriers will follow. I haven't any idea of how deep that river is, but once we've battered our way as far as the bridge, I want drivers to attempt to ford it on both sides of the bridge. Doesn't matter if you go under; Field Marshal Montgomery's got plenty more vehicles. The main thing is we get that bridge intact, even if we lose all our vehicles.' He paused momentarily and looked around their earnest young faces, hollowed out and looking much older in the hissing white glare of the petrol lantern. 'We lost some good lads yesterday,' he said, his voice taking on a softer tone. 'One or two of them had only been with us a short time, but they were good lads... Now, we're going to take this objective, have no doubts about that, but I don't want anyone to take any unnecessary risks. You old hands, look after the younger ones and see they don't do anything stupid.' At his side, Sergeant Hawkins was nodding his head in solemn agreement. 'Right,' Corrigan rasped. 'Any questions?'

Sanders put up his hand.

'Yes?'

'Do you think I can put in for an immediate transfer to the Royal Army Pay Corps, sir?' Sanders quavered in a mock frightened falsetto.

Corrigan laughed, and one or two of the men joined in, but the tension was still there. The Assault Troop was all too aware what might have to be faced this coming day.

Colonel Jones stood outlined a stark black against the faint white light of the false dawn, his gaze fixed on the green-glowing dial of his watch, his right arm raised. On the start-line the Red Devils tensed, licking their lips as if they were very thirsty. Any minute now they would start the attack. All was silent save for the faint hiss of the wind in the shattered trees and the chatter of the machine gun a long way off, like that of an irate woodpecker.

'Nine, eight, seven, six...' Colonel Jones started to count off the last seconds, the finger clutching the trigger of his flare pistol going white at the knuckle. '...five, four, three, two, one – *zero!*' He pressed the trigger. Plop! The red flare hissed into the sky and exploded in a burst of lurid crimson.

The Red Devils, disdaining helmets and proudly wearing their red berets, rose to their feet with a cheer, bayonets fixed.

'*Give them hell, lads!*' Jones cried – and then they were charging forward, straight into the first wild burst of machine-gun fire...

'*Start up!*' Corrigan yelled above the rattle of German machine guns, as the flare started to drop out of the sky to his right like a falling angel. Wolfers hit the starter button of the Crocodile and its huge motors burst into ear-shattering activity, thick clouds of blue smoke jetting from its exhaust. It seemed to act as a signal for the rest of the drivers. Engine after engine roared into life. The nervous replacements took a last leak into the ditch, their urine hissing and steaming in the cold, and clambered onto the half-tracks. In the jeeps the drivers stamped hard on the sandbags on the floor – extra protection against mines. All was controlled chaos, noise and activity. Corrigan took one last look at his little force, then cried above the racket; 'Wolfers – *ADVANCE!*'

Now spread out in two columns, with the great lumbering Crocodile in the lead, the Assault Troop rattled across the muddy fields, throwing up huge wakes of mud and grass. The race for the vital bridge had commenced.

Trouble started almost immediately. The first rocket from a *panzerfaust* hissed by them, trailing angry red sparks and only missing the Crocodile by feet. Sanders reacted immediately. He swung his Besa round and hit the trigger. White tracer sped towards the bushes from which the rocket had come. An elderly German came tumbling out, clutching his shattered stomach, and fell screaming to the ground.

'Hope that cured yer frigging stomach ache for yer!' Sanders yelled, as the German disappeared beneath a half-track, the whirling metal abruptly flushed a bright red.

Now slugs were pattering off the sides of the Crocodile like heavy tropical rain on a tin roof. Hawkins and Corrigan ducked inside the turret for shelter.

'That's fucking well torn it, sir!' the little Sergeant cursed. 'The buggers are everywhere!' He clicked off the safety catch on his Sten. 'Didn't bargain for this little lot.'

'Perhaps it's all to the good. It'll keep

those paras believing that their bridge is okay.'

'Ay,' Hawkins agreed grimly. 'I suppose yer right, sir. As long as those *pan–*'

'*Panzerfausts* don't get us!' Corrigan beat him to it. 'I know, Hawkins, I know – but don't bloody well go on about it!'

There seemed to be field-greys everywhere. The air was rent with cries, curses, commands and counter-commands. The Assault Troopers crouched behind their thin armour plating, firing to left and right, like pioneers in a wagon train attacking through hordes of Red Indians, cheering and cursing wildly, carried away by the heavy blood-lust of battle. But up front as the Crocodile got closer and closer to the iron-frame bridge, glimpsed every now and again through the smoke, Corrigan and Hawkins remained grim and silent. Every minute counted now. If the German paras spotted that the resistance to their front was breaking, they would blow up the bridge in an instant. Corrigan, his hands balled, his nails biting cruelly into the palms of his hands, willed them not to recognise the danger they were in.

The first German mortar shell hit the flying column in the very same moment that the men of the 'stomach battalion' threw in the towel and slipped back into the trees from which they had come. It howled down, right on top of the half-track to Corrigan's immediate rear. There was the great hollow boom of metal striking metal. The half-track rose several feet in the air, then plunged back to earth in a hail of shredded metal mixed with the flesh and gore of mutilated men. Suddenly the field looked like the yard of an abattoir, with steaming red offal piled on all sides.

Corrigan looked away, sickened. But more and more bombs were starting to rain down on the flying column, the air abruptly full of fist-sized chunks of gleaming silver metal.

'Oh my sweet Christ!' Hawkins moaned. 'My poor lads are being slaughtered!'

'*Shut your mouth!*' Corrigan bellowed harshly, lean jaw set and hard, a dangerous look in his light blue eyes. 'There's no time for that kind of twaddle now. Let's get this job over with.' He pressed the button of the head-set. 'Wolfers, give her all she's got. You, Sanders, prepare to flame!'

'But what you gonna do, sir?' Sanders gasped, instinctively knowing by the tone of Corrigan's voice that he was going to do something desperate.

'What am I going to do?' Corrigan echoed. He laughed madly. 'Why, what do you expect? I'm gonna crash through that bridge, that's all!'

FOUR

The white-glowing anti-tank shell came hurtling towards the Crocodile like a bat out of hell. *'LOOK OUT!'* Corrigan screamed as he saw the white blur zipping out of the black and grey smoke.

'SIR!' Wolfers shrieked, already snatching back the tiller bar.

The Crocodile lurched to the left in a sudden wild flurry of mud and gravel – but it was too late. The tank shuddered violently as if struck by a hurricane, groaning and creaking. They hung on grimly, nostrils already assailed by the acrid stench of molten metal. Then the engine went dead. In the sudden echoing silence, the awe-struck crew could hear the first greedy crackle of petrol flames.

'We've been hit in the rear bogie!' Sanders yelled in panic. 'We're burning! And there's all that frigging fuel–'

'BALE OUT, BELOW!' Corrigan cut in desperately. 'She'll blow in half a mo! *GO – GO – GO!'*

Wolfers needed no urging. With surprising speed and agility for such a big clumsy man, he abandoned the driving seat and wriggled towards the escape hatch below the tank, the searing heat already singeing the small hairs at the back of his head.

'Okay, Sanders,' Corrigan cried, 'We're leaving, too! Hawkins, give covering fire...'

But the little Sergeant had anticipated him, crouching in the turret with his Sten-gun at the ready. Veteran that he was, Hawkins knew that the machine-gunner attached to the anti-tank crew would be just waiting for the men of the stricken Crocodile to emerge from the turret, where they would present an ideal target. 'Ready, sir!' he barked.

'Okay, here we go!' Corrigan pulled the pin out of a smoke grenade with his teeth, mentally counted up to three, and then lobbed it as far forward as he could. It exploded with a sharp brittle plop between the Crocodile and the bridge. Thick white clouds of smoke immediately started to billow from it. He counted five more seconds, forcing himself to be deliberate, although the very metal of the turret was beginning to glow a dull scarlet with the heat. Any minute now the storage tank for the flame-thrower's fuel would explode and then they would be all covered with that terrible flesh-burning liquid. It was time to go. '*NOW!*' he shrieked.

Hawkins raised his hand and sprayed a wild burst to left and right.

There was an instantaneous response: the high-pitched, hysterical hiss of a Spandau. Tracer zipped frantically through the white fog. Slugs missed the turret by feet. But the smoke had effectively blinded the enemy gunner – for a while.

Corrigan waited no longer. He thrust Sanders forward. *'Out!'* he yelled.

The little Australian did a neat roll out of the turret, howled with pain as his back touched the red-hot metal, dropped over the side, and scurried to the cover of some bushes twenty yards away.

'Now you, Hawkins!'

'But sir – who'll give covering fire?'

Corrigan grabbed the little machine gun from Hawkins and fired a wild burst into the white gloom. 'Bugger off – *NOW!*'

So Hawkins did the same neat roll out of the turret, howled as Sanders had done when the searing metal burnt his back, and scurried for safety, slugs cleaving the white rolling cloud just above his head.

Now it was Corrigan's turn. He dropped the Sten, ripped off his black beret and pressed it to the turret. It immediately started to smoulder. *'Now!'* he commanded himself, swinging over the rim of the turret and dashing across the red-glowing deck of the dying Crocodile.

'Die hauen ab!... Ich kann sie jetzt sehen... Los, FEUER!' An angry German voice

issued a stream of commands as the smoke-screen began to drift away.

Corrigan's German was limited, but he had understood that word *'feuer'* well enough. Tucking his head between his shoulders, bending almost double, arms working like pistons, zig-zagging furiously, he ran for his life as tracer ripped the turf at his flying heels, encouraged by the wild yells and cries of the three soldiers already sheltering in the bushes.

But luck was on his side. A slug bounced harmlessly off his right-hand pouch – it was filled with hand grenades. One of them should have exploded, then the others, shredding his body. But it didn't. Instead, the slug saved his life. The impact knocked him to his knees, gasping for breath, in the very same instant that a vicious burst of fire ripped past his face. A moment later he was skidding to a stop in the bushes, his heart thudding crazily, the air whistling through his lungs like a pair of cracked leathern bellows. But he had done it.

'They're going through the water now!' Hawkins cried, cocking his head to one side.

'And they're boxing clever for once,' Sanders commented. 'Look, they're using their smoke dischargers.'

Weakly Corrigan nodded his agreement, still trying to regain his breath as he watched the Assault Troop's half-tracks floundering through the water, shielded from the German paras guarding the bridge by a thick screen of white smoke fired from their dischargers. Veterans and replacements, they were working like professionals, he thought, even though they were mostly commanded by junior NCOs, corporals and the like.

Then he forgot his men on the flank. It would be some time before they could seriously threaten the bridge. By then the Jerries might well have blown it. The time to act was now, while the German defenders didn't think themselves seriously threatened. He swallowed hard and finally stopped the painful stitch in his side.

'All right, lads,' he said. 'I know there are only four of us, but I think that's enough to do a mini-sized Remagen on this one.'*

'Remagen, sir!' Wolfers exclaimed. 'But they said in the *Daily Mirror* that the Jerries finally blew that one, *after* the Yanks were across–'

'Don't you bother to read the headlines, young Wolfers,' Hawkins scoffed. 'You keep yer eyes on Jane's tits and leave the intelligent bit to the officers.'

*Corrigan was referring to the famous capture of the bridge across the Rhine at Remagen, which had been taken by the Americans three weeks previously.

'She ain't shown her tits ever since she got into that ENSA strip, Sarge,' Wolfers retorted indignantly. 'In the last three bits I've read, she's only shown her step-ins once and her suspenders twice, and they weren't even black and frilly.'

'*Trooper Wolfers!*' Corrigan bellowed. 'Here we are in the middle of a bloody battlefield and all you've got in your mind is tits, knickers and garters. For Chrissake let's concentrate.'

Wolfers opened his mouth to protest but Hawkins shot him a warning look and he changed his mind.

'My guess,' Corrigan continued, 'is that they'll have a couple of explosive charges on both sides, near those buttresses. As soon as they scent danger, up she'll go. They'll blow her. *But*– he raised his finger – 'the bloke who'll make the decision and explode those charges will be on the *far* side of the river. That means–'

'If we can get to those charges before he spots us,' Sanders interrupted, 'we can knock 'em out – and he can do bugger all about it!'

'Exactly, you Aussie rogue,' Corrigan agreed with a brief smile. Over the water the smokescreen had started to drift away to reveal the half-tracks disappearing into the distance, obviously heading for the fir wood beyond; from there they would soon launch their flank attack on the bridge. They had only minutes left, Corrigan concluded.

'But they'll surely have somebody dug in on *this* side of the bridge?' Wolfers objected. His stomach was rumbling audibly, and he realised he hadn't eaten anything for well over an hour; the excitement and tension had been too much.

'That's a risk we've got to take,' Corrigan snapped. He ripped off his webbing pouches, opened them and gave each man two grenades. 'This is all we've got. They'll have to do. All right, no more blether. Let's get at it. Follow me at five-yard intervals.'

'You heard the officer,' Hawkins growled, keeping his voice low as if the paras on the bridge might hear him. *'Move it!'*

Corrigan had already started.

Now they could see every detail of the little bridge quite clearly, as they crawled ever closer to the machine-gun pit guarding the entrance to the structure. Pausing momentarily, his nerves tingling, Corrigan followed the course of the wires running the length of the bridge to a kind of concrete beehive on the far bank. (Later he would find out it was a one-man air-raid shelter used previously for the safety of the sentry guarding the bridge.) He frowned thoughtfully; that was where the engineer in charge of blowing the bridge would be posted. It was the ideal protected lookout spot. As soon as the machine-gun crew guarding the entrance to the bridge were endangered, the man in the box would detonate the charges. The obvious danger was alerting the machine-gun crew. But how were they going to sneak around them?

It was the big lumbering Yorkshireman who came up with the answer. 'Sir, I don't think we're gonna do much good against that Spandau with these here grenades and Trooper Sanders' revolver, like. They'd knock us off dead easy.'

'I agree, but what do you suggest, Wolfers?' Corrigan asked, automatically noting the scarlet stabs of flame to the rear of the German position, which indicated that the flanking attack was already meeting resistance.

'Them bushes, sir, at ten o'clock,' Wolfers answered eagerly. 'With a bit of luck, we could work our way over to them and then make a mad dash into the river and come up *underneath* the bridge, like.' He beamed at Corrigan winningly, pimply red face glowing.

'Of course!' Corrigan said excitedly. 'That's where the charges will be fixed anyway.'

'Hey, less of that mad dash stuff,' Sanders objected sourly. 'There's a good ten yards or more without cover. Those Jerry gunners could knock us off easy as pie, if they spot us between the bushes and the water. Now what do you say to that, Wolfers?'

Wolfers' face fell. 'I was just thinking like,' he said lamely.

'Yer – and you know what thought did! He *thought* he'd shat hisself and he *had!*'

'Hold it,' Corrigan interrupted. 'Wolfers' idea is all right. But you're right, too, Sanders. So we need a diversion for that mad dash – and you're it, Sanders.'

'*Me?*'

'Yes. You've got the revolver. Once we're in position, you open up and keep the machine-gunners occupied.'

The little Australian looked at Corrigan as if he suddenly had gone mad. 'Keep them frigging occupied with this ... this pissy little pea-shooter?' He stuttered incredulously. 'But ... you can't hit a shithouse door with this thing at five yards!'

Corrigan beamed at him. 'You'll have your nuisance value at least – as always. Now come on, Hawkins, you first, Wolfers next, and I'll bring up the rear.' He waited till the other two had broken cover and were crawling off to the left. Then he added: 'Good hunting, Sanders – hope you have a decent bag!' And with that he was gone after the others, leaving Sanders staring at the little service revolver in his hand in stunned disbelief.

'*NOW!*' Corrigan yelled. '*Fire like hell, Slim!*'

Like one of his native Australian jack-rabbits, Sanders popped his head out of cover and fired six quick shots in the direction of the sandbagged pit.

Someone howled with pain. Someone else cursed. An angry voice bellowed an order. Hastily Sanders ducked as the Spandau burst into frenetic life and a salvo of slugs ripped the length of his hide, showering him with broken twigs and earth.

Corrigan waited no longer. He doubled forward and dived straight into the river, gasping with shock as the icy water hit his body. Already numb with cold, he struck out for the cover of the bridge. Wolfers lumbered forward, preparing to dive after him. But he had been spotted. On the bridge a German wearing a camouflage cape and the rimless helmet of a *Fallschirmjager**** raised his rifle.

But Hawkins was quicker. 'Ye'll not croak one of my lads!' he yelled, furiously tugging the pin from one of his two grenades and tossing it through the air.

It exploded just beneath the para aiming his rifle. He went reeling back, both hands severed and dropping to the water below like abandoned white dress-gloves. Hawkins gasped with shock. Next instant he was pelting after the other two, tossing his helmet to

*Paratrooper.

one side as he made a shallow dive. He slammed into the river with such force that it seemed his stomach was being pushed sickeningly through his backbone.

The machine gun was chattering, but Sanders, rationing his ammunition, tried to keep it occupied and its crew's attention away from the three lone figures now swimming steadily for the nearest bridge support. Above them figures ran up and down the length of the structure like a bunch of startled ants, shouting to each other in confusion.

Corrigan was in the lead, striking out in a powerful breast stroke, using his last reserves of strength. He knew it would be only a matter of minutes now. They were preparing to blow. He forced his aching muscles to obey, ignoring the numbing cold, intent only on fighting the current that was tugging at his heavy serge uniform and boots, determined to reach the bridge and prevent the Germans blowing it.

And then there it was: the buttress, looming up in front of him, its base green and slippery with duckweed. But as he made a grab for it, the current swept him back. One of his fingernails ripped, and an excruciating pain shot up his arm. Stifling his yell of agony, he flung out his hand once more. This time his fingers found a better handhold. He managed to pull himself towards the buttress, then reached up and grasped a metal girder and swung himself out of the water. Choking for breath, numb to the bone with cold and dripping wet, at least he had made it: he had reached the bridge.

Two minutes later he had been joined by Wolfers and Hawkins. They clambered upwards among the girders, their ears filled with the clatter of heavy boots and rattle of gunfire above.

'Look, sir,' Hawkins hissed, looking more like an ancient wizened chimp than ever as he hung there among the dripping, glistening girders. 'Over there... *Primer wire!*'

Corrigan's eyes followed the little Sergeant's pointing finger eagerly. There was no mistaking the red wire leading up to a hole above their heads. It was the primer wire all right: the one that connected the explosive charges with the detonator. 'Come on,' he cried, 'let's get at it!'

The three of them leapt from girder to girder, not caring about the noise they made now, hoping that the water gurgling below might drown any sound they made, knowing that time was fast running out.

Corrigan grabbed hold of the double-stranded cable. 'Your jacknife, Wolfers!' he sobbed, chest heaving frantically with the strain.

The big trooper unhooked the clasp knife

from his belt and slapped it into Corrigan's hand. Above them, they could plainly hear the agitated voices and running feet.

'*Die sind unter der Brucke, Herr Hauptmann!*' someone was yelling. '*Wirklich, ich habe die gehort!*'

'*Sprengen!*' another voice cried urgently. '*Die Brucke sprengen!... Die Tommies sind da!*'

'They've spotted us – they're going to blow up the bridge!' Corrigan panted, desperately sawing at the cable.

'*Duck!*' Hawkins yelled.

A stick grenade came tumbling down at them, rattling from girder to girder. The three of them froze, heads tucked into their shoulders, squeezing their eyes shut like children trying vainly to blot out a nightmare. But the stick grenade clattered past them and dropped to the river, where it exploded with a muffled roar, throwing up a harmless fountain of water. Corrigan worked on...

A pair of heavy jackboots appeared. Hawkins didn't hesitate. He threw his second grenade. It hit the girder nearest to the boots and exploded in a scarlet ball of flame. Shrapnel pinged and whined. They caught a glimpse of a panic-stricken young face; then the German paratrooper, his right stump jetting bright red blood, was falling screaming to the river below.

Now, from the far end of the bridge where

the detonator chamber was, there came a series of angry blue sparks racing along the cable towards them, spitting and crackling, closer and closer.

'*They've done it!*' Hawkins cried, wizened face suddenly ashen with fear. 'They've blown the bugger!'

'Not yet they haven't,' Corrigan said grimly through gritted teeth, still sawing at the obstinate wire. 'Not yet...'

Wolfers threw up his hands as if expecting the bridge to explode in his face that very instant. Corrigan cursed, the sweat streaming down his forehead. The cable was heaving and twitching like a live thing now, as the sparks raced ever closer, like tiny blue demons intent on sending these bold mortals to perdition. On the bridge above them German boots were thundering to safety.

'*Los ... los, weg da!*' cried an urgent voice overhead. '*Wirsprengen!... Los, dalli... Weg... Wirsprengen!*'

The first strand snapped with an audible ping. The wild spluttering blue sparks were only five yards away now.

'Christ on a crutch!' Wolfers gasped. 'Not much time left, sir!' Shall we jump for it?' He turned to Hawkins, his eyes wild with fear. 'What d'yer say, Sarge – shall we?'

'*Shut your fuckin' mouth!*' Hawkins shrieked, while Corrigan continued to saw at the remaining wire, gasping for breath as if he were running a marathon race.

'Come on, you bastard ... *come on!*' he sobbed. The sparks were now only a yard away. 'For God's sake *COME ON!*' With the last of his strength, Corrigan pressed down with the knife.

Ping! The cable had snapped. The blue sparks ran harmlessly along the wire towards his hands, spluttered for an instant as if angry to be frustrated of their prey, and went out. He had done it. He had cut the cable. The vital bridge was safe. *The way for the breakout was free!*

BOOK TWO

WEREWOLF

ONE

General von Manteuffel's Third Panzer Division broke on the morning of April 1st, 1945. Just a few hours ago they had been an ordered, disciplined force, preparing routinely for another twenty-four hours of fighting retreat across the flat plains of Mecklenburg. They were low on petrol, food and ammunition, and the whole division was down to thirty-five 'runners' – tanks still capable of moving under their own power. But as the first pale light flushed the dawn sky to the east, the Third was still a fighting force to be reckoned with.

That had been at six o'clock. Within half an hour the whole might of Rokossovsky's Army had fallen upon them. Stormoviks came howling from the sky like steel hawks, hundreds of them, swamping the Third's forward positions with bombs. Minutes later the whole of Rokossovsky's artillery joined in. Using mortars, rockets, heavy guns, light guns, even anti-aircraft guns pressed into service in a ground role, the Russians flung a massive bombardment at the startled German tankers. With a hoarse exultant scream, flights of fiery rockets and shells ripped the still dawn sky apart in savage fury. The first angry sighs grew into a baleful howl. The noise mounted in intensity, elemental yet man-made. The whole horizon burned, a monstrous furnace belching flame and death. It was like some terrible Wagnerian cacophony.

The first line of the Third Panzer Division simply disappeared. Now the barrage moved to the Germans' second line. Great gaps appeared in their ranks as the shells exploded in their midst. A low hill began to burn. The Third's main petrol dump had been hit. Grey-clad bodies littered the fields, sprawling in ungainly heaps, their limbs thrown out in the extravagant fashion of those who have met a violent death. On and on, the terrible inhuman hammering continued as if it would never cease. Men went mad, tossing away their weapons, hands clasped to their ears, screaming senselessly, running about in the open until they too were caught by a slug or piece of shrapnel that sent them hurtling to the ground.

Then, as abruptly as it had started, the barrage ceased. Behind it, it left an echoing silence which reverberated back and forth from the amphitheatre of the low hills. But not for long. Suddenly the fur-capped soldiers rose from their hiding place in endless ranks, perfectly dressed, as if they were going on parade. Waving silver sabres, officers bellowed orders, breath fogging on the dawn air. Somewhere a brass band struck up one of those quick marches so beloved of the Red Army.

'*Slava Kransniya Armya!*' the General bellowed.

'*Long live the Red Army!*' came the response, roaring up from a thousand hoarse throats. '*Slava Kransniya Armya!*' And the flag-bearers swung their blood-red flags.

'*Urrah!*' the men cried. '*URRAH!*'

Horns blared. Drums thumped. Thousands of men surged forward, marching in closely packed ranks, the very ground trembling beneath that mighty tread of hobnailed boots.

It was too much for the German tankers. Here and there a lone machine-gunner fought to the last, cutting a swathe in the Russian ranks. But they still kept coming on, more and more of them, singing their bold marching songs and crying at regular intervals '*Urrah!... Urrah!*' in deep bass triumph, as if they knew that nothing could stop them now. The rest of the Germans broke. They abandoned their tanks and threw away their weapons, streaming back in disorganised panic. In vain their officers stood there with drawn pistols, trying to stop them. But the grey tide of fleeing, panic-stricken men simply swept them aside.

In their underground command bunkers, lit by hissing petroleum lamps, the German staff tried to stop the rot. Telephones jingled alarmingly. Staff officers, unshaven now and their faces pale and glazed with sweat, hurried back and forth. Runners raced outside to carry new orders to the hard-pressed companies. Clerks, their eyes wild and wide with fear, scribbled frantic requests for help on their pads. Harassed, tousled-hair radio operators tried over and over again to raise units that had long since been lost, vanished into the great retreat as if they had never even existed.

In the midst of all this feverish activity the General mopped his damp brow, monocle fallen from his eye and lying on his be-medalled chest, sobbing over and over again: 'My God, the whole front is disintegrating – *the whole front...*'

By eight o'clock that terrible April morning the General's own command post was under direct artillery fire. It swayed under the hammer blows of the heavy shells like a ship caught in a storm. The news got worse. Whole companies, even battalions, had thrown away their weapons and fled. By nine it was clear that the Third Panzer Division no longer existed. The staff officers gave up. As the earth trickled down like brown rain, as those terrible guns continued their pounding, they slumped in their chairs, eyes blank of any emotion, smoking cigarette after cigarette. A few sat dolefully with their heads in their hands. One sat at his table, fists clenched, fighting to restrain his rising hysteria. Another stared at the dancing naked light bulb, eyes ablaze, teeth bared wolfishly as if he were already mad. And the General kept sobbing aloud: *'The whole front is disintegrating... The whole front...'*

By nine thirty they could hear the hiss of approaching flame-throwers as the Russian infantry started to infiltrate their position. The first casualties – bloody broken men, their faces contorted with pain, eyes blank with shock – began to arrive. The very air stank of death. The bunker was rocking wildly, the dirt tumbling from the earth roof with every fresh shell. Now the radios went dead. They were cut off!

The sobbing General made his final decision. 'Gentlemen,' he announced, 'the Third Panzer Division no longer exists. I hereby release each and every one of you from any further duties. Thank you, gentlemen. Now would you please excuse me.'

He stalked into his private latrine, while his staff officers and radio operators, clerks and casualties, all stared after him in blank confusion. The hiss of the flame-throwers came ever closer.

One moment later there came a muffled

shot – from the direction of the latrine. The General's suicide seemed to act as a signal. Men fought and clawed their way out of the bunker, panic-stricken, screaming, throwing away their weapons. Some crouched in their chairs, crooning or moaning to themselves, or laughing dementedly. Others followed the example of their commander and shot themselves while there was still time.

And then they arrived: the men in earth-coloured blouses with little round-barrelled tommy guns in their hands, some of them not more than children, but highly dangerous children, grabbing the proud Knight's Crosses from the staff officers' throats, slashing through their belts to obtain the prized automatics, ripping off their gold-plated watches, and killing – killing without any compunction or mercy. The Red Army had broken through.

That long April Fool's Day, Colonel Piotr's rats from the concentration camps probed far and wide behind the lines of the shattered Third Panzer Division, raping, plundering, terrorising, as they sought to find the German stop-line, the next position of organised resistance, barring Rokossovsky's progress westwards to the sea.

Everywhere they caught the Fritzes, civilian and military, by surprise. They rampaged through a huge German supply dump.

The fat bespectacled Quartermaster had tried to defend his precious supplies single-handed, but they had riddled his belly with tommy-gun fire so that he now lay spread-eagled over a pile of salami sausages, soaking them with his own blood.

Now the Gulag rats went wild, looting the German stores, ransacking shelves, shooting padlocks off doors, crying out in delight at every new discovery, stuffing sausages, bread, jam and tinned fruit down their throats in sickening profusion, whooping and yelling all the time like drunken Red Indians looting a pioneer settlement.

Then they found the great fifty-litre carboys of *Wehrmacht* schnapps. It took two men to lift each heavy carboy protected by its wicker basket. They hoisted it shoulder-high and poured the fiery spirit down the throat of one of their comrades coughing and spluttering as the schnapps ran down his gullet. Then it was someone else's turn.

Soon there were whole mobs of them, singing drunkenly, swaying from side to side and staggering out into the streets. *'Frau, du schlafen!... Schlafen!'* they cried, breaking down the doors of the little peasant houses with their rifle butts, dragging out the German women, grannies and little girls, rutting with them on the wet cobbles, ears deaf to their screams of agony and pleas for mercy. There was to be no mercy this day for the hated Fritzes.

It was at the height of their drunken excesses that Colonel Piotr, riding on a looted German stallion, found his rats. Some of them had broken into a German military hospital. Outside in the courtyard lay a good dozen of his men, drunk to the world, sleeping heavily where they had fallen. Another four, naked save for jackboots and helmets, rifles tossed carelessly to one side, were assaulting a screaming German nurse; three of them were holding her naked writhing body while the fourth, as drunk as the rest, tried vainly to mount her.

With a cry of rage, Piotr spurred his horse forward. His whip flashed, the light reflecting from tiny steel wires embedded in the leather. His cruel lash stripped the flesh from their naked backs in crimson streaks and they fell back, howling with pain and rage. Piotr urged his mount onwards, digging his spurs hard into its sweating flanks and keeping a tight rein. It whinnied with pain as he forced it up the marble steps of the looted hospital. Just inside the entrance hall one of his rats lay slumped against a wall, drinking schnapps from his helmet. He seemed to recognise the Colonel, for he raised the helmet in a kind of drunken salute. Again Piotr's whip flashed. The drunk howled with agony, a bright red strip right across his face. He dropped the helmet, flooding the floor with schnapps, and tried to push himself upright as Piotr swung down from his mount and approached him.

'Corporal!' Piotr roared. 'Get outside *now* – if you value your life – and get those drunken pigs out there organised. *Davai!*' He raised his cruel whip once again.

The man was rapidly sobering up. He grabbed his helmet, a trickle of schnapps mingling with the blood on his face, and placed it on his head. 'Yes, Comrade Colonel ... at once, Comrade Colonel!' he muttered and stumbled outside.

Piotr slapped his whip against the side of his gleaming boot. His rabble was getting out of hand just when he needed them most. Only two kilometres away, von Manteuffel had organised a stop-line for the broken Third Division. Piotr knew of old what the cunning, undersized Fritz commander would do next: he would order an immediately counter-attack to stop the rot spreading. So Piotr's First Guards Punishment Battalion had to be in position, and soon, or they in their turn would be overrun. And he had no illusions about what the Fritzes would do to his men if their counter-attack were successful. They'd slaughter the lot of them.

He clattered up the marble staircase to the second floor, aiming a savage kick at a man who squatted there defecating, a bottle of schnapps in his hands. The man tumbled down the steps, breeches around his ankles, exhibiting his naked rump, but bottle still clutched in his hands. Turning into a corridor, Piotr found a dead German soldier, still in hospital pyjamas, sprawling in the centre of the corridor. He had been beaten to death with his own crutches. Next to him lay a dead nurse, skirt thrown up about her thighs, cotton knickers ripped down to her feet. Dark red blood still trickled down the inside of her legs. Piotr grunted. He had seen it all before and no doubt he would see it all again. Such things no longer moved him. All he was concerned with was getting his rats out of the hospital and supply depot and back into the line.

He flung open the nearest door and was suddenly blinded by an incandescent white light blazing from the twin emergency lanterns hanging from the ceiling. He blinked, eyes narrowed against the harsh glare. Then the room came into focus. In one corner there were five or six unconscious Fritzes stretched out on benches, their arms attached to the life-giving drip-drip of plasma, snoring with the heavy, rasping grate of men under deep sedation.

In the centre of the room, directly under the twin lanterns, a German surgeon was working at the operating table, assisted by two very nervous blonde nurses. Crowding round them was a group of Piotr's men, watching the surgeon's performance with every appearance of total fascination. There was complete silence in the room. Even as the Colonel approached, the men just stared down at the table. Not by a flicker of an eyelid did any of them reveal their awareness of his presence.

Piotr peered over their shoulders. The surgeon was slicing into an unconscious soldier's thigh with swift deft strokes. Bright red blood jetted from the wound. One of the nurses hastily reached for a swab and attempted to stem the bleeding, while the other selected a surgical saw from the tray of instruments and held it ready for the surgeon.

In spite of the urgency of the moment, Colonel Piotr found himself fascinated, too. He stood watching with the others as the surgeon accepted the saw into his gloved hand and began to cut through the bone. The saw made a sickening grating sound as it bit into the bone. Piotr gritted his teeth. He couldn't tear his eyes away...

Now the Fritz surgeon had almost finished. He lifted up the nearly severed leg, which was still attached by some bloody gristle, and completely detached it from the scarlet mess of the stump. He sighed and paused to mop his damp brow with the back of his hand. Then he was at work once more, sewing up the flap of skin he had left dangling below the gaping wound. A few moments later the job was done.

The spell was broken. Abruptly the surgeon became aware of his drunken, dangerous audience. He let the severed leg fall to the blood-stained floor and thrust up his mask. 'What ... what are you doing in my surgery?' he demanded, his voice a mixture of defiance and fear; but his Russian was good.

'*Your* surgery?' Piotr recognised the speaker as Katukov, one of the many murderers in his battalion. '*Our* surgery! We are the masters now, Fritz – aren't we, mates!'

There was a chorus of agreement from the others. The operation already forgotten, they were now eyeing the two blonde German nurses pressed back against the wall in terror, licking their lips as if they were hungry. But it wasn't food they wanted and the German surgeon knew it.

'Stop that!' he commanded, with the voice of a man who was accustomed to giving orders and having them obeyed. 'I am not going to have any of that kind of thing in my ... in *here*,' he corrected himself quickly. And he reached out his gloved hands as if he were going to stop the rape personally.

'Fine pair of hands you've got there, comrade doctor,' sneered Katukov, swinging his sabre up.

'*No!*' Piotr commanded.

Too late.

The blade came hissing down. The doctor stared in horror. Next moment he was howling and shrieking at the ceiling as the keen edge swept through flesh and bone as efficiently as one of his own surgical instruments. His hands dropped onto the table, rolled across the body of the unconscious soldier and fell to the floor.

Katukov threw back his head and roared with laughter till his eyes began to stream. 'Fine pair of hands you *had*, comrade doctor,' he choked, tears spilling down his evil face. 'Now I suppose *I* shall have to play the surgeon! *Boshe moi*,' he gasped, 'what fun!... Now, girlies, let's be having those clothes off you...'

But Katukov was not fated to enjoy the favours of any more 'girlies'. In the very same instant that Piotr reached forward to grab the murderer by his dirty collar and shake the life out of him, the first German shell slammed into the wall opposite. It came tumbling down in a thunderous roar of metal and brick and dust.

Katukov's head had disappeared. For one long moment he stood there swaying, blood spurting from his neck, while his head lay at his feet, staring upwards as if mocking the body to which it had once belonged. Then he crumpled and fell to the littered floor.

'*Out ... out!*' Piotr bellowed. '*It's the Fritzes – the counter-attack!*'

At last his men awoke to the danger. They streamed out of the room, stopping on the way to collect their weapons, and clattered down the stairs just as another German shell burst against the wall and sent more debris flying across the room.

For one moment Colonel Piotr paused, taking in the ghastly scene: the dying surgeon, the headless body on the floor, the unconscious man on the operating table, the hysterical screaming nurses cowering to-gether in a corner. It seemed to him that his whole past life had been made up of just such terrible tableaux. He had never known anything else but butchery and horror. Then, with a trace of his old crazy gallows humour, he blew a kiss at the sobbing nurses.

'Goodbye!' he cried. 'Goodbye, ladies! Your honour has been saved for another day!' And with that he pelted after his men, ears already full of the snap-and-crackle of the small-arms battle below.

The race for the Baltic had been inter-rupted yet again.

TWO

Beret at the back of his head, battledress blouse ripped open, rifle over one shoulder and sackful of tins over the other, Slim Sanders barged into the queue of eager, excited American infantrymen outside the big German villa, followed by a reluctant Wolfers nervously munching a corned beef sandwich.

'No naked light within twenty yards, mates!' Sanders yelled at them, grinning. 'I'm up to the gills in frigging rum. We'll all go up in flames! Ha, ha...'

'Shit in yer hat, Limey!' cried a burly American, carrying a light machine gun over his shoulder and a carton of cigarettes lodged under his arm. 'Ya wait in line like the rest of the guys! We all want get our rocks off, ya know.'

'I ain't no Limey,' Sanders said happily. 'I'm an Aussie. Now *piss off!*' He let the heavy brass-bound butt of his rifle drop on the unsuspecting American's toe; then, as he opened his mouth to screech with pain, Sanders slammed his elbow into his stomach and he flew into the gutter, dropping both machine gun and cigarettes. Above him, there was a cackle of laughter from two German whores leaning out of the window, taking a breather, and the other GIs joined in.

'Good for you, Limey!' one of them yelled.

Sanders leered up at the whores. 'You'll be laughing on the other side of your face, frauleins, when you see what I've been saving up for you since we crossed the Rhine!' He grabbed the front of his khaki trousers, rolled his eyes, and moaned dramatically. 'A real blue veiner. You could cut diamonds with this one!'

The whores hadn't understood a word, but the little soldier's meaning was clear enough. They cackled even more and one of them pretended to hide her gaze, as if she were some modest, virginal country lass shocked by such things.

Now the two troopers pushed their way into the house, discreetly set back in the unbombed suburbs, away from the prying eyes of the British and American MPs who were roaming everywhere in newly captured Munster on the watch for soldiers infringing the new Non-Fraternisation Ban imposed by Eisenhower.

Wolfers drew yet another corned beef sandwich out of his pack and started munching it. 'Do you think it's safe, Slim? I mean, if the Redcaps nab us they could sling us in the glasshouse, like.'

'Stop bellyaching,' Sanders said easily, eyes

fixed on the door to the brothel; at that moment it seemed to him like the gate to Heaven itself. 'They'll never find us. Besides, they'll never put *us* in the glasshouse! They want our bodies still for the fighting, never you fear, Wolfers... Oh my bloody Christ!' His voice suddenly took on a note of rapture. 'Will yer get a butcher's of that one!'

A huge blonde, naked save for a pair of red silk panties and high-heeled shoes, was pushing her way through the crowded interior, smoking an American cigarette between bites at a Hershey bar, breasts like two over-ripe melons bouncing up and down delightfully with each step.

Wolfers swallowed his sandwich in one gulp, eyes bulging out of his pimply face.

Sanders gave a piercing wolf-whistle. 'I could put my poor old head between them udders, Wolfers, and not hear a thing for a month of Sundays! Holy cow, they breed 'em in Germany!'

The two lone British Army troopers, among the crowd of American paratroopers from the 17th US Airborne Division, could see the place was doing boom business. Fat middle-aged *hausfraus* dressed as maids were hurrying back and forth, carrying bottles of wine and boxes of contraceptives. Flushed whores in various stages of undress were moving up and down the stairs with their excited or satisfied clients. Somewhere above, rusty bed springs were squeaking frantically and an excited Mid-Western voice was crying over and over again, *'High-ho, Silver!'*

It was almost their turn. The two of them fumbled with their tins as they came ever closer to the madame; another fat, middle-aged *hausfrau,* with dyed blonde hair wrapped in a plait around her head, she sat behind a desk at the bottom of the stairs surrounded by piles of cans, tins of coffee, mounds of cigarettes, even a pair of men's boots.

'What you have?' she asked in hard clipped English. 'What you have for girl?'

Sanders leered at her, grabbing the front of his trousers again. 'Can't yer see, missus?' he chortled.

Madame was not amused. 'No piggery!' she snapped. 'What have you to pay?'

Wolfers nudged Sanders. 'Go on, Slim, no messing. Give her the stuff and let's get on with it.'

Sanders unslung his pack. 'I've got a tin of M & V,★ a tin of bully, a tin of compo tea, two bars of chocolate, a fifty tin of Capstan fags – *and a gross of french letters!'* He up-turned the sack and poured out its contents,

★Rations were called 'compo rations'. They included 'M & V' which was a can of meat and vegetables.

108

grinning hugely.

Madame nodded her approval. '*Gut.* You take that one.' She indicated a plump blonde clad in black underwear with a bandage soaked in vinegar around her head.

'That one?' Sanders exclaimed indignantly. 'Why, she's shop-soiled! Here, missus...' He dug into his pocket and brought out a handful of small cans of margarine. 'That lot's best Kiwi butter. Gimme two fresh ones.' He held up two fingers. '*Versteh!* Two ... *deux* ... *zwei!*'

Madame eyed the 'butter' for a moment, then nodded. '*Gut,*' she said again, and, clapping her hand around her mouth, called upstairs. '*Gerda und Heidi, der Kunde braucht zwei!*'

There was a whistle of envious approval from the assembled Americans. 'You'll be sorry, brother,' one of them called. 'Two Veronika Dankeschoen,' another cried. 'VD for short!... Brother, are you a glutton for punishment, man!'

Sanders smirked at the Americans and gave a little bow. 'Gentlemen, let it be known, in all modesty, that whores have been known to give *me* money!' And with that he was gone, racing up the stairs two at a time, rifle bobbing up and down on his back, followed by Wolfers and the cheers and hoots of the waiting Americans.

A mile away at the outskirts of the newly captured German city, Corrigan and Sergeant Hawkins sat idly outside the farmhouse that was now the Assault Troop's home, enjoying the warm spring sunshine and watching the steady stream of American and British armour rolling north. The line was endless. Ever since dawn there had been the rumble of heavy tanks, packed tail to tail, heading for the front – wherever that might be now – taking no protection whatsoever against enemy air attack.

Hawkins took his cold pipe from his mouth. As always he was saving his tobacco to send home to the 'missus', so that she could sell it on the black market for extra food. 'Look at them tanks, sir,' he breathed. 'Does yer good just to see 'em. By Christ, sir, if we'd only had all that equipment back in '39, we could have wiped the floor with old Jerry!'

'But we didn't, Hawkins,' Corrigan remarked, not taking his eyes off the massive Churchill tanks of some Hussar regiment now rolling by, their decks piled with infantry, their aerials whipping the sky like lashes of silver. 'The politicians saw to that before the war. It'll probably be the same the next time.'

Hawkins glanced at Corrigan's face, with its bitter disappointed mouth and corrugated frown. *Next time?* he echoed. 'Don't say that, sir!'

Corrigan shrugged carelessly. 'People never learn. We've about finished off old Jerry, as you call him. Next it'll be the Russians or someone else. They say that wherever there's a vacuum something moves in to fill it. Central Europe is a vacuum, now the Germans have about bought it. Who'll fill that vacuum? With the Americans moving back home, it'll be the Russians, no doubt.'

'What about us, sir?' Hawkins protested. 'In all my years in the Kate Karney★ I've never seen a bigger or better equipped British Army than the BLA.★★ We could do it with one hand tied behind our backs.'

Corrigan shook his head. 'I don't think so,' he said. 'Now the war's nearly over, the parlour pinks and liberals will be playing their silly political games again. Mark my words, Hawkins: within the decade they'll have thrown the Empire away, cleared us out of Europe and turned us into little England, an insignificant island off the coast of Europe. Then the Russians and Americans will be top dogs.'

Hawkins whistled through his ill-fitting Army teeth. 'Ain't fair, sir, if it turns out like you say it will. I mean, all the lads who've

★Kate Karney: slang for Army.
★★BLA: British Liberation Army (official title of the British Army in Europe).

bought it over here since the Invasion... Think of our Iron Division alone. I bet that in the rifle companies there's been a hundred per cent turnover due to casualties. Think of the Assault Troop – there's only you, me, Slim Sanders and young Wolfers left of the old gang who set off on June 6th, 1944. All the rest have gone for a burton, long ago.'

Corrigan nodded sombrely. 'All in vain, all in vain...'

'You don't sound too happy with yourself, sir, if I may say so,' Hawkins commented.

'You may – and I am not.' Corrigan indicated a cheerful group of drunken paratroopers, heads shaven save for a single central tuft like Mohicans, who were trotting past in a looted German horse-drawn carriage, one of them twirling an umbrella and wearing an old-fashioned top hat which he kept taking off and waving as if he were a nineteenth-century swell. 'Look at the Yanks,' Corrigan went on. 'They're swanning around all over the place, bashing down into Saxony and Bavaria, while the Russians are aiming at Berlin. As for us, what the hell are we supposed to be doing here in Westphalia? I can't see any sense in it. We should be aiming at Berlin.'

Hawkins nodded. 'I always fancied meself marching into Berlin with the bands playing, rifles at the slope and the old Union

Jack waving at the head of the column.' His wizened old face broke into a sad smile. 'They told us in the old war that we'd march into Berlin and hang old Kaiser Bill, but we didn't. And then what happened? This little lot came along. Now they're gonna get away with it again, I suppose.' He sucked at his pipe a little angrily.

Corrigan gave him a sideways look, noting automatically that it was about time Hawkins dyed his hair again – what little there was left of it. The 'grey lads', as he called them, were showing through pretty badly. But then, cold tea was never the most effective dye.

For a while they sat in silence, still watching the flood of armour and infantrymen moving north towards the fluttering pink of the horizon. That was the front. It was so far away now that Corrigan had to turn his head to the wind and strain his ears to catch a faint rumble of the permanent barrage.

'Wonder if the old Iron Division'll ever catch up with it again?' Hawkins asked idly, putting into words Corrigan's own thoughts at the moment.

'You mean go back into the line?' Corrigan shook his head. 'Doubt it somehow. It's the armoured boys who're doing all the running now. The Jerries are retreating too fast for any infantry division to catch up with them. Look at the Sixth Airborne.

They've been sitting on their bottoms doing nothing but get drunk and fret for days now, while their general cries out for action. No, I think the Iron Div, the Sixth, and naturally the good old Assault Troop have seen their last action.'

'Garrison duties, sir?' Hawkins said. 'So it's all over. This is the end of the road for the Assault Troop, eh?'

'Yes – the end of the road, Hawkins,' Corrigan echoed sadly. 'It's all over...'

But for once Captain Corrigan was wrong. There was still fighting to come – and plenty of it – for the Iron Division's Assault Troop.

Slim Sanders was lazily guzzling weak wartime German beer while the two half-naked whores bent over his lower body, delightfully trying to rouse his flagging potency yet once more, when the crunch of heavy steelshod boots in the corridor and sudden shrieks and cries of alarm disturbed his pleasure. The blonde one raised her head – but he pressed her down again.

'Nothing to worry about,' he said. 'When Slim Sanders is happy everybody is happy.'

Next door a woman screamed and a harsh north country voice yelled angrily, 'Get off me frigging back ... I was just about to frigging come!'

'Yer,' a tough official voice sneered. 'You're frigging *coming*, all right. Back with us to the frigging lock-up. Now, get yer duds on – at the double!'

'Sod it – the Redcaps!' Sanders was alert to his danger at once. 'Hey, missus, get yer teeth out of my dong. I'm in trouble!' He slung the beer bottle in a corner, pushed the two whores aside and slammed his foot against the opposite wall connecting with Wolfers' room. 'Hey, you big git, get off the job! *The rozzers is here!*'

Sanders flung himself into his clothes – not forgetting, however, to palm the fifty tin of cigarettes he had promised the two whores 'for a little something special'. He'd had his 'something special'. *Fuck 'em!*

He was tugging on his boots when the door flew open. Two hard-faced Redcaps, hands on their white-blancoed pistol holsters, stood in the doorway, their peaked caps almost touching the top of the frame they were so tall. Both were sergeants, wearing the sand-coloured ribbon of the Africa Star. They'd been around, Sanders realised. It would be no use trying to sweet-talk them.

'All right,' the older one snapped. 'Yer've had yer fun. Get them boots fastened up. And let's see yer paybook.'

'Yes, Sergeant,' Sanders answered tamely, eyes fixed on his bootlaces, hiding an expression of sudden resolve and deter-mination. He finished lacing them up, then flashed his hand to his battledress pocket as if he were going to bring out his paybook for examination. The brass knuckles he always carried for such emergencies appeared on his hand as if by magic.

'Hey, what the hell–'

The older sergeant's cry ended in a yelp of pain as the cruel knuckle-duster slammed against his blue-black chin and sent him reeling out into the corridor.

The other sergeant grabbed for his pistol. The blonde whore, carried away by excitement, sprang forward, her naked breasts quivering, and thrust her knee right up into the soldier's crotch. He staggered back, hands holding his burning genitals.

'The bitch kneed me!' he moaned in agonised surprise. 'The Jerry bitch kneed me...'

Sanders burst out of the room and into the corridor. He flung himself through the door to Wolfers' room, ignoring the naked whore lying on the rumpled bed, smoking a cigarette and staring blankly at the ceiling, as if completely bored by the whole business.

'Come on,' Sanders yelled, grabbing hold of a bewildered Wolfers and shoving his rifle at him. 'It's the bulls! Don't just stand there looking bloody useless, like a dildo in a convent. Can't you hear the buggers? They're right down the corridor – millions of the muckers!'

'What we gonna do, Slim?' gasped the big Yorkshireman, buckling on his belt and taking his rifle.

'Run! Run like hell!'

Sanders flung open the window. Down to the right, a group of sheepish Americans, some of them still trying to drag up their pants, were being herded into waiting trucks. The white-helmeted American MPs were lashing out with their clubs to make them get a move on. 'Haul ass, you guys!' they cried. 'Haul ass, willya!' Beyond them were the British Redcaps, some of them carrying Sten machine pistols as if expecting trouble. But to the left, Sanders saw, there was a narrow alley, which had been bulldozed through the ruins – and it was empty.

'Quick, Wolfers – out you go! *Move it!* They'll nab us in half a–'

'*Open this bloody door!*' a harsh voice cut in, 'or we'll bloody well knock, it down! Come on now... Let's be having yer!'

On the bed the naked whore raised her body slightly and farted contemptuously in the direction of the voices.

Sanders grinned cheekily. 'That's the stuff, fraulein! Damn well fart on the buggers!' And then he was clambering out of the window after Wolfers and dropping to the bomb-pitted road below.

THREE

The Major slapped his little swagger stick down on the table in front of Corrigan, eyes ablaze with anger.

'I have had just about enough of you frontline wallahs!' he shouted. 'Just because they have a bit of shit flung at them every now and again by the Hun, they think they have a right to do whatever they please. Well, I can tell you this, Captain ... er ... Corrigan. *They are not above the law!*'

Corrigan stared coldly at the fat little officer with a plum-coloured face and then at the line of MP jeeps outside, filled with heavily armed Redcaps. 'Major – er–'

'Jenkins!'

'Yes... Well, Major Jenkins, why am I the recipient of this lecture?' Corrigan asked, apparently bewildered, though by now he had guessed why this company of MPs had suddenly descended on the Assault Troop's farmhouse base this afternoon. His men had been sneaking back into the barns all afternoon, most of them drunk, and all of them wearing the smug smile of conquest which indicated that they had been success-fully 'fratting'. And Sergeant Hawkins had reported, only minutes before the MPs' arrival, that Slim Sanders and Trooper Wolfers were missing. There had been trouble in Munster, probably with women, and undoubtedly his Assault Troop were involved in it. Now Corrigan waited for the explosion to come.

'Why? *Why?*' Major Jenkins spluttered, hitting the table again with his swagger stick and making the mess tins rattle. 'I'll tell you why, sir! Because we found *this* in the brothel where two of my noncommissioned officers were assaulted.' He opened his gloved hand to display a barbed-arrow badge resting there. 'This is the regimental badge of the Assault Troop, is it not?'

'Of course it is,' Corrigan answered, trying now to control his own rising temper. He had met many Major Jenkinses in the last five and a half years. Fat, pompous base-wallahs who had never heard a shot fired in action and never would. 'But remember, Major, the Reconnaissance Corps is very large. There are at least five regiments of the Reconnaissance Corps in North-West Europe at this moment. So I repeat: why my Assault Troop – *sir*,' he added through suddenly clenched teeth, his lean jaw hardening ominously.

With the air of a conjuror about to produce a rabbit out of a top hat, Major Jenkins stalked to the farmhouse door and flung it open. 'Bring them in, Sergeant-Major,' he barked. 'Bring the rogues in here!'

'Sir!' A big sergeant-major out in the courtyard slapped his hand hard against the canvas of the nearest truck. 'All right, you two – out! At the double now!'

Behind Corrigan, a worried Hawkins stifled a groan. Trooper Wolfers had just come into sight, his tunic torn and sporting a beautiful black eye, handcuffed to two MPs, both of them looking the worse for wear. And he was followed by Sanders, similarly chained to two Redcaps, his head heavily bandaged, but a cocky grin on his face all the same.

Major Jenkins tapped his cane impatiently on the table as the sorry little procession hobbled into the farmhouse watched by the rest of the Assault Troop outside, too awed by the presence of so many military police-men even to cat-call.

Corrigan tugged the end of his nose. He supposed that this was going to be his future until they finally kicked him out of the Army: dealing with the meaningless, petty crimes of the peacetime Regular Army. Sentencing men to punishment in military prisons for having their bootlaces the wrong way round; for not having the regular number of studs in their boots; for failing to call a lance-corporal 'sir' – the whole absurd routine of the British Army at peace.

'Halt!' the sergeant-major barked. 'Prisoners – hats off!'

Awkward with their manacled hands, Wolfers, looking very worried, and Sanders, still trying to appear defiant, pulled off their caps. The sergeant-major threw Major Jenkins a tremendous salute. 'Prisoners all present and correct, *sir!*' he yelled, as if he were back at the depot at Aldershot.

'Thank you, sergeant-major,' Jenkins snapped back, acknowledging the salute with his brown-gloved hand.

Inwardly Corrigan groaned. The base-wallahs were taking over again.

Jenkins looked at the two prisoners contemptuously. Suddenly he lashed out with his cane. Sanders ducked, as if expecting a blow. Wolfers stood white-faced as the Major's cane picked at the open flap of his battledress blouse, then poked into its open neck, then prodded at his loose belt.

'Look at it!' Jenkins snapped, face almost puce-coloured with rage now. 'Absolute shit order! Tunic undone, pockets, belt – the whole lot!' He swung round on Corrigan. 'I don't know who it was – I think Napoleon – who said there are no bad soldiers, only bad officers. And it's damned true. I have been looking into your record, Corrigan. You have committed one crime after another since the outbreak of war. Striking a superior officer, stealing government property, acting in

121

a way that amounts virtually to mutiny...'

As Jenkins reeled off his past crimes, which had ensured that while most of his Sandhurst contemporaries were colonels, Corrigan himself had remained a humble captain, he tapped his gloved hand with that absurd cane of his. Somehow it made Corrigan's blood boil; his face started to flush. Next to him Hawkins tensed, recognising the signs. Any minute now, Corrigan was going to explode.

'God knows how you managed to escape being cashiered years ago,' Jenkins rumbled on. 'You have certainly deserved it. No matter. What concerns me today is the riotous behaviour of your men. If you feel you can't handle–'

'Have you ever killed a German?' Corrigan interrupted suddenly, his voice icy.

Jenkins almost dropped his cane with surprise. 'What ... what did you say?' he stuttered.

Corrigan quietly repeated his question.

'What in God's name has that got to do with this business? I think you are being insubordinate and impertinent, Corrigan.'

'Well ... did you?' Corrigan persisted, his voice still controlled and icy, though a vein was now throbbing at his temple. He knew he was on the point of losing his temper altogether. But what did it matter? His career was ruined anyway.

Major Jenkins licked his lips, nervously watching the big man's face. 'I must warn you, Corrigan, that you are being insubordinate to a superior off–'

His words ended in a surprised yelp of pain. Corrigan had punched him straight in the mouth. He went reeling backwards against the MP sergeant-major's bulk, while Hawkins grabbed Corrigan's right arm, anxious to prevent a further attack.

The sergeant-major picked up the Major's dress cap, which had tumbled to the ground, dusted it and handed it back to Jenkins, face impassive, though there was a malicious sparkle in his eyes as if he were enjoying the scene. 'Your cap, sir!' he snapped.

Jenkins made a show of putting it on, dead straight across his forehead, not knowing that a thin trickle of blood was escaping from the side of his mouth and that his lip was already beginning to swell. 'So, Corrigan,' he said ponderously, 'now you really have blotted your copybook – for good! Striking a superior officer in front of witnesses.' He tried to grin, but didn't quite succeed. 'There will be no getting out of this one I can assure you. I am afraid – for you – that all your powerful friends at court have vanished. They'll sling you out on your ear for this one. Without a pension,' he added, as if that was the most important point.

'Fuck the pension,' Corrigan said tonelessly, his eyes fixed on some spot behind the fat Major's right shoulder, known only to himself.

'There's no need to be obscene as well, Corrigan,' Major Jenkins said, obviously savouring the situation now. 'You are in trouble enough already... And have the common decency to look at me when I speak to you! I presume that you were brought up as a gentleman at least.' He suddenly frowned. 'What the devil are you looking at?' he demanded.

Behind him, his men were already beginning to stiffen to attention. For there was no mistaking that camouflaged pre-war Rolls Royce with a Union Jack fluttering proudly at its bonnet, adorned with the five stars of a field marshal.

Jenkins sensed something was happening to his rear. His frown deepening, he turned to look out of the window – and gasped aloud, his mouth falling open stupidly as he recognised the car. A familiar figure in a battered old duffle-coat was standing upright in the back, casually saluting the rigid military policemen.

'Oh, my God!' he whispered huskily. 'It's *Monty!*'

Miserably Major Jenkins swung Field Marshal Montgomery one of his depot salutes.

All the ebullience had drained from him. He had tried more than once to tell the Great Man about the heinous crimes that Corrigan and his men had committed. But each time he had been overruled. In the end he had submitted tamely as Montgomery laid down the law, telling him that all charges against Corrigan and the two troopers had to be dismissed at once. They were needed for a 'highly secret mission of great national importance'. Jenkins did not believe one word of it. What use would they be, this bunch of insubordinate sloppy civilians masquerading as soldiers? But Montgomery was Montgomery. So, thoroughly deflated and not a little nervous about his own future in the British Army, Jenkins had been forced to accept the Field Marshal's decision, irregular as it was. In the British Army one simply didn't erase crimes from a man's crime sheet. But then Montgomery had always been a law unto himself.

Casually Montgomery acknowledged Jenkins's salute, then flung out one skinny hand like a man wanting to rid himself of the unwelcome attentions of some domestic animal.

Jenkins turned to his MPs. 'Mount up!' he cried, but there was no real fervour in his tone. He started to march back to his jeep. As he passed Slim Sanders, holding his hand to his bandaged head, the little Australian

125

whispered out of the side of his mouth so that only the two of them could hear his words: 'See what it got yer, old piss-and-vinegar? Nobody pushes the old Assault Troop around as long as we've got Captain Corrigan.' He leered at the red-faced Major. 'Now yer on Field Marshal Montgomery's own personal shit-list. There'll be no promotion on this side of the ocean for you, cobber.'

Jenkins stopped, gasping and spluttering like a stranded fish, but already Montgomery had turned and was walking Corrigan back to his waiting car, deep in animated conversation. There was no help to be had from that quarter. Angrily he kicked a stone out of his path and strode on. Behind him Slim Sanders began to sing a taunting song.

'Where was the engine driver when the boiler bust?... They found his ballocks – and the same to you! Ballocks...!'

Thus the frustrated MPs drove away to that mocking chorus, as the men of the Assault Troop joined in heartily. *'BALLOCKS!... AND THE SAME TO YOU!... BALLOCKS!... BALLOCKS!'*

Above the happy young men, enjoying these few minutes of triumph in their battle with the hated Redcaps, the sun was beginning to disappear as dark threatening clouds started to roll in from the east.

Standing there listening, half-amused and half-anxious, Sergeant Hawkins glanced up at the sky and shivered. Like a copper coin glimpsed through the green scum at the bottom of a pond, the sun had just vanished behind the bank of clouds. A storm was brewing. But not only in Nature. Whenever Monty made an appearance there was trouble in store for the Assault Troop. Hawkins gazed round at the cheerful young faces of his troopers, then glanced at Corrigan's back as he stooped slightly to hear the little Field Marshal's words. He shook his head. 'No good'll come of it,' he muttered to himself. 'No good at all. We've got another mission...'

Slowly the first hesitant drops of rain began to fall.

FOUR

'*Kaugummi,* you got chewing gum?...
Cigarette for papa?'

The little foreign voice startled Hawkins.
He had been sheltering with Sanders and
Wolfers in the lee of the dripping, over-
hanging thatched roof. All three men swung
round to look.

A small boy was standing there, wrapped
in a soldier's camouflage gas cape which
came down to his ankles, looking up at them
winningly, hand stretched out for whatever
they might have to offer him. He repeated
his chant, the same one they heard from all
the German kids they had met since crossing the Rhine: 'Chewing ... gum ... choco-
lates ... cigarettes for papa?' It was always
the same, as if someone had hurriedly
instructed them how to say the litany in the
new language of the conquerors.

'I'll give yer a cigarette for yer sister, kid!'
Sanders sneered, and made an explicit,
obscene gesture with his thumb and forefinger, '*Ficki-ficki, schwester* fer cigarettes!'
He laughed maliciously at his own humour.

'Give it a rest,' Wolfers said at his side.

'Stop it, Sanders,' Hawkins snapped. 'It's

128

only a little 'un. I don't like that kind of muck with little kids. Here, sonny...' He reached into the pocket of his greatcoat and brought out a handful of compo ration acid-drops. 'Some *bonbons* for you.'

The little boy gave him a huge smile, the whole of his innocent face lighting up. '*Danke, Herr Feldwebel, vielen herzlichen Dank,*' he said warmly and pocketed the sweets hastily.

'How about that?' Hawkins exclaimed, beaming too. 'That kid even knew my rank! Isn't that something?'

'Well, yer bleeding stripes are big enough! Even a Jerry kid knows that three stripes make a sergeant,' Sanders sneered.

But neither Wolfers nor Hawkins was listening to him. Both men were still gazing down at the boy, raindrops glistening in his blond thatch. He pointed a skinny hand at Montgomery's Rolls and said, 'And that is car of *Feldmarschall? Ja?*'

'Field Marshal,' Hawkins prompted. 'Yes, that's right, son, that's Field Marshal Montgomery's car. By gum, you are a smart little bugger! Hey, look what I've got for you here – a bar of real chocolate!' He held it up for the little German boy to see.

'Stop it, Sarge,' Sanders protested. 'You're ruining the black market, you know, frigging well giving the stuff away like that!'

'*Schokolade!*' the boy breathed, as if he

129

could not believe his own eyes. Suddenly and surprisingly, he took Hawkins's hand and kissed it tenderly.

The old NCO blushed furiously and gave the boy the blue-paper bar of ration chocolate. 'Now off you go, son,' he said. 'Back home to your mother. Nobody should be out in this kind of weather. Off you go...'

'*Vielen Dank, Herr Feldwebel!*' the boy cried once more and then he was off, skipping happily through the puddles, heedless of the pouring rain, watched by a doting Hawkins and a cynical Sanders – and, from two hundred yards away, by another pair of bright blue eyes, carefully assessing the set-up in the little rain-drenched farmyard through a powerful pair of *Wehrmacht* binoculars...

Montgomery took his time. This wet April day, he was unusually hesitant and circumspect. The two of them were sitting on folding Army-issue wooden chairs in what had once been the best room of the little farmhouse, its walls decorated with yellowing photographs of bearded nineteenth-century worthies and plump housewives dressed in black. In one corner stood a battered old clock, ticking away the minutes of their life with grave metallic inexorability.

'You see, Corrigan,' the little Field Marshal emphasised again, while the rain continued to pour down outside, lashing against the windows, 'I am faced with a very complicated military and political situation – one that our American ... *friends* simply do not understand, I'm afraid.' His gaunt face wrinkled up at the thought and he tugged the side of his beaky nose as if he were angry.

'I see, sir,' Corrigan said politely, though he did not see at all.

'At the moment, for want of more troops to carry my attack forward, the Army is coming to halt on a line below Hamburg and Bremen and right up to the Elbe. It looks as if the Boche are going to defend that particular line, too, which won't help things. So if I am going to see the Hun off there I shall need all my strength. That's the military side of it, Corrigan.' Montgomery frowned again. 'But that is not my major problem. One way or another we'll soon knock the Hun for six. His innings is virtually over. No, my major problem is the Russians.' Abruptly he turned his piercing blues eyes on Corrigan as though searching for something in the younger man's face.

Corrigan tensed. So that was it. Monty wanted the Assault Troop for one of those unorthodox missions of his, which probably wouldn't meet with official approval in Whitehall and which could have a decidedly lethal outcome for him and his men if things went wrong. He leant forward expectantly. Outside the rain was still gusting against the windows, streaming down like tears.

'Eisenhower in his wisdom,' Montgomery continued, and there was no mistaking the bitter note in his voice now, 'has decided that the Allied Armies will not march on Berlin. We are to stop on the other side of the River Elbe until the Russians link up with us. No one, however, has told the Russians where *they* are to stop! So what will they do?' Montgomery poked a bony finger at Corrigan. 'I shall tell you. They will keep charging on, right into Schleswig-Holstein and into Denmark itself – while I, thanks to Eisenhower taking the Ninth US Army away from me, am marking time on the Elbe. The result?' The little Field Marshal shrugged eloquently. 'The Baltic will then be in Soviet hands, with disastrous political and military consequences for the post-war world. That I cannot allow to happen. Do I make myself clear?'

'Yessir,' Corrigan answered a little help-lessly. For the life of him he could not visualise how anyone could stop the might of the victorious Red Army.

'So, this is what I am going to do.' Montgomery's voice rose; suddenly he was his usual chirpy self again. 'While I prepare an assault crossing on the Rhine and an attack on Bremen-Hamburg – can't play a good game of cricket on a sticky wicket, you know, Corrigan! Got to have the team assembled, pads and all the bats ready before we can go out to play, what?'

'Yessir.' Corrigan smiled to himself: Monty was back in his usual form now, making war sound like a game of cricket.

'Well, while I'm doing that, I want you and your chaps, Corrigan, to cross the Elbe.'

'*Cross the Elbe!*' Corrigan exploded, sitting suddenly upright. 'By ourselves? Just the Assault Troop?'

'That's right,' Montgomery beamed, as if it were the most enjoyable treat in the world for a handful of men to tackle Germany's last surviving natural barrier.

'But the Yanks have twice been beaten back on the Elbe, sir,' Corrigan protested, '*in divisional strength!*'

'Yes, yes, I know Simpson's chaps got a bloody nose up there the other day. But I mean to say, Corrigan,' Montgomery waved his hand airily, 'they aren't the Iron Division's Assault Troop, are they? Nor did they have the advantage of surprise – which you will have, what?'

'Yessir,' Corrigan responded weakly.

'So you will cross the Elbe – say somewhere in the region of Salzwedel, just below Magdeburg, where the Yanks took a pasting the other day. Then you will head due north to the Baltic, trying to find out just where the Russian vanguard is. Must know where the Russkis are before I get my chaps moving. Soon as I have the details and the assault across the Elbe is successful, I am going to send the Sixth Airborne cracking towards the Baltic coast between Wismar and Lübeck, to seal off Schleswig-Holstein and Denmark from the Russkis.' He beamed suddenly at Corrigan, as if he was well pleased with himself, and paused momentarily.

Corrigan waited, his mind racing. Outside, the storm continued with increasing force, erupting in vicious little spurts of rain on the farmyard cobbles. Wisely his men were sheltering, Corrigan noted through the window. Even the men of Montgomery's bodyguard had abandoned their open scout car and sought refuge within the farmhouse.

'You see, Corrigan,' Montgomery went on, still beaming happily, while the younger man swiftly took his eyes off a civilian youth, lugging what looked like a pole on his shoulder as he trudged through the pouring rain some two hundred yards away, 'I have a shrewd idea that *if* and *when* we seal off the Schleswig-Holstein peninsula, it is going to produce some jolly surprising results indeed.'

'In what way, sir?' Corrigan asked, knowing that it was expected of him, for Monty was now looking like the proverbial cat that had just swallowed the cream.

'The Hun knows that he has lost the

match. That is exceedingly clear, Corrigan. So why does he continue fighting up there in the north? I shall tell you. Because he wants to gain as much time as possible to rescue his chaps – and civvies – fleeing from the Russkis in the east. There's nearly half a million of them over on the eastern side of the Elbe desperately trying to flee west to the safety of our lines. Old Hun knows what the Russkis will do to him if he's captured, so he's running and fighting to save his precious neck. Once we block the Russkis' path, and there's no more chance of saving those in the east, what will those in authority do, eh?' Montgomery cocked his head to one side and looked quizzically at Corrigan like a cheeky town sparrow.

'Pack up, sir,' Corrigan ventured, 'because there's no point going on fighting?'

'Exactly, Corrigan,' Montgomery agreed heartily. 'And with all authority now in the hands of the military, it will mean a tremendous mass surrender of all German forces in North-West Europe. They are all controlled by Grand Admiral Dönitz and his generals up there in Schleswig-Holstein, now that Hitler is trapped and powerless in Berlin.'*

*Dönitz had been designated Hitler's successor as well as commander-in-chief of all Germany's Armed Forces.

Suddenly it dawned on Corrigan what the little Field Marshal was about. Insufferably vain and headstrong as he was, Montgomery wanted the kudos of final victory for himself. If he couldn't capture Berlin and thus conclude his long fighting career on this supreme high note, he at least wanted to take the surrender of the German Army personally. It wouldn't be the Americans, at present swanning around in Southern Europe, who would win that prize – in spite of the fact that they fielded three times as many fighting men as the British – it would be Bernard Law Montgomery with his pitifully small British Liberation Army!

'You see what I'm getting at Corrigan. There are over one and a half million soldiers under Dönitz's command alone in the North. It would be a really fine achievement. Good Egg, you know.' His eyes glowed. 'The surrender of the Greater German *Wehrmacht*, what?'

Corrigan returned his smile. Whatever the conceited little commander's faults were, he seemed to be the only senior British officer who knew that Britain's real interest was not solely the conquest of Germany, but the preservation of her Empire and her status as a world power. Britain must be seen to be *winning* the war, not America – and certainly not the probable new danger to world peace, the Soviet Union.

'It certainly is an important mission, sir,' he said with new enthusiasm. Outside the boy with the pole had stopped and was simply standing there, in spite of the pouring rain. Perhaps he was worn out from his load and was resting. Corrigan dismissed him from his thoughts as Montgomery completed his briefing.

'Remember, Corrigan – especially with your notorious temper – that this is a very delicate mission. Not only will you be fighting Germans, but you could easily bump into the Russians with disastrous consequences on the other side of the Elbe. And Winnie* wants no trouble with Uncle Joe** – not *yet* at least. Then there is this damned Werewolf movement of the Germans to take into consideration. From what Intelligence tells me they could be more of a problem than the regular German soldier. Fanatics to a man – or should I say *boy?*'

'Werewolf, sir?' Corrigan echoed in bewilderment.

'Yes – aren't you in the picture yet?'

Corrigan shook his head.

'Well, back in November last year, when it was clear in Berlin that we were going to push over Germany's frontier and occupy their territory, the word was given out in

*Winnie: Winston Churchill.
**Uncle Joe: Joseph Stalin, the Soviet dictator.

Berlin – it's believed by that monster Himmler* – that a new secret organisation should be recruited primarily from the fanatics of the Hitler Youth and the German Maidens. Mostly, it appears, they are teenage kids. But they are all ready to die for their Führer. There have been several attacks already on our rear echelon units and only last Sunday they murdered the Burgomaster the Americans had appointed to govern Aachen. The problem with them is, of course, they wear civvies–'

LOOK OUT, SIR!' At the very last instant Corrigan realised what it was that the boy outside was putting to his shoulder. *'PANZERFAUST!'* With a mighty heave Corrigan sent the little Field Marshal flying to the floor as the hurtling projectile crashed through the window and exploded in an ear-splitting burst of scarlet flame against the opposite wall, showering the two men with debris and dust.

From outside there came cries of alarm and yells of rage. Heavy feet pounded over the slippery wet cobbles. There was the hectic crackle of a Sten gun. Someone screamed, high and hysterical. A whistle shrilled.

But for a long moment, as the running feet approached, the two officers remained

*Head of the SS.

motionless on the floor among the smoking rubble. Then, slowly, as a heavy shoulder barged against the jammed door, Montgomery raised himself. His face was paler than normal, but his eyes were firm and his voice was steady when he spoke. But then, Corrigan told himself, Monty had seen his fair share of action in his time; he was used to being under fire.

'Well, there you are, Corrigan. Now you know what you will soon be facing. Not only the German *Wehrmacht,* and perhaps also the Red Army, if things go drastically wrong, but those young buggers who have just tried to murder us – *the Werewolves!'*

FIVE

'*Idiot! Verdammter idiot!*' Reaching out one pudgy paw, *der Dicke* slapped Klaus right across the face. Klaus Kaufmann stood his ground, his handsome face flushed and his eyes burning, but he said nothing. *Der Dicke* was always right. He wasn't a person to be trifled with.

Next to the handsome youth stood a little blond boy, still clutching his bar of English chocolate, nervously waiting for his turn.

Ponderously, the sweat already streaming in glistening rivulets down his plump piglike face from the exertion of slapping Klaus, *der Dicke* now turned to him. 'You little piece of apeshit!' he gasped, short of breath as always. 'Why didn't you shitting well report more exactly where the English swine were located? Here we had this wonderful chance of croaking no less a person than Montgomery himself and you make a shit of it!'

'I ... I'm sorry,' the boy quavered, tense with anticipation.

'There is no room for apologies in the Hunting Commando,' *der Dicke* wheezed, his cheeks crimson, his monstrous chest heaving. 'I want results, not apologies.'

140

The boy waited, while the others stood around watching fearfully. Behind the boy, his sister Gerda bit her bottom lip anxiously. Ever since that morning two weeks ago when *der Dicke* had felled her with one blow of his fist, ripped off her knickers, then smothered her with his monstrous bulk and raped her wordlessly and brutally, she had been scared of their new leader's unpredictability.

Der Dicke took his time. He always did. It seemed to the watching girl that it took things longer to penetrate his thick hide than it did with other people. And yet, as she well knew, he was capable of swift savage action, once that fat addled brain of his had come to a decision.

Suddenly their leader's face lit up in a smile, though his small red eyes remained angry. 'So you failed this time,' he said softly, his chest heaving again, as if the very effort of speaking was too much for him, 'but we won't fail again, will we, kid?'

Dutifully the little blond boy shook his head, as *der Dicke* reached out and gently grasped him by the genitals.

The boy gasped, but dared not pull away.

'We didn't get the damned Tommy leader, but there are others. For instance, those men at the farm.' Slowly he increased his pressure on the boy's genitals.

Gerda bit her bottom lip to stifle a scream.

The boy's eyes flooded with pain and he went an ashen white, but he didn't cry out.

'*Gelobt sei was hart macht, eh?*'* The fat man was increasing the pressure even more, forcing the boy to stand on tiptoe. 'Those other Tommies must be important, too. Why else should a field marshal visit them? So you, kid, and you, Klaus, are going to find out more about them for me, aren't you, kid?... *Answer me!*'

'*Jawohl, Kommandofuhrer!*' the boy managed to gasp through gritted teeth, tears streaming down his pain-contorted face.

'Then get on with it!' *Der Dicke* squeezed the boy's testicles with all his strength, a look of savage pleasure on his fat glistening face, and let go.

The boy fell to the ground writhing with pain, vomit streaming out of his mouth, hands clutching his tortured testicles.

Der Dicke rose to his feet and looked coldly at the stricken child, tossing back and forth on the ground in a ball of sobbing agony, then at the other members of his *Jagdkommando*.** 'Let that be a lesson to the rest of you,' he announced slowly. 'At this, the eleventh hour, there can be no slip-ups, no weaknesses, if we are to help save

*'That which makes hard should be praised': a motto favoured by the Nazis.
**Hunting commando.

142

our beloved Germany and our leader Adolf Hitler.' He raised his right hand. *'Heil Hitler!'*

In an instant the tortured boy and his humiliated companion were forgotten. Fanaticism glowed in their eyes as the young boys and girls who made up the 'Hunting Commando Himmler' stiffened to attention and barked in unison: *'Heil Hitler!'*

Der Dicke watched their faces for a moment. Then, satisfied with what he had seen there, he turned and ambled off to his own room in the abandoned country house, leaving the rest of them to stare after his monstrous bulk, their eyes still glittering with fanaticism – and fear.

Hunting Commando Himmler had been formed exactly five months ago, on the same day that the German High Command launched its last great offensive against the Western Allies in the Ardennes. All of its members had been eager volunteers from the Hitler Youth, boys and girls, none of them older than sixteen but all of them with years of para-military training behind them.

To begin with they were prepared for operations in the German-speaking part of Belgium. But when the Ardennes Offensive failed and the German Army was pushed back into the Reich, their mission was changed. They were then smuggled behind

Allied lines in the Rhineland to sabotage rear-area installations, signal units, supply dumps, vehicle parks and the like, terrorising the local German population so that they dared not offer aid or assistance to the new conquerors.

Once the Allies crossed the Rhine, their mission was changed again. They were pulled back to this remote rural area between the Rhine and the Elbe and instructed to prepare secret arms caches and food dumps in the thickly wooded hills. And there they were told to wait for a new leader, being sent from Werewolf HQ in Berlin, who would give them their new orders. That leader was *der Dicke*.

They laughed when they first saw him. Hardened by years of outdoor living and training, the lean, bronzed boys and girls could hardly believe their eyes. Yet here was this grossly fat young man, who seemed likely to burst out of his civilian suit at any moment, waddling into their camp to announce: 'Klugmann is my name. I've been sent by Berlin. I am your new leader.'

Gerda actually giggled, but Klaus, who had been their temporary leader, just managed to stifle his own burst of amazed laughter in time. 'Did you say *you* are our new leader, Herr Klugmann?' he gasped.

The stranger nodded, small piggy eyes watching them carefully but revealing nothing. 'My authorisation from Prutzmann...'* he panted, handing a document to Klaus. Then as if exhausted by the movement, he slumped down on his haunches and pulled out a sandwich, devouring it greedily.

'*Impossible!*' Klaus proclaimed to the others, who were now passing the document around and examining the stamp with the half-cross of the Werewolves, and puzzling over the scrawl at the bottom: *General der SS und Polizei Prutzmann*. 'They must have made a mistake,' Klaus went on, 'they must be out of their minds in Berlin, to send us – *that!*'

'Why, he's fatter even than Fat Hermann!'** Gerda's brother declared, shaking with suppressed laughter. 'I wouldn't like to buy him by the kilo!'

'But he's disgusting!' Face contorted with revulsion, Gerda watched how their new leader slobbered over his sandwich, cramming it in till his fat cheeks bulged and licking his thick blubbery red lips at intervals with almost sexual delight. 'How can a thing like that lead a hunting commando?'

'How indeed?' Klaus echoed, staring down at the document miserably.

*SS General Prutzmann, commander of the Werewolves.
***Reichsmarschall* Hermann Goering, the enormously fat head of the German Air Force.

145

'*Der Dicke*', as they were soon calling him, after the contemptuous nickname given to Goering, was apparently unmoved by their sneers. He just slumped there, chewing and slobbering, his whole attention devoted exclusively to his sandwich.

Soon their initial contempt for their new leader changed to fear, however. On his second day in the camp at the abandoned country house, he raped Trudi, at thirteen one of the youngest members of the Hunting Commando. Completely naked, his monstrous body gleaming with sweat, breasts big as a woman's jiggling as he walked, swollen organ thrust out in front of him like a truncheon, he pushed his way into the room that she shared with Gerda. Without a word, he threw back the blankets, stifling her screams by thrusting a pillow over her face, ripped her skinny child's legs apart and plunged himself cruelly into her virginal body, while Gerda just screamed and screamed and screamed.

Naturally there was a commotion. Gerda's wild terrified screams had roused the others. They came blundering and rushing into the room to find Gerda in hysterics and Trudi sobbing broken-heartedly into the pillow.

'Holy strawsack!' Klaus cried, taking the scene in with wild staring eyes. 'What in heaven's name are you about, Klugmann?

Answer me!' He grabbed *der Dicke*'s pudgy white shoulder and heaved him up from his victim to reveal the blood trickling down her leg beneath the faint puff of pubic hair.

Der Dicke stared up at the angry young Hitler Youth, his pig-like eyes revealing no emotion, blood dripping from his now flaccid organ. 'What ... did ... you ... say?' he asked, pausing after each word as if it required an effort of will for him to speak.

'You've raped her!' Klaus shrieked. 'Heaven, arse and cloudburst, don't you realise she's only *thirteen!* Why, you ... you filthy *swine!*' Beside himself with rage, he swung a punch at the fat naked figure on the edge of the bed.

But *der Dicke* moved with surprising speed. His dimpled knee flew up. It caught Klaus completely off guard, striking him in the crotch. He dropped as if he had been poleaxed. *Der Dicke* did not even look down as he stepped over the unconscious body to waddle back to his own room, his white belly trembling like blancmange.

Now he was the undisputed leader of the *Jagdkommando*, greatly feared, but grudgingly respected, too. For he had proved himself a born leader and organiser – and a fanatical opponent of the Allied conquerors. Within the first week he had attacked two Allied supply convoys, personally shooting the captured Negro drivers. Once he had ambushed a small party of English infantrymen single-handed, and taken them all prisoner; then he lined them up and ambled from man to man, blowing the back of their heads off with his pistol, obviously enjoying himself hugely, according to the boy who had raced to help him and instead found him chanting in English, *'Fee, fie, foe, fum, I smell the blood of an Englishman!'* And by the end of that little massacre, there had been blood enough undoubtedly.

Even his own countrymen were not spared. One day *der Dicke* had a German priest nailed alive to the door of his own church for flying the white flag from its steeple; he left the scene with the cynical comment: 'Well, priest, now you can feel what it was like to be Jesus...' Three deserters from the *Luftwaffe* who blundered into his camp were taken to the nearest road, where he personally garrotted them, then had them hung in line from telephone poles, each bearing a placard on his dead chest announcing *'WE ARE FOLK PARASITES WHO WON'T FIGHT. THIS IS THE FATE OF ALL WHO RUN AWAY!'* A woman who attempted to hide her soldier husband until the Allies overran her village was ceremonially raped by *der Dicke* in front of her husband and the rest of the village; then, when he had finished with her, he committed the final atrocity: he thrust the shaft of her husband's rifle into her vagina crying, 'Is that all the good his weapon is for?' And one minute later he blasted the man's head off.

While the much vaunted One Thousand Year Reich crumbled and fell apart, *der Dicke* ruled his little command with a rod of iron, sparing neither the enemy nor his followers; and so, as Klaus and the Kid trudged off miserably into the pouring rain once more, to report on the movements of the Assault Troop, both of them knew their lives were forfeit if they made another mistake. This time their gross monstrous leader would show no mercy.

Back at the house, lying on his bed and listening to the raindrops beat against the window, the Fat One, completely naked now, looked lovingly at the massive tumescence poking up from beneath his hairless white belly and wondered which of the girls he would take this night...

SIX

Dawn came reluctantly, as if God himself hesitated to throw light on what had happened in this terrible place. Slowly, very slowly, the sky started to flush an ugly white to the east and the men of the Assault Troop could finally see what lay to their front: death and destruction.

'A refugee convoy,' Corrigan said, his voice low and husky. 'Our fighter bombers must have caught them in the open, probably yesterday.'

'Bastards!' one of the awed Assault Troopers hissed vehemently. 'Rotten bastards!'

At a gesture from Corrigan, Hawkins swung out and stood on the road, silently staring at a dead German propped against a shattered tree as if he had been placed there deliberately. He had a typical farmer's face, Hawkins thought, heavy and muscular, with that expression of clever stubbornness and surface servility common to his kind. Now the upper plate of his false teeth hung out of his dark face giving a mocking aspect to it, as if to say 'You won't catch me out!' But Allied fighter-bombers had caught him out. His upper body was shattered; Hawkins

150

could see his lungs through the white-flecked gory flesh of his rib cage.

Beyond the dead farmer there were dead animals and human beings strewn everywhere on the cratered road, their pathetic possessions scattered all about them. They were all too visible in the growing light of day – a day that none of them would see.

Hawkins moved forward a few steps, the only sound being the steady throb of the half-track's engine. He passed a little girl, her face ripped off, still clutching a rag doll in her skinny arms. Sombrely he stepped over an old woman, with her skirts thrown up and her legs opened to reveal her faded patched bloomers in the kind of obscene sexual invitation she had probably never known in life. He stopped and stared at the horizon, straining his ears.

The Assault Troop was entering no man's land now. They knew from Intelligence that regular German resistance was patchy in this area, scattered pockets of the defeated *Wehrmacht* more likely to throw away their weapons and surrender than fight. But there might be others, lying in ambush and waiting to take a crack at any small isolated convoy of Allied vehicles, such as theirs was – and there were these Werewolves that suddenly everyone was talking about in hushed fearful tones.

'They sound like something out of a

bleeding horror film,' Wolfers had snorted. 'Bela Lugosi and Boris Karloff – that kind of thing, like!'

So Hawkins was taking no chances.

Neither was Captain Corrigan, as he waited in the cab of the half-track, gazing fixedly at the road ahead and watching Hawkins, gripping the half-inch machine gun mounted there.

'Bloody spooky, ain't it,' Wolfers commented, a corned beef sandwich lying among the bandoliers of ammunition and loose grenades beside him. He shivered dramatically. 'What with all them stiffs and this Werewolf lark. Fair gives yer the creeps.'

'Don't cream yer skivvies,' Sanders sneered from the wheel. 'Daddy'll see you get a night light tonight so that you don't have no bad dreams.' But even the cynical little Australian had no heart for banter this day. The sight of a dead woman suckling a dead baby at her worn flabby breast, lying in the ditch beside the vehicle, had sobered even Sanders.

Hawkins was waving his hand. That meant the road ahead was clear. Corrigan snapped out of his gloomy reverie. 'All right, Sanders, advance!' he barked, his breath fogging on the cold dawn air.

'But the stiffs, sir!' Sanders protested.

'Yes sir,' Wolfers added his plea to that of his pal. 'We can't run over...' He trailed off, extending his hand to indicate the road littered with the refugees' corpses.

'Yes we can.' Corrigan forced down his own revulsion. 'I'm not taking any chances that the fields on both sides are mined. I know the road *isn't* mined because the stiffs, as you call them, came down it. Now move it, Sanders. No more chat. Advance!'

Sanders muttered something rebellious under his breath as he engaged first gear. The five-ton truck moved forward with a series of rusty creaks. Wolfers closed his eyes as the tracks started to churn over the first bodies, willing himself not to be sick, trying to ignore that dreadful sound of limbs snapping and flesh squelching under the half-track's weight. Behind them came the next driver, his face an ashen white. Slowly the whole convoy began to crunch its way over the slaughtered civilians, turning the whole road into a sea of gore and pulp, the wheels and tracks of their vehicles splattered with a deep loathsome crimson.

Wordlessly, his wizened old face as pale as the others, Hawkins clambered up on the half-track's running board, trying not to see the head trapped by its hair in the tracks of the following vehicle, swaying back and forth, an inane grin on its dead face.

Corrigan nodded to the little fir wood looming up to their right. 'Keep your eyes on … on that wood at three o'clock, Sergeant,' he commanded, his voice not quite

153

under control. 'If they're anywhere, they'll be there.'

'Yessir,' Hawkins answered, swallowing hard to stop the vomit from rising. Behind him one of the vehicles had caught a severed arm in its towing hook; it was moving up and down as if waving encouragement to them.

The long armoured snout of the half-track suddenly smashed into a wooden cart that barred the road. The cart splintered and fell apart like match wood. Sanders gasped and nearly lost control as a dead baby fell from the back of the cart and disappeared beneath the roaring scarlet tracks.

'Oh, God in heaven!' Wolfers moaned, then he could stand no more. The hot vomit flooded his mouth. He sprang to the side of the vehicle and began retching violently, big shoulders heaving as if he were sobbing his very heart out.

The first harsh crack, followed an instant later by that great roaring whoosh like a huge piece of canvas being torn apart, came almost as a relief. Next moment the half-track was rocking from side to side as the 88mm shell rushed by like an express train roaring through a station. It exploded in a huge spout of flame and erupting earth in the field to their left.

'It's in the wood, sir!' Hawkins yelled above the sudden racket. 'Spotted the muzzle fl–' The rest of his warning was drowned by the screech of another shell, immediately followed by a burst of machine-gun fire erupting the length of the little fir wood.

The corpses littering that terrible road were forgotten now as the Assault Troopers crouched low behind the frail protection of thin steel sides, slugs belting against them in a deafening tattoo.

As yet another shell tore the dawn air apart and exploded between his number two and three vehicles, Corrigan rapidly took stock of his situation. To stay on the road was suicide. They were sitting ducks here, clearly silhouetted against the rising sun: a perfect target. But which way was he to go? To the right he'd be heading straight into their fire. To the left there was a sheer drop through dwarf firs growing on poor thin soil and naked rock. Their ambushers had picked the site well.

'Got us by the short hairs, sir, eh?' Hawkins yelled, then ducked instinctively as machine-gun fire ripped the length of the half-track, ricochets howling off the steel.

Corrigan made a snap decision. The slope would offer some hold at least, and the Whites⋆ were half-tracked. Praying he was

⋆The name of the US firm which made the half-tracks.

not making the wrong move, he yelled above the clatter of machine guns: 'Hard left, Sanders!'

Sanders shot him a wild look. 'Strewth – did you say left, sir?'

'I did!

'Hold bleeding tight then!' Sanders swung the wheel round and the five-ton vehicle shot off the road. With a great lurch and howl of protesting metal, it went over the side in a slither of pebbles and mud, while another shell went roaring harmlessly past.

Grimly, face glistening with sweat as if it had been greased, Sanders held on with white-knuckled hands as the half-track went roaring down the rough slope, dark green twigs slapping and smashing at its sides, its wheels quivering frantically. One wrong move now and they would be completely out of control, crashing into the deep ravine below.

Behind them more and more half-tracks swung off that bloodied road, pursued by an angry enemy fire, attempting to follow 'Waltzing Mathilda' as they'd nicknamed Corrigan's vehicle. Jerricans rattling merrily, every rivet screaming out in protest, they lurched and rocked in crazy progress down the treacherous scree.

'*LOOK OUT!*' Hawkins shrieked suddenly, as a drop of at least six foot loomed out of the blinding green foliage.

Sanders swerved frantically to the right – and then they were zooming out into space, the little Australian gripping the whirling wheel with all his remaining strength, body tensed for the impact to come.

They hit the ground with a dreadful smash. For one awful moment Corrigan thought they had snapped an axle, but then they were moving again, a twig slashing him across the face like the lash from a whip. He didn't even notice it, he was so tense.

Behind them one of the jeep drivers had lost control of his vehicle. It leapt into the air, smashed nose-first into the base of the drop and burst apart, scattering injured men and shattered metal to all sides. A moment later it was a mass of searing blue flame, as the petrol tank exploded, dousing the injured with burning gas. Corrigan moaned out loud as one of them staggered a few feet, a living torch, only to collapse and die a terrible death, writhing frantically as the flames consumed him.

Now they were sliding down the slope through the dwarf pines as if they were on a bobsleigh, the scared Assault Troopers instinctively leaning to one side while Sanders cursed and fought to keep the White from overbalancing.

Suddenly there was a sickening thump. Corrigan gasped and held on for dear life as the half-track shuddered and shimmied alarmingly. But seconds later they were moving forward once more – on even ground, while vehicle after vehicle struck the bottom of the ravine behind them. They had made it. They had escaped the ambush!

Slowly the gross leader of the Hunting Commando lowered his glasses and the camouflaged vehicles slipped away from the gleaming circles of calibrated glass. This time Klaus and the Kid had not failed. They had correctly assessed the route the Tommy pigs would take to reach the river. After that it had been easy to convince even those white-livered gunners, who were probably at this very moment abandoning their positions, that there was a nice fat target on the way to them, theirs to have for the taking. The fact that the *Wehrmacht* ambush had failed did not entirely displease him. At least it had forced the Tommies into the terrain of his choosing. For a moment longer he lay there behind the rock like an old dog in the sun, panting softly, the sweat trickling down his fat red face as he considered his situation.

They would now follow the narrow secondary road below to the Elbe, for he had reasoned that was their objective. Being soldiers, they would have to make a production of crossing it; boats would have to be found, crossing sites reconnoitred, a crossing timetable worked out. Unlike normal people, soldiers always did things by the book, he told himself contemptuously, wasting time instead of plunging boldly ahead and getting the job done. No matter. By the time they had organised things it would be dark – and then they would cross. So he would have to be in position by nightfall too. He chuckled softly to himself, as he lay there in the warm grass, the insects buzzing about his sweat-glazed face; but there was no mirth in the sound. They hadn't a hope of success. Fire to their front and water to their rear. Not one hell of a hope!

A maybug zoomed in low, fat, black and stupid like all its kind. *Der Dicke*'s pudgy hand shot out with amazing speed for such a normally sluggish person, and he caught the beetle in mid-flight. Slowly, almost pleasurably, he crushed it in his fist. Finally he opened his fingers, each one like a plump port sausage, and stared intently at the sticky mess of blood and black glistening matter in his palm with the fascination of the monstrous, overgrown child he was, but with none of a child's innocence. Suddenly his broad pasty face lit up, saliva dripping from his slack mouth. *'I shall crush them,'* he panted, staring at the dead beetle's remains, *'I shall crush them – just like that...'*

SEVEN

'Like the dreaded werewolves of the Middle Ages that came out of the night to spread terror and disaster,' the prissy female voice intoned out of the pear-shaped radio high up on the wall, *'so shall we, the immortal underground soldiers of Adolf Hitler, spring from the night to deal out death and destruction...'*

Wolfers, squatting in the cramped German kitchen listening to the upper-class voice of the Berlin radio announcer, hastily swallowed down the last of compo ration pilchards. 'Fair puts the creeps up yer, don't it, Slim?' he muttered. 'All that talk about werewolves coming out of the night, like.' He glanced out of the window to the darkening River Elbe, as if he half expected to see a monstrous vampire bat winging its deadly way towards them. ''Orrible it is. Puts a bloke off his bleeding grub, even.'

'Strewth!' Slim breathed in mild disgust, still rubbing the spoons he had looted from the abandoned house to check if they were really silver. 'What a bleeding nervous Nelly you are, Wolfers!'

'Beware Americans!... Beware Englishmen!' the radio announced persisted. *'For soon you*

shall feel the death grip of our fangs. We are everywhere. Unseen but waiting... Beware of the Were—'

Wolfers snapped off the catch and the radio fell silent, leaving behind a loud echoing silence, broken only by the moan of the wind in the trees outside.

Nervously, hardly aware that he was doing so, he scooped his dirty hands into a can of peaches and ladled a dripping syrupy mouthful down his throat, staring first at the door and then back at the window in undisguised apprehension. 'Do you really think they're everywhere, Slim?' he asked, wiping the sticky juice from his unshaven chin. 'I mean ... *really?*'

Sanders tossed back his head and let loose a bloody-curdling shriek like a beast in agony.

Wolfers jumped visibly. 'For Chrissake, Slim, don't fucking well do that!' he gasped. 'You know my nerves are all shot. I'm trembling all over. You scared the shit outa me!'

'And I'll *kick* the shit outa yer,' Hawkins' voice cut in harshly from the suddenly open door, 'if yer don't grab yer bondhook and get outside, young Wolfers. Yer late for stag by exactly two minutes. Now grab yer rifle and hop it!'

'Yes Sarge... Sorry Sarge...' Wolfers stuttered. Then, seizing his rifle and helmet, he dutifully 'hopped it' outside just as the first

161

dark shadows began to creep along the river.

Captain Corrigan was standing by himself near the little collection of armoured vehicles grouped in a defensive laager, staring thoughtfully at an old ferry which they found that afternoon. All was silent save for the muted sounds of the men inside the house, eating, resting. Whiling away the time until they crossed the river at midnight.

Shivering a little in the cold air, Wolfers cleared his throat softly and said, 'Good evening, sir.'

Corrigan swung round, hand falling to his rifle-sling automatically. 'Oh, it's you, Wolfers,' he said and dropped his hold. 'Thought you might be one of those werewolves that seem to worry you a lot.'

'Well, there is a lot of talk, sir...'

Corrigan smiled encouragingly at the pimply-faced young giant with nervous eyes. 'That's what it is, Trooper Wolfers. Just talk. Old Jerry's about beaten. I don't see what a bunch of boy scouts in short pants can do about changing things, do you?'

'I suppose you're right, sir,' Wolfers admitted, shivering again as the shadows grew ever darker.' But it is a bit scary, like.'

'Scary – for a hairy-arsed veteran like you, Wolfers?' Corrigan said heartily. 'A bloke who's been through Normandy, the Ardennes and the Rhine? What could frighten

162

you after all that, eh?'

'Oh, that was only shot and shell, that kind of shit,' Wolfers asserted. 'But this is…' His ugly young face contorted as he tried to find the words to express the depth of his feelings. 'This is sort of spooky, sir. Unnatural, like. Things that come up from the grave at midnight, things that you have to kill by thrusting a stake through their heart … and garlic and silver crosses…'

Corrigan held up his hands to halt the sudden flow of words. 'Wolfers, Wolfers, Wolfers,' he pleaded, *'cease!* You're going to turn yourself into a nervous wreck if you go on like that. Your trouble is that you have too vivid an imagination – or seen too many films. Now just you walk up and down keeping your eyes on those vehicles and the ferry. Believe you me, things that go bump in the night simply do not exist. Good evening.' As Wolfers stiffened to attention, Corrigan touched his hand to his helmet, then settled his rifle into a more comfortable position against his shoulder and started to walk slowly back to the house, leaving Wolfers alone.

'Great Crap on the Christmas Tree!' *der Dicke* hissed at his boys and girls, labouring with the heavy hoses of petrol bowsers. 'Are you made of sugar, you lot? Hurry it up. *Dalli, dalli!'*

Klaus muttered angrily under his breath, while Gerda flashed a venomous look at the gross figure of their leader lolling on a rock overlooking the silver ribbon of the Elbe below. But no one dared point out to him that he was doing nothing to help. They continued with their labours, dragging the heavy steel tubing from the stationary vehicles and laying it in a line down the slope to the river.

They had already set up the explosive charges; now it was time to check the detonator. Slowly *der Dicke* touched the leads of the detonating wire to a little galvanometer, straining his piggy eyes in the dim light to check the reading. The green needle flickered to the right. He muttered his approval. It was working. Those young brats had been well taught; they had wired up the splices correctly.

He peered at the leads while another group laboured past panting with the strain of carrying the heavy steel hoses, and his nostrils were assailed by the stink of petrol. 'Careful,' he warned them. 'Don't spill any more. One mistake and the whole lot'll go up, taking us with it.'

They mumbled their understanding and he turned his attention back to the leads. Good; they were all right, too. He twisted them around the poles of the detonator and screwed them in tight under the wing nuts, as he had been taught to do at the SS Explosive School – but that of course was before they kicked him out for 'perverted sexuality', as *Reichsfuhrer SS* Himmler called it; he had narrowly missed death on the executioner's block only by volunteering for the Werewolves. He taped the wooden handle of the plunger. That was also functioning smoothly. He sat back satisfied, suddenly remembering the girl who had caused all the damned trouble.

It had been while he was training at the Explosive School outside Berlin-Lichterfelde. Due to the shortage of manpower, the kitchen and mess halls had swarmed with kids in the black and white uniform of the Hitler Maidens, all jiggling little tits under artificial silk blouses and plump arses in black skirts. He had walked around with a permanent hard-on, scarcely able to concentrate on the instructors and their training. But he had been strong-willed enough to remind himself that they were just kids, all of them under fourteen and therefore jailbait.

That was until Uschi had come into his life. She giggled a lot and had the habit of sitting down *too* carelessly, her short black uniform skirt riding up her slim bare legs to reveal simple white panties below. She was simply panting to be done. He had known all along that she was only thirteen, although at his court-martial he pleaded that he had always taken her to be over sixteen. And in truth she had acted like it, ogling him all the time with her 'bedroom eyes', touching his hand seemingly carelessly, always bending down low whenever he was near. She left little to the imagination. She had simply been a child-whore, deliciously corrupt, exactly the way he liked them – and she had not laughed once at the sight of his gross naked white body when he finally succumbed to temptation.

He had taken her cruelly and violently. How she had screamed and struggled! But she'd liked it all the same. By God, *how* she'd liked that piece of hard salami! She'd told him so afterwards, panting, laughing, crying, all at the same time. Then she had begged him to do it again, in spite of the fact that she was bleeding like a stuck pig. So he'd thrown all caution to the winds. He had half carried her to his little cubicle, knowing that he could be discovered at any time, but too overwhelmed by lust to care.

She had screamed. She had struggled like a trapped animal. She had ripped her nails the length of his back. But he had forced her legs high above her head and ploughed into her, gasping with the effort, grunting in noisy satisfaction.

It was thus that they had been found. Naturally she had screamed rape, in the very moment that she had arched her spine, digging her nails deep into his fleshy buttocks till blood was drawn and she had had first real experience of sexual pleasure. Naturally – rape. They always said that ... *afterwards.*

The SS chaindogs⋆ had beaten him to a pulp. So severely, in fact, that they had not dared court-martial him until he was at least partially recovered. The verdict had been a foregone conclusion: death by the axe.

'*Kommandofuhrer!*' It was Klaus calling, interrupting his thoughts. Uschi's white breasts and delightfully writhing thighs vanished from his mind's eye.

'Yes?' he called back.

'We have finished. All the hoses are in place, *Kommandofuhrer.*'

'Good,' he wheezed, mopping his face as he leant back against a rock. After this operation was completed, he told himself, he would take one of the young ones. Perhaps Thea. She still had the figure of a boy, delectably unripe. He licked his slack lips in anticipation. 'Take five minutes rest. Then prepare for action.' And with that he sat back once more, already feeling the faint stirring in his loins that heralded pleasure and depravity to come. He smiled in the darkness...

⋆Nickname for the military police on account of the little silver plates they wore around their necks.

A thin mist writhed back and forth across the river, curling itself around the anchored ferry like a skinny grey cat. A night owl hooted eerily. Otherwise there was no sound save the soft lap-lap of the river and the muted chatter coming from within the house. Wolfers shivered. He might have been the last man alive on the whole bloody earth.

He cast another sudden look over his shoulder. It was only a matter of seconds since he had done so before, but he couldn't help it. Ever since this bloody werewolf business had started, he had felt that there were weird things lurking in the bushes behind him; and he simply couldn't take his mind off that damned old Spencer Tracy film, in which Tracy had been transformed one night in his study into a monster – a werewolf. Even now, standing on the banks of the River Elbe, deep in the heart of enemy country, Wolfers could see that scene in the film: Tracy staring in horror at his hand changing into a hairy paw, complete with the razor-sharp claws of a wolf; then glancing into the big mirror above the ornate fireplace and seeing his face taking on an evil vulpine look, teeth growing long and yellow, being transformed into the fangs of the beast as he became that horror of horrors – the werewolf.

'*Wolfers!*'

168

The young sentry nearly jumped out of his skin. 'Christ, it's you, Sarge!' he gasped, as he saw Sergeant Hawkins emerge from the thickening mist, a cup in his hand, Sten gun slung carelessly over his shoulder.

'Who did yer frigging well think it was – Betty Grable?'

'Sorry, Sarge. Bit on edge, that's all. Bit spooky out here, what with the fog and everything.' Gratefully he accepted the cup of tea that the Sergeant thrust into his hand.

'Better get a grip of yerself, son,' Hawkins said, voice gentle again. 'Can't have yer going windy on me, yer know. There ain't many of you veterans left. Now get a sup of that char. It's real sarnt-major's. Made it meself. Put some of that evaporated milk in it, special like. Yer couldn't get a finer cup of char this side of Dover.'

Wolfers took a sip of the thick brown mixture, letting the steam warm his cold nose, glad that he had company and could forget those damned werewolves. 'Do you think there'll be any Jerries on yon side, Sarge?' he asked after a while, as the wizened old NCO who could have been his father watched him sip his tea, full of concern.

'Well, the CO doesn't think so. I had a good butcher's earlier on, but I couldn't see a thing. More than likely they've gone and hoofed–' He stopped suddenly and sniffed

169

the air like an old gundog picking up the scent with difficulty.

'What's up, Sarge?' Wolfers asked.

'Can't you smell nothing?'

'Like what?' Wolfers lowered his mug of tea and turned, staring at the horizon and straining his ears. But there was no sound now save that of their own breathing. 'Can't say as I do–' He broke off abruptly and sniffed hard. 'Smells like petrol, Sarge,' he said after a moment.

'That's what I was thinking,' Hawkins agreed. 'I hope none of the lads has been frigging around over at the vehicles and left one of the jerricans open.' There was suddenly urgency in his voice. 'Come on, young Wolfers, put yer char down. Yer can drink it later.'

'What's up?'

'Somebody could be sabotaging the vehicles!'

'You mean ... *werewolves?*' Wolfers breathed, dropping the mug to the ground and unslinging his rifle, as if he could already see a transformed Spencer Tracy about to pounce on him with those hairy claws of his.

'Something like that. At the double now, Wolfers!'

Sergeant Hawkins broke into an awkward run, heading for the circle of silent vehicles. But he didn't get far. Abruptly, all along the hilltop above the river bank, there was a series of blue crackling sparks like the opening salvo of some fireworks display. Hawkins stopped in horror. Up above him the whole top of the hill had begun to tremble and shake. Bright spurts of scarlet flame were stabbing the night.

Wolfers lumbered to a stop next to him. 'What the fuck's going on, Sarge?' he gasped.

Hawkins didn't answer. He simply stared at the hilltop display, the lurid light transforming his old face into a death's head, his nostrils sickened by the ever more powerful cloying smell of escaping petrol.

Suddenly it happened. Like a gigantic blowtorch, a huge jet of burning bright flame seared the darkness and in an instant the whole hilltop was burning, with a wall of flame, ten foot high, racing down towards the river.

Hawkins was already raising his Sten gun. *'Warn the others!'* he shrieked at the petrified Wolfers. *'For Chrissake, get them out of that house before it's too late!'*

'But what's happening, Sarge?'

'What's happening?' There was near hysteria in the little sergeant's voice now. 'I'll tell you what's fuckin' happening – they've set the whole hillside on fire and it's coming straight at us! *NOW MOVE!...'*

EIGHT

'Abandon the vehicles!' Corrigan bellowed above the great baleful hiss of the holocaust descending upon them. The startled men milling around the jeeps and half-tracks needed no urging. They dropped the starting handles at once; they'd never start the vehicles in time.

Crouched at Corrigan's side, Sten gun at the ready, Hawkins watched in horrified fascination as that tremendous wall of roaring flame came ever closer. 'What we gonna do, sir?' he bawled, already feeling the searing heat sucking the air from his lungs.

'Back to the river – to the ferry!' Corrigan shrieked. 'It's our only chance. Everybody, *BACK TO THE FERRY!* Come on, it's everybody for himself... *RUN!*'

As one they started to pelt for the water, racing through the eerily glowing night towards the anchored ferry, while the fire chased after them like a live thing pursuing its prey.

The flames swept round the first of the vehicles. Next moment its petrol tank was exploding with the crump of a high explosive shell detonating. The evil blue flames leapt ever higher. Another half-track exploded. And another. Showers of sparks and burning metal rained down on the panic-stricken running men. Corrigan felt a tremendous blow at the side of his head. For one awful moment he thought he was going down. But his rifle butt saved him. It hit the ground first as he crumpled to his knees, but it steadied him, and an instant later he was running again, that thundering roar and long searing hiss of flames getting ever closer.

Then the ammunition truck went up. White, green and red tracer exploded, zig-zagging into the dull-pink sky, whizzing lethally through the air. A running trooper flung up his arms and clawed the air frantically, as if he were climbing the rungs of an invisible ladder. Hawkins hesitated, his whole body screaming out for him to continue running and not go to the aid of the kid. Suddenly the trooper pitched face-forward to the ground and the greedy all-consuming flames swept over him. Hawkins caught a horrified glimpse of the dead man shrivelling up to the size of a charred pygmy... Then he was running again, the wall of fire hard at his heels.

The water was now only twenty yards or so away, but the flames were gaining on them all the while. Corrigan spurred his men on to even greater efforts. *'Keep going!'*

he gasped fervently. *'Keep going ... straight into the water!... Keep going!'*

A trooper stumbled. He started to pick himself up. *Too late.* He shrieked in terror as the flames caught him. For one long moment, he writhed and fought them, clawing at the fire as if to tear himself free from the deadly embrace of those voracious flames. It was not to be. Next instant he sank back like a weary lover surrendering.

Now Corrigan was only five yards away from the water. He propelled himself forward in a shallow dive, gasping with shock as the cold water struck him. On all sides his men were doing the same, screaming and shrieking in fear. Corrigan struck out for the ferry, knowing he had to get it moving before the holocaust swamped it.

There was a blood-curdling howl. *'It's got me, it's got me!'* someone screamed piteously. Corrigan flung a glance over his shoulder. One of his men was posturing wildly on the bank, as if engaged in some wild lascivious dance, while the flames crept ever higher up his young body. He cursed and swam on.

The great wall of fire hissed and steamed as it hit the water. For a moment it recoiled, then a fresh flood of petrol came spurting down the hillside. It ignited immediately. With renewed fury, the wall of fire spread on.

Sobbing for breath, Corrigan reached the ferry and swung himself aboard. Fighting off the temptation to just lie there helpless as a child till he regained his breath, he forced himself to his feet and staggered to the primitive wheel house, his heart thumping madly at his rib cage.

Now the flames were spreading across the water, running over the surface film of petrol while the troopers swam frantically towards the ferry. Some of them were already clambering aboard as Corrigan searched for the instrument panel. There it was – the starter button! As more and more terrified men flung themselves on board, sobbing and choking for breath, absolutely exhausted, Corrigan hit the button.

Nothing happened.

Frantically he tried again.

Again nothing!

'It's too cold!' Slim Sanders shrieked, pushing Corrigan aside. 'There must be a choke!' With fingers numb with cold he fumbled at the instrument panel.

The hiss of that horrific, all-consuming flame grew louder as it seared across the steaming water, getting closer and closer.

'*Got it!*' Sanders yelled. 'Try again!'

Corrigan tried again.

There was a long low groan, like some eerie dirge played on the Highland bagpipes. Corrigan kept his finger pressed down hard on the button, the sweat streaming down his face, a nerve ticking at the side of his temple.

'*Come on yer bastard ... come on!*' Sanders cursed, his face turning bright red as the scarlet wall of flame hissed towards them, sending up clouds of thick white steam.

Black smoke was streaming from the exhaust. The ferry was going!

Wildly Hawkins hacked at the tow-rope with his bayonet. Here and there, men lay sobbing on the wooden deck as the flames raced towards them. Others prepared to throw themselves over the far side of the boat. Already the paint was beginning to melt and bubble under that awesome heat.

The ferry was shaking and shivering as if it might fall apart at any moment. Its motor backfired like a burst of rifle shots. The flames were only ten yards away now. Corrigan could smell his hair beginning to singe, and the sleeve of his jacket was smouldering.

White smoke flooded up from beneath. Suddenly the engine exploded into life with a violent roar. Corrigan did not waste a second: he thrust open the throttle. Hawkins severed the bow rope with one final slash and slumped down on his knees, exhausted.

'*We're moving!*' Sanders shrieked. '*WE'RE FUCKING WELL MOVING!*'

They were slowly gathering speed, leaving the wall of flame to hiss and splutter impotently behind them, as the current took hold, bearing them ever more swiftly into the darkness of the Elbe.

But even as Corrigan slumped over the controls, not seeing, not hearing a thing, totally drained of all energy, he knew they had lost their vehicles, most of their heavy weapons, and all their rations. They were now completely at the mercy of this remote fast river, sailing into the unknown.

BOOK THREE

COLLISION COURSE

ONE

An uneasy stillness lay over the land. It was like a premonition of impending danger – so thick, Colonel Piotr told himself, that you could almost cut it with a sabre. There was a strange smell too: a kind of raunchy stench that he vaguely remembered from the zoo at Kazan which he had visited with his father so long ago.

To another eye, the trees, green and sparkling in the early spring sun, the clean invigorating April air, the immense blue wash of the sky might have seemed beautiful: a scene of peace and new promise, as might have been painted by a nineteenth-century artist. But not to the tall Cossack who crouched there beside the vehicle surveying the landscape through his binoculars. He was a veteran. He could smell the danger that was waiting for him and his men as they finished off their breakfast of black bread and dried fish, washed down with ration vodka, and prepared to advance westwards once again.

He lowered his binoculars and nervously touched that leather bag of native earth slung round his neck, his usual bold grin

181

absent. Like all Cossacks he was a superstitious man, only one degree removed from his warrior forefathers – brave fighters, but basically savages who believed in spirits and omens. Something was going to happen today and he knew it. If he had been his own grandfather he would have heeded his own intuition and taken to his bed until the portents for the future looked better. But he couldn't, not with Marshal Rokossovsky breathing down his neck, urging him, almost hourly, to ever greater speed so that he reached the Baltic before the treacherous, cunning English. He sighed and tossed down the last of his vodka, shuddering with pleasure as the fiery spirit slammed against the wall of his stomach.

'Horoscho!' he bellowed, waving his fur cap in the air. *'Davai, davai!'*

All along the column his officers and senior sergeants took up the cry, waving their arms, rounding up the men still defecating in the ditches or lingering over their precious vodka and booting them into the trucks. Drivers started up their motors. Suddenly the dawn calm was shattered. The air filled with noise and blue fumes. Men cursed angrily, grabbing their weapons, and boarded the trucks. In the trees, the crows rose hastily, squawking in angry protest at the racket.

Piotr's second-in-command raised his

green flag – in the Red Army they had no time for new-fangled gimmicks such as radios: all signalling was still done by flag, just as in the eighteenth century – and dropped it. Colonel Piotr's armoured command car lurched forward. They were moving again; and this morning Colonel Piotr knew, with superstitious conviction, they were heading for danger.

Igor, his second-in-command, was first to spot it. They had just rolled through an empty village, the doors and windows of the little white-painted cottages securely closed, all the inhabitants and their animals fled, not even a stray dog left behind, when he cocked his shaven Mongol skull to one side, his slanting eyes narrowed to slits.

'Aircraft,' he announced in that peculiar hissing Russian of his.

'Where?' Piotr snapped, alert to the danger immediately.

Igor pointed his finger, the nail exceedingly long in the fashion of his Asiatic ancestors to prove he was not a worker but a member of the select upper class. 'There, Comrade Colonel!' he answered.

Piotr peered upwards. A dark V-shape had appeared over the horizon. But this beautiful spring morning it was not a peaceful formation of geese making their way southwards, as he had so often seen in his youth over the River Don. No, there was something very definitely lethal about the purposeful, deliberate flight of these mechanical birds.

'Scatter!' he yelled. 'Everyone hit the dirt!'

Next to him, the driver hit the brakes hard and the command car shuddered to a violent stop.

'But Comrade Commander, we do not know they are the enemy!' Igor protested.

Piotr taped the side of his nose and glanced at the squat, yellow-faced Mongol. 'You have eyes, Comrade Major. I have a nose – and I smell danger. Now, let's get the hell out of here!'

Seconds later they were over the side and running for the shelter of the nearest ditch, where already the men of the First Punishment Battalion were crouching expectantly, while that sinister drone grew closer and closer.

'*Stukas!*' Piotr breathed in awe, lowering his glasses as gull-winged German dive-bombers hovered above the abandoned convoy like metal hawks. '*Boshe moi,* I haven't seen them in action since forty-two! In the devil's name, where have they dug those old crates up from?'

Igor opened his mouth to answer, but the words froze on his lips. The first of the dive-bombers had waggled his wings in a signal to the others, still hanging there seeming not to move, stark black and sinister against

184

the bright blue morning sky.

'Here they come!' Piotr yelled, rising to his feet to call his warning. 'Tuck in yer turnips and keep yer arses to the rising sun, brothers!'

There were yells of amusement from the men cowering in the ditches. Some of them took off their conical rimless helmets and placed them over their genitals for protection, as if the latter were more important.

Piotr ducked back into his hole as the first dive-bomber suddenly fell out of the sky. In an instant the heavy brooding silence was transformed into hideous, ear-splitting noise. Sirens howling frantically, the wind shrieking through their air brakes, plane after plane came racing down at an impossible angle.

Piotr watched in fascination as those evil hawks of death came closer and closer, filling the whole world with their banshee-like shriek. It seemed nothing could stop them plunging straight to their own destruction. Surely their pilots could not pull out now?

Suddenly, when it seemed nothing could save the pilot of the first plane, he pulled back at the throttle. Piotr caught one mad glimpse of him as he wrenched at his stick, face purple, eyes bulging from their sockets as the tremendous G-force pressed him back against the seat. Then he was gone, soaring upwards into the perfect blue, and the shriek of the sirens was replaced by the whistle of the bombs, those evil black eggs tumbling from its belly.

'NOW GOD HIMSELF SHITS ON US!' Piotr screamed, carried away by wild atavistic excitement as all about him the world went mad, rocking and shuddering under the impact of the bombs, scarlet flames erupting everywhere, sending huge spurts of whirling earth and severed limbs flying high into the air.

On and on it went. Plane after plane came hurtling down in a death-defying dive to drop its bombs, shrieking afterwards in shrill, stomach-churning whistles. Piotr lay there helpless, feeling the ground shudder beneath him. Then the blast hit him, the hot acrid blast of the explosive. It dragged his breath away. He sobbed and choked, blood spurting from his nostrils and ears. All around him, fist-sized chunks of red hot metal hissed back and forth, severing frail human bodies; everywhere there were piles of what looked like offal, the work of some crazy bloodthirsty butcher armed with a blunt cleaver. Time and time again. On and on. Until it seemed the survivors must surely be swept away in this maelstrom of wild metallic death.

'Why us, Comrade Colonel?' Igor croaked,

staggering to his feet, ears still roaring with the echo of that terrible bombing. He stared blankly around at the transformed world: the huge mounds of smoking fresh-brown earth like the work of giant moles – and the dead, the dead sprawled on all sides like piles of broken, abandoned dolls. 'Why us? Why not an armoured column? We're just a bunch of Gulag Rats... Why, Colonel?' There was a note almost of pleading in his cracked, broken voice.

Piotr wiped the earth off his sticky face and noted that his hand was still trembling. That was a bad sign. Unconsciously he touched that bag of earth hanging round his neck for reassurance. 'I don't know, Comrade Major,' he said huskily. 'I just don't know.' He too was staring around in horror at the awful scene. Just one arm's length away lay the body of one of his men, severed head staring at the headless body as if in anger. Propped up against the ditch beyond him lay a fat old soldier whose belly gaped open, intestines hanging out, still steaming slightly. A boy lay near him as though asleep, hand under his right ear, not a mark on him.

Impatiently Piotr shook his head. The buzzing in his ears vanished. Suddenly he was acutely aware of the moans, the curses, the angry calls on all sides. His battalion had suffered badly. There would be much work for the gravediggers this day. He turned to Igor. 'Get the men sorted out ... I want you to–'

He stopped short. Igor was not listening. 'What in the devil's name are you staring at, Comrade Major?' he demanded, flushing with anger.

'There, Comrade Commander... There... What do you make of that?'

Piotr stared in the direction indicated. Silhouetted against the horizon was a sight he had not seen these many years: cavalry, at least a regiment of them. Their pennants fluttering, the spring sun glittering on the drawn sabres that they bore over their shoulders, the riders and horses trotted towards them.

'Fritz?' Igor asked.

Piotr shrugged his shoulders, puzzled. 'No Fritz could ride like that, Comrade Major,' he said after a moment, staring hard, trying to make out the banner borne at the head of the leading troop. 'They're Cossacks all right...' he added hesitantly. But a dreadful thought was beginning to uncurl in his brain.

'But we have no cavalry on this front, Comrade Commander,' Igor objected in bewilderment.

'I know ... I know,' Piotr said softly. 'But Vlassov has.'

'*Vlassov!*' Ivor hissed in that strange

Asiatic manner of his. 'That traitor!'

'Yes, that traitor...' Piotr shook his head almost sadly. 'Today, Comrade Major, Cossack is going to have to fight Cossack.' Then his voice rose urgently. 'Sound the alarm – they're going to attack! *Sound the alarm!'*

They rode at ease, the soft turf muffling the sound of their horses' hooves, relaxed in their saddles, slumped slightly forward like the expert riders they were, sabres jogging up and down on their shoulders, fanning out on each flank in a horn formation, automatically, without a word of command being spoken.

Piotr, crouched along the ridge-line with his men, watched them with a mixture of anger and pride. They belonged to his own people, perhaps he even knew some of them; but all the same they were traitors who had volunteered to fight for the Germans under that renegade Colonel-General Vlassov. He knew, too, that they had not volunteered simply to curry favour from the Germans or to receive extra privileges. No, they had honestly thought that the Fritzes would honour their promises and give them back their old lands, stolen from them by the Communists in the thirties, in the Kuban and along the Don. Yet, he told himself as they came ever closer, their pace increasing now, they had fought and killed their own people, just as they had ridden down the working-class mobs back in the old days at the Little Father's command.*

'Now?' Igor hissed, as everywhere the survivors of the bombing raid squinted along their weapons, ready to fire.

'No, not yet.' Piotr found himself answering in a whisper. 'They are cunning, the Cossacks. Give our position away now and they will simply melt away, then hit us later from another direction. No, wait awhile, Comrade Major – and watch those flanks. That horn as we Cossacks call it, can extend itself –' he grinned suddenly – 'quicker than the horn on a man who hasn't seen a woman for a year!'

But Igor's slant-eyed yellow face failed to light up in response. Piotr told himself that the Mongol had the infantryman's instinctive fear of the horse soldier, who from the infantryman's perspective looked enormous and unstoppable.

'Don't worry,' he said heartily, raising his voice, 'we can beat them – beat them easily. If they try a simple head-on charge they're sunk. Now, prepare to fire!'

'Prepare to fire, comrades!' The command ran from man to man and the Gulag Rats squinted along their sights, each selecting

*Name for the Czar.

his own target, clicking off his safety catch and shifting into a position of readiness.

As Piotr watched, the Cossacks changed pace from trotting to cantering. He could see how the riders moved up and down more quickly and how their horses' hooves beat a faster rhythm on the grass, scattering little clods of earth and turf. Any minute now their commander would order the gallop – then they would charge.

For a few moments his gaze lingered on the commander, clearly visible at the front of his men. He wore the old uniform, the one Piotr remembered from the days of his youth on the Don: long black fur-trimmed coat with silver cartridge cases dangling on both sides of his chest; black fur cape set at a rakish angle on his carefully curled and oiled black hair; the inevitable dagger thrust into his broad leather belt. It was a picture that tugged suddenly at Piotr's heart. Why was he fighting a brother Cossack, he asked himself suddenly. Why were they all fighting for a system that had disgraced them, imprisoned them, used them as contemptible cannonfodder time and time again? *Why, why, why?* For the first time in all the many years since they had released him from the Gulag, his spirit broken, willing to do anything they commanded, Piotr asked himself the painful question. Why was he fighting for *them?*

'They're extending out to the left flank, Comrade Commander!'

Igor's urgent warning broke into his reverie. He shook his head like a man coming out of a heavy sleep. 'Rush the machine guns up there – *davai, davai!* Quick now!'

Sabres flashed silver to his front. The steady drumming changed to thunder. The horses' hooves flew. A hoarse cry rose from a thousand throats, a well-remembered cry that sent a shiver running down Piotr's spine: *'Forward to the freedom of the Homeland!'* It was the age-old Cossack motto. They were charging!

Piotr hesitated no longer. Once they came within striking distance and started laying about them with those silver sabres of theirs, they'd be lost; the Gulag Rats under his command would break. *'FIRE!'* he shrieked at the top of his voice. Then, springing up from his hiding place, he fired a wild pistol-burst at the galloping line of men and horses.

'CHARGE!' the tall Cossack commander bellowed. His standard-bearer swung the black banner of the Don Cossacks to and fro. His men leant forward, crouched low over the flying manes of their mounts, sword arms extended, their sabres parallel to their horses' necks, shrieking obscenities, carried away by the wild, mad ecstasy of the charge.

The first volley slammed into their packed

front rank with devastating effect. Abruptly the field was transformed into a chaotic scene of murder and mayhem. It wasn't war; it was a massacre. Men and beasts went down everywhere, the horses rearing and plunging, snorting with terror as great scarlet patches appeared suddenly on their gleaming, sweat-lathered flanks, throwing their riders, trampling them underfoot as they struggled in panic to rise again, being swamped by ever more wounded and dying men and mounts.

'Keep firing!' Piotr screamed, near hysteria himself, and sick at heart at this great slaughter. 'Don't let them get within sabre distance!... Here they come again – *FIRE!*'

The tall young commander was waiting slightly to one side, coolly smoking a long cigarette as if he were attending a Cossack *krug** in peacetime, while the second wave pushed its way through the gory carnage of the first, then closing ranks and urging their mounts into the gallop once more.

Suddenly he flung away his cigarette, nodding to his wounded standard-bearer, whose face was now a bloody mess as if someone had thrown a handful of red jam at it. Weakly he waved the heavy banner. The commander rose high in his saddle and

*Krug: an assembly (or meeting place).

swung his sabre, glinting a bright silver in the sun. And then they were thundering forward again, bent low over their horses' flying manes, yelling their wild Cossack cries as they came in for the kill.

Piotr took careful aim, hating himself for doing so. But it had to be done. The handsome face of the commander was dissected by the black sight of his pistol. He tried to control his harsh breathing. Knock out their commander and the Cossacks would break, he knew that. *'One ... two ...'* he started to count under his breath, his hand and arm as steady as a rock now as he watched the young cavalry commander riding towards his death.

'THEY'RE BEHIND US ... BEHIND US!' Igor screamed.

Piotr fired. A Cossack riding to the right of the commander rose high in his saddle, screaming in agony, a purple hole where his right eye had been, then slumped forward over his horse's mane, dead.

Now the Cossacks were everywhere and Piotr forgot the tall young commander. The Battalion was fighting for its life. Once again the proverbial Cossack cunning had triumphed; they had arranged to slip a company to his rear while the Gulag Rats had been congratulating themselves they could slaughter the rest of the regiment easily.

Infantryman against rider, rider against

infantryman, no quarter was given or expected. The Cossacks milled around little pockets of infantrymen, hacking and slashing with those cruel sabres, while the Gulag Rats fought back with their bayonets and entrenching tools.

Piotr flung away his empty pistol with a curse. He reached up to grab at the nearest Cossack's arm, and gave one enormous heave. The man came tumbling down to disappear beneath the flailing hooves of his own terror-stricken mount. Meanwhile Piotr had grabbed his sabre and was hacking away now at another who had fallen when his horse was shot beneath him. He was a brawny young man, but no match for Piotr. They clashed sabres once, twice, three times, Piotr easily parrying the other's thrusts, then with a quick flick of the wrist he sent the Cossack's sabre flying. The young man reeled back, face contorted with fear. Piotr had no mercy. Carried away by the bloodlust of battle, he aimed a mighty blow at the defenceless Cossack's face. The keen blade cut through flesh and bone – and the Cossack fell dead, his face split diagonally from temple to jaw.

'*Dog!... Red dog!*' an angry voice cried behind him.

Piotr swung round, sabre at the ready.

It was the young commander on his horse, towering above him, eyes blazing with fury, blood trickling from a deep wound in his forehead. 'Now die, you dog!' he roared, tugging fiercely at the reins. Then as the horse rose high on its hindlegs, its forelegs pawing the air, he raised his sabre to bring it down on Piotr's head.

The Colonel reacted with surprising speed, pulling an old Cossack trick he remembered from the days of his long dead father. His opponent, he knew, was expecting him to react with his sabre in his right hand. But, equally dextrous with both hands, Piotr flung his sabre from his right to his left hand. The move caught the other man completely by surprise, throwing him off balance. He hesitated for one fatal second.

Piotr grunted and brought his weapon down – *hard*. The keen blade sliced into the young commander's right knee, deep into the bone. As the bright red blood jetted from the tremendous wound, he doubled up and screamed with agony, losing his hold on the reins. The horse dropped its forelegs, and as it did so Piotr lashed out again. The blow caught the Cossack right across his throat. One moment his head was there; the next it was gone, spinning away to disappear among the hooves and shuffling feet. Behind it the headless body slumped off the white horse, smearing its hide scarlet with the blood of its slaughtered master...

Five minutes later it was all over. The Cossacks were retreating, slashing at their horses with their whips, even with the blades of their sabres in order to escape, leaving behind them a shocked, exhausted handful of Gulag Rats, drooping over their weapons among the piles of dead men and horses; and Colonel Piotr staring as if for ever at the head of the man he had killed, the tears streaming unchecked down his face, his nostrils assailed yet again by that strange smell, as what looked like charred fragments of burnt paper started to drift by in the gentle spring wind...

TWO

It looked like all the camps that Colonel Piotr had ever seen since he first entered the Gulag, a prisoner, a broken man, dishonoured by his own ungrateful country. It was the usual half-a-dozen hectares of hard-packed, naked farmland shaped into the form of a great hexagon by the high triple wire fence surrounding it.

Inside there was the customary collection of dreary brown wooden huts, grouped around a parade ground dominated by the usual swastika flag hanging from the flagpole. At regular intervals there were the typical stork-legged wooden towers, manned by guards with machine guns and searchlights, hanging about in morose boredom as they eyed the emaciated wretches below. If it had not been for the crooked cross of Nazi Germany, this could well have been the same camp in which he had spent four miserable years in Siberia, until the war came and they released him to form the Punishment Battalion.

But there was one big difference. Piotr frowned and lowered his binoculars, while Igor and his surviving officers waited tensely for his orders. How did one explain the sickly smell of gas that suffused the spring air and made his stomach turn? And what was one to make of the strange, unwholesome, pale-yellow colour of the vegetation outside the camp? Had it something to do with the gas? But what was the gas used for? The jailers down there certainly wouldn't use it to heat the place up for those emaciated wretches in their drooping striped pyjamas!

'What are your orders, Comrade Commander?' Igor asked. He had been badly shaken by the attack of the previous day and did not want to linger anywhere long, in case those evil metal birds appeared once more to drop their deadly eggs.

Piotr fumbled with his bag of native earth for reassurance. 'I don't know, Comrade Major,' he said, frowning. 'I don't know. But I have been thinking … and I have come to the conclusion that the Fritzes wasted all the effort on us yesterday to stop us reaching that camp down there. That is why they sacrificed my brothers from the Don.' His frown deepened and his face took on a sudden bitter look. 'But why? What is so important about that place?'

Igor nodded his shaven head in agreement. 'Yes, indeed, Comrade Commander. It looks just like any other camp.' He hesitated momentarily and cast a quick look over his shoulder as if he had half expected a Green-cap* to be standing there, taking notes of what he said. 'And we all know about camps, don't we, Comrade Commander?'

'We do indeed,' Piotr said grimly.

A heavy silence fell upon the little group of officers crouched on the hillside overlooking the strange camp. Once again Piotr's nostrils wrinkled at the peculiar sweet smell wafting up from the camp; once again he noted the parchment-thin fragments of matter drifting by in the faint breeze.

He lifted his binoculars and surveyed the place for the umpteenth time, lingering on the six chimneys from which thin grey columns of smoke were ascending. Whatever it was that was drifting in their direction obviously came from the huts below those chimneys.

Suddenly he made up his mind. 'Comrade Major, get the men on their feet!'

'*Da, da, Tavarovitch!*' the little slant-eyed officer snapped, eager to be on his way. They were too exposed out here on the hillside. 'Where are we going?'

'We are going to attack the camp, Comrade Major,' Piotr answered. 'Something strange is happening down there and I want to know what it is.'

*A member of the Russian secret police, the NKVD, who wore green caps.

'But Comrade Commander, our orders were to stop for nothing. The Marshal–'

'Damn the Marshal,' Piotr said easily. 'We are here and he is far away – undoubtedly stuffing his face with caviar and good vodka, or tumbling in bed with that plump pigeon of his. Remember the old saying? What you don't know doesn't make you hot!' He grinned suddenly. 'We'll inform the Marshal of our actions, all right, – but *afterwards!* Now, *move it!*'

Igor jumped to obey.

Doctor Dietrich was nervous, very nervous. Head *Kapo** Bruno could see that, as he carefully packed the Doctor's 'souvenirs' under Dietrich's supervision. And he knew why. The good Doctor's world was falling apart. After nearly ten years of being undisputed master of the camp and its inmates, he had now been reduced to the level of a common criminal on the run, with every man's hand against him. For there was no denying the fact that the Nazis had lost the war, and soon the victors would be hunting down the Doctor to make him pay for his war crimes.

'The lampshade,' Dietrich demanded, taking a drag at yet another cigarette – the

---

*A trusty, a prisoner who took charge of a group of other prisoners in the concentration camps.

ashtray was already overflowing – 'have you packed my lampshade, Bruno?'

'*Jawohl, Herr Doktor,*' Bruno sang out hastily. Finished as he almost was, Dietrich was still dangerous. Most of the older guards had already fled, but the young fanatics of the SS were still holding on.

'Good, good... It was made from the skin of that Yiddish professor from Poland. Almost as dark as a nigger he was, d'yer remember? It'll go very well with the décor of my house near Hamburg.'

'I am sure you're right, *Herr Doktor,*' Bruno answered, though privately telling himself that Doctor *shitting* Dietrich was *shitting* well kidding himself! He'd never see Hamburg again.

Dietrich stubbed out his cigarette with a shaky, fevered movement and immediately lit another. 'Pity about that Polack's tit,' he said, flashing a quick look out of the window as if to reassure himself that all was still well. It was. The smoke was rising from the chimneys in steady grey curls; obviously the ovens were functioning properly.

'You mean the one they're curing for you in the workshop, *Herr Doktor?*' Bruno asked, dutiful to the last.

'Yes...' Dietrich smiled suddenly at the memory, his ugly yellow teeth bulging out between his pale, bloodless lips. 'That Polack wench had a remarkable bosom. One tit as big as a pair on most women. I was struck by them at once.' He shook his head a little sadly. 'If we'd had time to cure the skin, that tit would have made a wonderful tobacco pouch – and a rather nice little conversation piece at parties as well.' He puffed on his cigarette, enjoying the daydream. What a nice opening gambit it would have made back in Hamburg when once again he was mixing with the great port's *prominenz* – shippers and lawyers and the like: 'Rather remarkable history, this tobacco pouch... Made from the left tit of a Polish communist, you know.' How they would have gaped and laughed! But he dismissed the pleasant little scene from his mind and concentrated on the task in hand. 'All right, Bruno, carry on packing – and for God's sake be careful. Some of those things are priceless. Their like won't be seen for another thousand years or more, I'll be bound.'

'*Jawohl, Herr Doktor!*' Bruno snapped, springing to attention as Dietrich reached for his cap, decorated with the gleaming silver skull and crossbones that still made him shudder even after all these years in the camps.

Dietrich lifted his riding crop, slapped it against his highly polish jackboot and then swaggered out of the door, every millimetre a senior member of the Master Race.

He was barely gone before Bruno spat on

the scrubbed wooden floor. Thank God, he told himself, no one would see such things, such horrible perverted things, for another thousand years. Then he got on with his job, only vaguely conscious of the distant rumble of motor engines...

Dietrich stalked through the camp ignoring the walking scarecrows with staring, cavernous eyes, still just strong enough to get out of his way. He acknowledged the salutes of the teenage SS men with a gay flourish of his riding crop, occasionally slashing it through the air as if practising the ritual flogging to death of yet another victim.

He would miss this place, he told himself, heading towards the barracks where the women were kept. Another year, perhaps even as little as six months, and he would have completed his research. It would have meant a professorship, a chair at a really good German university, and then he would have been set up for life. He smiled ruefully at the thought. And he would miss the fun and games with the women, too. Black, white, yellow, he had had them all, in ones, two, threes, even fours, from all five continents. My God, he must have had sex with women from virtually every country in Europe. By now he knew more than even the most scholarly professor of sexual relationships!

He passed under that mocking legend, painted in white on the arch leading into the women's compound, *'WORK MAKES FREE'*, and acknowledged the salutes of the sentries. It was here that he had carried out most of his experiments. Women were tougher than men. They had been able to stand up to pain amazingly well.

One of the women was shuffling towards him now, her feet wrapped in filthy rags and a potato sack wrapped around her skull-like face, skinny leathern dugs hanging out of her pyjama jacket. Dietrich stopped and frowned. He liked women with breasts like balloons, not shrivelled up paps like that. The woman sickened him. She ought to be taught a lesson for offending his eye like that.

'You!' he barked at her, suddenly noticing the rumble of approaching motor engines, but ignoring them while he dealt with the woman. 'What are you? Polack? Ivan? Cheesehead?...' He ran through the litany of contemptuous nicknames, thwacking his crop against his boot at the mention of each nationality. 'Well, speak up, woman – what are you?'

Strangely enough the woman did not seem aware of the mortal danger that she was in. Instead she was staring at something beyond him, what appeared to be a kind of twisted smile on her wizened face.

Dietrich flushed with rage. Was she smiling at *him?* 'Do ... do ... do you know who I am, you whore?' he spluttered, raising his cane and pointing it at her threateningly. 'Have you any idea what happens to wretches like you when they keep me waiting?... *Have you?*' He was so overcome by anger that bubbles of saliva were forming at the corners of his thin cruel mouth.

The woman's expression did not change, save that now he seemed to discern a look of longing in her faded eyes. *'Krasnaya Armya,'* she quavered suddenly, as the noise of many motors rumbled ever closer, *'Krasnaya Armya...'* She reached out one dirty, shaking hand to point, tears of joy streaming down her sunken hollow cheeks.

Dietrich swung round and almost dropped his stick at what he saw there.

On the heights above the concentration camp was a long column of vehicles moving slowly down, with men in earth-coloured blouses springing to the ground everywhere, already raising little round-barrelled tommy guns at their chests ready to fire; and there was no mistaking the red star adorning the side of each camouflaged vehicle.

'The Red Army!' he gasped, ducking as the first angry salvo cut the air. *'The Red Army!'* And then he was running for his life, zigzagging across the compound where once he had ruled supreme.

THREE

Now they were taking their revenge.

The surviving SS guards were being mercilessly beaten to the death by the crowds of roaring, mocking, shouting ex-prisoners, wielding sticks, broom handles, iron bars, indulging themselves in a wild frenzy of revenge. Those who were too weak to wield a club simply squatted on the dying SS men and urinated on their ghastly, gory faces.

Another group had almost finished the crucifixion of Doctor Dietrich. He was being nailed to that sign over the women's compound, *'WORK MAKES FREE'*, his riding crop thrust deep up his anus, his skinny body naked and covered with bloody slashes from his own whip. Now one of the women he had tortured, breastless and minus most of her inner organs thanks to him, was sharpening a long butchers knife looted from the kitchen.

Colonel Piotr knew what was going to happen next. The woman would sever Deitrich's penis and thrust it into his dying mouth. They always did that. In life they had been rendered sexless by the torturers;

accordingly the torturers invariably went to their deaths in the same fashion – emasculated!

Piotr turned away from the frenzied scene outside his window, trying not to notice that there were still prisoners dying in the midst of their liberation, sinking into the mud helplessly, perhaps even unaware that they were free at last.

'All right, bring the bitch in,' he ordered.

At the door to what had once been Doctor Dietrich's bedroom, its walls covered with the coarsest of pornographic photographs and instruments of torture, Igor clicked his fingers at the waiting guards, most of them drunk on looted schnapps. They thrust the chief wardress inside roughly and she staggered to a halt just inside the room.

When they had arrested her, after slaughtering most of the other SS female guards, she was in bed with a simpering little Polish blonde. She laughed at them when they threatened her. Her beating she accepted without a mutter. Then they gang-raped the little Polish girl, who screamed and pleaded for mercy before finally sinking into unconsciousness. Still the woman remained unmoved. She stoically accepted her own savage raping in the same manner. *'Do ... do what you wish,'* she croaked at them in accented Russian. 'What does it matter?... What does anything matter any more?...'

She did not cry out even when the last of the Gulag Rats was thrusting brutally into her.

Now she stood there, swaying slightly, one eye blackened, uniform hanging from her shapely body, sensual lips set in a mocking smile.

Colonel Piotr looked at her in repulsion. She had been directly responsible to Doctor Dietrich, his trusted assistant who selected female victims for his sadistic experiments and later disposed of the evidence in the ovens. She was a monster, he thought. Yet she did not look like the rest of the female guards – big ugly peasant girls. She was petite and dainty, and her one open eye revealed interest and intelligence and not one bit of fear.

'Why?' Piotr asked, tossing away his cigarette and slowly beginning to open his breeches.

'Why what?' Her voice was low and educated.

'Why this – this horror camp?' Piotr snapped, growing angry again. 'How could a woman – a woman like *you* – help to run such a place?'

She did not answer.

Igor slammed his fist brutally into her kidneys. 'Answer, Fritz cow!' he rasped. 'Answer the Comrade Colonel, *quick!*'

For a moment she winced with the pain of

that savage blow but she recovered herself quickly. She even forced a weary, cynical smile. 'Why the questions, Colonel?' she said huskily. 'You are going to kill me... Well, get it over with.' She shrugged her shoulders slightly. 'When the world has fallen apart, what does the fate of one individual mean?'

'But this c-camp...' Piotr stuttered furiously as he undid his flies. 'The things you and the others have done... How could you?'

The woman smiled a cynical smile. 'Do you think you are different, Colonel? You have camps, too, don't you? The only difference is that we are ... we *were* just a little more efficient–'

'Damn you, *stop it!*' Piotr yelled angrily. 'Comrades, prepare her!'

The waiting Gulag Rats didn't hesitate. They grabbed the unresisting woman by the arms and flung her face forward on Dietrich's bed, holding her down.

With one hand Piotr ripped the rest of her clothing from her battered body to reveal her neat white rump, while with the other hand he tore open his breeches. His organ sprang out, swinging in front of him like a militiaman's club.

For a moment he towered above her, while she lay there motionless, legs forced apart by the leering soldiers eyeing those plump inviting buttocks. Suddenly he struck her hard. She bit the pillow to prevent herself from screaming out.

'Pleasure and punishment,' he growled, dark Cossack eyes blazing with anger and lust. He hit her again right across the buttocks; they immediately flushed scarlet with the marks of his fingers. 'Punishment and pleasure ... *NOW!*' And he suddenly plunged forward, dwarfing her with his massive male hulk.

'No – you cannot do that to me!' she gasped. *'No ... no ... no man has ever done–'* Her wild protest ended in a hysterical, gurgling scream, coming from far down within her, as her spine curved taut like a bow and he thrust himself with all his savage strength deep between her taut fearful haunches.

Five minutes later he thrust his pistol deep into her vagina and pulled the trigger. But just before he managed to blow her apart, she opened one mocking eye. *'Soviet morality!'* she sneered. Then she died.

Marshal Rokossovsky frowned and took a deep drag at his cigarette. The drunken ex-prisoners and the men of the First Punishment Battalion were dancing wildly around the bodies of dead German guards, slowly turning black as they dangled from wires above the merrily crackling fires. Their revenge had turned into a kind of perverted game. Someone – a Polack, Piotr guessed from the accent – had suggested playing 'ovens and going up the chimney', as he had called it, and the others had taken up the suggestion with alacrity.

Everywhere prisoners and Russian soldiers were roasting the dead Fritzes over fires. It made Piotr think of peasants smoking dead pigs for the winter back on the Don.

The Marshal abruptly threw away his cigarette, grinding it out under the toe of his elegant, gleaming boot. 'Why have you wasted so much time with this place, Piotr?' he asked, steering the tall handsome Colonel away from the rest of his staff, as if he wanted to hear Piotr's explanation alone.

'They were prisoners, many of them our own people, Comrade Marshal. I had to help them. It is as simple as that.'

'Is it?' Rokossovsky raised one eyebrow.

'Yes, Comrade Marshal,' Piotr replied stoutly. 'We have come as liberators!' He frowned suddenly, as if the word reminded him of something unpleasant. 'We could not deny them that freedom, whatever it cost us in terms of lost time – if that is what you are concerned about, Comrade Marshal.'

Rokossovsky did not take up the point immediately. 'You have changed, Piotr,' he said, half seriously, half in jest. 'You are thinking now – which is something that you didn't do a few weeks ago. What do you say to that?'

'Perhaps this is the time for thinking, Comrade Marshal, now that the war is virtually over.'

'Yes? Thinking about what?' The Marshal had lowered his voice, as if even he were afraid that he might be overheard by the Greencaps.

'Oh, *why* we are fighting... And for *whom* we are fighting...'

'For our country, for the glory of Mother Russia.'

Piotr shook his head. 'No, Comrade.' Deliberately he omitted the 'Marshal', as if he wished to emphasise the solidarity of two fighting men. 'We are fighting for Old Leather Face and the creed of communism. Mother Russia, as we knew it as young soldiers, no longer exists. It disappeared in those years of the Great Purge, when you and I both were sentenced to the Gulag as traitors.'

Rokissovsky lowered his gaze, but said nothing.

'Our kind of Russia has not existed these ten years. What *does* exist is a country that is run by a despot. When you say we fight for Mother Russia, you really mean we are fighting to keep Stalin and his rotten gang in power, to ensure that the Gulags of this world – just like this death camp – continue to exist. We defeat one tyranny and help to maintain another.' He licked his dry lips.

'For me it was more important to liberate these poor wretches than to carry out the mission for – *Stalin*.' He spat out the hatred name venomously.

The tall Marshal frowned a little helplessly. 'But what can we do, little brother? What?'

Piotr shrugged, his shoulders slumping as if he were suddenly very tired. 'I don't think I know, Comrade Marshal. But this I do know–' He looked at his superior officer as if for the first time, noticing his pale, clever face. 'I do know that it's time we refused to go on fighting just to keep that monster in the Kremlin. Once the Fritzes are finished, then there has to be an end to it.'

'But Piotr,' Rokossovsky breathed, 'that is treachery! They would shoot you out of hand like a rabid dog.'

Piotr forced a laugh. 'Don't you think they will do anyway? Oh yes, one day they will. Once a Gulag Rat, always a Gulag Rat. Old Leather Face needs us now – but as soon as he doesn't...' Piotr crooked his right forefinger as if he were pulling the trigger of a pistol.

Rokossovsky sighed. 'What will you do, Piotr?'

'Never fear, Comrade Marshal, I shall soldier on,' Piotr said lightly. 'I shall try to achieve the objective you have set for my battalion, even if I do it only for you, Comrade. But the day I find an alternative...' He paused.

'An alternative?' The Marshal looked puzzled.

'Vlassov found one,' Piotr said softly.

'But he sold out to the Fritzes!'

'I know, he sold out to the wrong people for the right cause. All he and those poor swine who died yesterday ever wanted was their rights as Russians. Unfortunately they believed the lies of the Germans. But there must be an alternative, Comrade Marshal. *There must!*' But Piotr's voice held a note of despair.

'And if you find it?' Rokossovsky asked softly, suppressing a shudder; for if the question ever came to the ears of the Green-caps, even his life would be forfeit.

Piotr hesitated only a moment, his mind racing as he realised the full import of what he was going to say. 'Then, Comrade Marshal,' he said, looking hard at the other man, 'I shall vote with my feet.'

'And what in the devil's name is that supposed to mean, Colonel Piotr?' Rokossovsky barked, his pale cunning face flushing abruptly.

Piotr did not answer. Instead he turned and strode to the door. Suddenly he remembered what the Fritz woman had cried at him just before he blew her evil body apart. She had been a pervert and a sadist, but all the same she had been brave and honest in her last moments on this earth. 'Soviet morality!' she had sneered, staring at him mockingly even as he reached for his pistol to shoot her. And he had known exactly what she had meant. He and all he stood for was just as corrupt as the German system had been. She had died, but he was carrying on the same terrible, depraved order of things: the brown-shirted cruelty of the fascist system under a different flag and a different leader, but still the very same thing.

'Igor!' he bawled, completely ignoring Rokossovsky. 'Round up those Rats of ours – we're moving out! *Davai, davai...!*'

Ten minutes later they had vanished, leaving the camp to the drunken riotous inmates and the dead guards. Slowly and thoughtfully, Marshal of the Soviet Union Konstantin Rokossovsky walked out to his waiting staff car. Wordlessly he clicked his elegantly manicured fingers at the driver, and they moved off with a little cavalcade of staff cars following them.

As they left the camp they passed under the arch with its mocking legend *'WORK MAKES FREE'*. Above them the mutilated body of *Herr Doktor* Dietrich swung back and forth in the faint wind, the mouth wide open and sucking its monstrous lollipop of flesh, while sprawled in the mud nearby,

Bruno, the lampshade made of the skin of the Yiddish professor clamped on his head, precious bottle of Dietrich's schnapps clasped to his chest, laughed and laughed and laughed...

FOUR

To Corrigan and his weary men, marching doggedly up the roads that ran parallel to the River Elbe, it seemed that the whole of Eastern Germany was heading westwards. Refugee columns blocked the roads everywhere, crawling painfully towards the river, fleeing the advancing Red Army, which was slaughtering, burning, raping and pillaging its way across the great plain of Mecklenburg.

Many were on foot, their possessions piled high on their shoulders. Some came from further east; they had set out on this great trek back in the winter from their homes in Silesia and East Prussia, driving westwards in farm carts covered with tarpaper roofs through which stove pipes stuck, so that they looked like pioneers of the Old West in their prairie schooners.

Nearly a thousand years ago, the forefathers of these Germans had migrated eastwards from this self-same Elbe plain lured by the promise of the rich Slavic lands. Now a millennium later the Slavs were reclaiming that land, forcing the hated *Nemets* – 'the silent ones' – as they called the Germans, back to where they had come from so long before.

The refugees no longer cared that they had lost their farms and homes for ever. They were motivated solely by one over-whelming desire – to survive, to escape the terrible revenge that the Russians would exact from them if they overtook their long weary columns. Time and time again, marching through the German *treks*, as they called them, completely disregarded by the shabby frightened civilians, the Assault Troopers observed the tragedies of their weary progress. A skinny old nag led by an equally skinny old woman, collapsing in the middle of the road, with the column sweep-ing past in unreasoning fear, leaving the old woman behind to weep, stroking the dying animal's neck with her ancient withered claw. A baby born dead and flung out of a passing cart wrapped in newspaper. An old man going mad, tearing off his clothes, running naked about the fields until he finally slumped down at the side of the road, white head resting on his hand, watching the carts trundle by like some country yokel of a Sunday evening watching the big-city traffic returning from a peacetime country outing. Tragedy after tragedy...

'They're finished, sir,' Hawkins had com-mented. 'The whole of Germany is packing up for good and making a run for it, before the Russkis nab them.'

And Corrigan had been forced to agree. More than once they had encountered heavily armed German infantrymen, obviously survivors from shattered units, who had not even glanced at these strange khaki-clad figures in their midst. Their gaze had been fixed almost hypnotically on the far horizon to the west, as if they were following a vision of the Holy Grail itself. They passed their English enemy without a single challenge.

And yet, on this second day since they crossed the Elbe on the wildly drifting ferry, Corrigan was worried. Their luck would run out sooner or later. In the end they'd meet the fanatics of the SS – and that would be that. Besides, he told himself, as his weary men armed only with their personal weapons slogged up the dusty road, what good was an armoured recce unit without vehicles? If he were to carry out the mission that Montgomery had entrusted to him, he needed wheels and weapons – and needed them *soon*.

Later that afternoon Corrigan spotted the opportunity he had been looking for. They were approaching a small Mecklenburg village, a group of white-painted, one-storey houses huddled around the little local church, its slate-covered onion steeple glistening in the sunshine. But unlike the other villages they had passed through so far, this one was definitely inhabited. He could see the smoke curling upwards from a few of the houses and there was a distinct flash from underneath the onion-domed steeple, as if someone up there might be using binoculars to survey the area to the east. A few minutes later he noticed the first heavily camouflaged vehicles, their bodies draped with netting, parked under some apple trees to the right of the little settlement.

'Wheels!' he hissed.

'What, sir?' Hawkins stuttered, waking up from that self-induced reverie which is the old soldier's way of forgetting the weariness of a long march. 'What did you say, sir?'

'Forget it,' Corrigan snapped. 'Pass it on. The men will drop out, one by one, making it casual. We want to be taken for part of this lot. Nice and casual…'

Hawkins hissed the command out of the side of his mouth at the man directly behind him, while Corrigan hurried on to catch up with a lumbering farm cart pulled by two oxen in front of him, tossing his helmet into the ditch to his right as he did so. The typical pisspot shape of the British Army's tin hat would be a dead give-away if anyone were observing the weary column of human misery from the church steeple.

Now as man after man flopped out into

the ditches on both sides of the road as if they were completely exhausted and could not walk another yard – which wasn't far from the truth – Corrigan put the ancient farm wagon between himself and the nearest houses, eyes suddenly gleaming as the adrenalin pumped new energy into him.

He could see the shapes of the camouflaged vehicles quite clearly now. They were six-wheeled German armoured scout cars, the open-turreted kind, which he remembered the enemy using back at Dunkirk in what seemed another age now. They were old, that was for sure, but they would suit the Assault Troop's purpose ideally: they were German and they were fast; and his men, he knew, had had their bellyful of marching. The question now was how could he nobble them without casualties.

They were passing through the village now, apathetic civilians paying no attention to the lounging German soldiers who whistled at the girls and made improper suggestions; they had only one thing in mind – to reach the Elbe! Corrigan shuffled past with the rest, his rifle concealed in the side of the bullock cart, his gaze apparently cast down on the dusty ground. In reality his mind was racing as he took in the sights and sounds all around him in the little village street.

They were the elite, he could see that. Fit

young men in their early twenties, their black tunics heavy with the enamel and tin that the German Army handed out in such profusion to its combat soldiers. These were veterans, he told himself. Veterans in good heart, who were not prepared to flee in terror at the sound of the first shot. They would fight it out – and that was the last thing the Assault Troop wanted at this stage of the game: a pitched battle with heavy casualties.

They crouched in the shelter of a wood while darkness fell on the village below, watching the first night shadows creeping across the plain towards the houses and munching their 'iron ration'– a bar of hard bitter chocolate – washed down with careful sips from their waterbottles, while Corrigan explained the situation.

'Of course we could outflank the village and escape north without a fight. It would mean a detour of – say – five or six miles. But where would we find vehicles again, I ask you?'

'You're dead right there, sir,' Sanders said with a moan. 'My dogs are slaying me. Let's find some wheels. Mrs Sanders' handsome son wasn't cut out for the infantry. No sir!'

'Point taken, Sanders,' Corrigan said, as Hawkins glared warningly at the little Australian. 'But I'm not prepared to pay any kind of butcher's bill for those wheels. I want them as cheap as possible.'

Hawkins sucking his dead pipe, took his eyes off Sanders and nodded his approval. The CO was right; they wanted no more losses in the Assault Troop, especially with the war almost over.

'So, how do we do it? I'll tell you. We do it by stealth.' Corrigan let the words sink in before taking up a twig and drawing a line in the dry earth in front of him. 'This is roughly the line held by the Jerries, running to the front of the village, with their vehicles hidden against the church wall – *here.*' He marked a cross in the dirt. 'And *here* is the village stream, in other words between their line and the vehicles. Got it?'

'Got it,' they chorused, weariness forgotten now as they craned forward in the growing darkness to look at the rough sketch map.

'Now I checked that stream out,' Corrigan went on. 'The water itself is only a couple of feet deep, but the banks offer ample cover. So–'

'So we can use it as cover to get in behind the Jerries.' Sanders beat him to it.

'Yes, that's right. We could get almost to those vehicles, with a bit of luck, and not be seen.'

There was a soft murmur of approval from the men, as the night wind started to blow and the last rays of the sun faded on the horizon to the west.

'But sir...' Wolfers was holding up his hand like a schoolboy asking to be excused, his mouth brown with chocolate to complete the picture.

'Yes, Wolfers?'

'There's a catch though, sir, like,' he said in his ponderous Yorkshire fashion.

'How do you mean, Trooper Wolfers?'

'Well, yon stream ends about twenty-odd yards, as far as I can make out, from the armoured cars. We'd be dead out in the open from it to them.'

Sanders moaned. 'Christ, Wolfers, ain't you just a little bundle of frigging fun!' he sneered. 'You can put the frigging moppers on anything, you can.'

Corrigan nodded as if agreeing with the earnest-faced young soldier, however. 'I've already taken that into consideration, Wolfers. You see, most of these one-horse German villages, as you know by now, have no real sanitation. It's the piss-bucket and the outside privy for most of the houses.'

'You can say that again,' Sanders snorted. 'Even in the Outback they do better than these Jerries. Talk about Jerry frigging culture!' He spat in disgust.

'Only the bigger houses have some form of real sanitation – and where does it run off to?' Corrigan answered his own question.

'Into the nearest stream. Not very hygienic, but cheap and practical.'

'So the lesson is, mates–' Sanders seized his opportunity quickly – 'never drink water. Besides, fishes fuck in water!'

There was a rumble of laughter. Corrigan smiled tolerantly. In spite of their weariness and hunger, the Assault Troop was in its usual good form. The boys wouldn't let him down now, he knew that.

'Now *here*,' he said as he drew another line on the ground, 'is the church ... and beside it is a large eighteenth-century house, which I think is probably the rectory. It is my guess that the house will be linked to the stream by a sewer. If we can find it and get into the house, we're quids in. We'd only be a matter of yards away from where those wheels are parked next to the church wall.'

Corrigan fell silent, waiting for their reaction as they digested his words.

Slowly Hawkins took his cold pipe from his mouth and said, 'Begging yer pardon, sir. But there seem to be a lot of "ifs" in your plan.'

'Yer,' Slim Sanders agreed quickly. '*If* there's a sewer. *If* we can find it. *If* we can get into the house. *If* it ain't packed with Jerries. *If ... if ... if...*' He grinned suddenly and added: 'But it's better than frigging hoofing it any frigging day, sir!'

Corrigan returned his grin. He knew he

had them. They wouldn't let him down, even if the plan was, as Hawkins and Sanders had pointed out, decidedly shaky. 'All right, chaps, that's it. Let's get our heads down for a bit of kip. Sergeant Hawkins will post the sentries.' He yawned wearily. 'We go in at the witching hour – midnight.'

Wolfers shuddered dramatically. 'Oh Christ, sir,' he quavered, 'not them bleeding werewolves again...!'

FIVE

With a grunt, Wolfers took the strain and heaved, as all around him the others crouched in the stream, the burbling noise it made drowning the sound of Wolfers' bayonet grating against metal and stone. Five yards away, facing to the rear of the German line, Corrigan and Hawkins tensed, weapons at the ready. Now they were really sitting ducks. A couple of stick grenades over the side of the stream and they would be finished, bunched together as they were around the entrance to the sewer. Corrigan felt the nerve at his temple begin to tick electrically. He told himself to stop it; he was getting too tense.

Behind him the giant Yorkshireman grunted again and levered his little bayonet between the stone and the ancient rusty grid that closed the mouth of the sewer. 'Come on, yer bugger,' he cursed through gritted teeth. 'Give, won't yer!'

It was a plea that could have come straight from Corrigan's tortured mind. It only took a patrol to look over the side of the stream and–

Behind him something grated. Even at

that distance Corrigan's nostrils were assailed by the stench; it struck him an almost physical blow. He gagged.

Wolfers had ripped the lid off, tearing at it with his big hands, the rusty metal giving easily now. Within a couple of minutes it was open and they were able to peer into the tunnel. It was higher than a man and had a small channel running down its centre, filled with a nauseating brown liquid.

'Shit!' Sanders commented in disgust. 'Now they're gonna turn us into bleeding shit-shovellers!'

'Dead ones, if you don't keep it down to a low roar,' Corrigan growled, pushing Sanders to one side and flashing on his torch, his nose wrinkled up at the stench. Ahead there was the sudden scampering of clawed feet and, for an instant, the shadows of a handful of rats scuttling away, grotesquely magnified by the white light.

Wolfers stifled a yelp. 'Get a grip of yerself, lad,' Hawkins urged. 'Yer allus bloody well doing that. It puts years on me!'

'All right,' Corrigan whispered urgently. 'Let's get on with it. I'll go first. Sergeant Hawkins will bring up the rear. No noise and no heroics. I want those wheels with the minimum of trouble. Here we go!'

Wolfers licked his lips nervously as he followed Corrigan into the evil-smelling tunnel with nauseous dripping walls. Great black cockroaches were swimming in the seepage below their feet as he and the rest fought to keep their balance on the slippery flags, which probably had not been trodden since they had been first laid a couple of centuries before. Christ, he told himself, was there never going to be an end to it? First the bleeding werewolves and now this traipsing around under the earth at midnight. God knows what they might be meeting down here. It was just the setting for the living dead – and worse!

Corrigan's thoughts were much more prosaic. Flashing his torch from side to side he checked there were no sudden drops or hidden drainage chambers. He estimated that it might be a hundred yards to the rectory, and that probably the tunnel passed right under the old house with perhaps an inspection chamber in the middle of the cobbled yard behind it. The problem was, however, would there be a sentry posted in the yard? It was obvious that the rectory itself was occupied. He had seen smoke emerging from its chimney stack and it would be the likely place for the company guarding the village to set up its headquarters. Grimly he plodded on, trying to ignore the heavy cloying stench and the clatter of hobnailed boots on the stone flags which echoed and re-echoed hollowly the length of the tunnel. More than once he shivered at the sound of fat black cock-roaches squashing under his own boots and then the eerie pitter-patter of rats scuttling about busily in the shadows.

Now he could feel a cooler breeze on his face, driving away the stink a little, and he reasoned that they were coming closer to the exit. He quickened his pace and cursed inwardly as one of his men slipped and fell, clattering down on the flags.

'Get yer finger out, you idle 'orrible man,' Hawkins hissed.

Wolfers' voice quavered: 'But Sarge, I'm covered in shit!'

'Serves yer right, yer pregnant penguin,' Hawkins answered unfeelingly.

Corrigan grinned in spite of his inner tension. Of course, it would have to be the big clumsy Yorkshireman!

They were creeping round a corner in the tunnel. In the flickering light Corrigan caught a fleeting glimpse of a masonic mark – calipers and hammer and an arrow pointing in their direction – placed there by some long dead mason. What all the masonic mumbo-jumbo meant, he did not know. But somehow it seemed a sign of hope and encouragement. He pushed on even more eagerly. Now the air was quite cool; he knew they were almost at the exit. He said a sudden prayer that there would not be a German sentry waiting for them at the other end.

A minute later they were grouped at the bottom of a ladder below the grating, through which shafts of silver spectral moonlight shone down on their pale upturned faces.

Corrigan waited till the whole troop had closed up, then he whispered: 'I'm going up first. With luck we'll get out without being noticed. But whatever happens, from now on in, there will be absolutely no talking whatsoever. Is that clear?'

There was a murmur of agreement.

'Right, safety catches off, everyone. Check your bolts.'

With quick deft movements the men carried out his instructions, checking whether their weapons had been affected by the dampness and mire of the tunnel.

Corrigan waited impatiently, staring at their pale strained faces, and then hissed: 'All right, I'm turning the torch off now. Here we go!'

He flicked it off and stood there, blinking his eyes for a moment, trying to become accustomed to the thin silver moonlight. Then he was off, clambering up the rusting rungs of the dripping iron ladder. He placed his shoulder against the grating at the top of the ladder and pushed gently. Surprisingly enough, the heavy iron lid gave immediately; he almost knocked it over onto the cobbles outside. But at the very last moment he seized it with his right hand, then gently lowered it to the cobbles. Cautiously he stuck his head out and looked around.

There was nobody in sight. The house beyond, squat and silent against the light of the crescent moon, was totally blacked-out; it might well have been abandoned these many years.

He dropped inside again and whispered to Sanders, 'Pass it on, the coast is clear ... I'm going out!'

With nerves tingling Corrigan crawled out. He paused, still on his knees, the hand which held his rifle wet with sweat, eyes peering into the silver gloom. It was hardly believable, but it was true. The whole place seemed deserted. Luck was on their side. The Germans had apparently posted no sentries to protect the rear of their line.

The Assault Troop wasted no time. Like grey ghosts they crept silently out of the sewer. Apart from the soft scrape of their boots on the cobbles, the only sound was the faint rustle of a breeze in the trees around the churchyard.

The camouflaged enemy armoured cars were tantalisingly close. Six of them, clearly visible under the netting, each one capable of taking ten men or more. The whole Assault Troop could be accommodated in them, Corrigan told himself happily. Naturally once they started the engines there would be all hell to pay, but by then they would have the protection of the steel plating – and they would have heavy weapons, the vehicles' Spandau machine guns. With a bit of luck, they'd be started up and gone before the Germans could bring whatever artillery they possessed to bear. He hurried on, already attempting to visualise the unfamiliar controls of the enemy armoured car in his mind's eye.

Suddenly there was a heavy footfall. Corrigan froze. Behind him his men did the same, pressing themselves against the church wall, hearts thudding painfully, hardly daring to breathe.

A black shadow had detached itself from the shadows in the corner – and there was no mistaking that coal-scuttle helmet. It was a German sentry all right, and he was coming straight towards them.

Even before Corrigan could begin to think straight, Slim Sanders left cover boldly, whistling, of all things, as he moved right into the centre of the street and began to advance on the sentry.

'My Christ,' Corrigan cursed, 'what the devil is he doing?' But suddenly he recognised the tune. *Sanders was whistling the German Army's favourite tune – Lili Marlene!*

With studied carelessness, the little Australian halted in the middle of the street, scraped a match and proceeded coolly to light a cigarette.

The sentry growled something angrily. But Sanders, not understanding the warning, pretended to be occupied with his cigarette, puffing at it hard as the sentry came over to him.

Corrigan tensed. If the damned little Aussie didn't nobble the sentry first go, all hell would be let loose.

But Corrigan need not have worried. In one and the same movement, Sanders dropped his cigarette and thrust forward his trench knife. The sentry gave a gasp, followed by a thick-blooded gurgle, raising the hairs at the back of Corrigan's neck, as the Australian's knife penetrated his throat. His knees started to sag at once.

Sanders was taking no chances, however. He stabbed the man again, feeling the hot blood gush out and wet his knuckles. His other hand shot out and grabbed the dying sentry, tugging him closer in a lover's embrace. In the silver light, Sanders could see how the German's eyes were beginning to roll upwards, his mouth gaping like that of a stranded fish. 'Come to mother, you bastard!' he gasped, and then, still clutching the handle of the knife, buried it deep in the sentry's throat and lowered him gently, almost lovingly, to the ground. Next moment he had withdrawn the blade with a horrid sucking sound and was wiping it clean on the dead man's tunic. 'Sucker!' he sneered. Then, straightening up, he waved the others to come on.

Five minutes later they were in position, the camouflage nets thrust back, gunners manning the armoured cars' machine guns, drivers poised behind the unfamiliar controls, all waiting tensely for Corrigan's signal.

The big officer threw one last glance over his little column. Still all was peace and silence, the little village looking almost romantic, in a Gothic kind of way, in the pale light of the moon. But in a minute, he knew, all hell was going to be let loose, once they started the motors. He took a deep breath, praying that every motor would start at once.

'*START UP!*' he bellowed.

As one, his drivers hit the buttons. Corrigan and Hawkins looked up and down anxiously. The first armoured car engine burst into life with a roar. Jets of blue smoke streamed from its exhaust and suddenly the night air stank of petrol. Another followed, then another. *'Ready to roll, sir....! Ready to roll, sir....!'* Driver after driver yelled the information above the ever-increasing racket.

Somewhere up at the German line was a chorus of angry voices. They had been spotted.

Corrigan waited no longer. *'DRIVER, ADVANCE!'* he roared at Wolfers down below in the green gloom at the wheel.

Wolfers needed no urging. As the first red flare hissed into the night sky, followed by the sound of running feet, he thrust home first gear and let out the clutch. The armoured car lurched forward. Behind him, driver after driver did the same. Although Corrigan knew their formation was terrible – they were packed together like sardines, the ideal target for an anti-tank gunner– he was overjoyed to see that every vehicle had started. They were on their way!

Trouble began almost immediately. In the lurid light of enemy flares, shooting into the night sky everywhere, they were barrelling down the little cobbled street when the first stick grenade came sailing into the open turret of Corrigan's armoured car. For a moment he was paralysed, unable to move.

'Duck!' Hawkins screamed, grabbing at the grenade and flinging it outside. It exploded in mid air, sending a burst of shrapnel through the night.

Now they were being fired on from all sides, as the off-duty Germans sprang to the windows to take up the battle. The gunners in the armoured cars answered the challenge. Tracer, red and white, glowing angrily, zipped back and forth lethally. Slugs stitched the cobbles all about them and rattled against their armoured sides. In an instant, all was noisy confusion and violence.

Half-blinded by the flames and the flares, Corrigan peered over the edge of the turret and spotted a little track leading off to the left. He kicked Wolfers' left shoulder hard. The big Yorkshireman reacted immediately, swinging the wheel round. The armoured car groaned and creaked in protest; its tyres squealed, and there was a stink of burning rubber. Then they were bouncing up and down the rough earth track followed by car after car, the frustrated Germans redoubling their efforts to knock them out before they escaped.

But Corrigan knew they weren't out of trouble yet. To their immediate right on a low hillside he saw the first angry spurt of purple flame, followed an instant later by the hurrying white-glowing blob of an anti-tank shell. *'AP coming in!'* he screamed frantically. *'Watch out, Wolfers!'*

Wolfers hit the brakes instinctively. The armoured car shuddered to a stop, rocking like a boat on a stormy sea.

Metal pattered heavily against the turret – and Corrigan yelped with pain as a small steel splinter ploughed into his hand. 'Driver *reverse!*' he bellowed in the same instant that

Wolfers did just that, swinging the big armoured car to the left into a side lane. But behind him, the rest of the column had stalled as the driver of the second armoured car fumbled noisily with his gears.

'*Sort them fucking gears out!*' Hawkins shrieked back desperately, as the German anti-tank gun belched smoke and flame once more and another terrible blob of death and destruction hurtled towards the packed vehicles.

Wolfers drove like a maniac. They barrelled through a wooden fence and smashed into what seemed to be a series of greenhouses, glass cracking and flying everywhere. Behind them the shell slammed into the second armoured car with a great hollow boom. Slowly, dramatically, it began to keel over, frightened men tumbling out, running towards the next vehicle which was now moving again.

Corrigan groaned out loud and then concentrated on holding on, while Wolfers charged forward down the dark track, swerving madly to left and right to avoid potholes.

'*Jerries!*' he gasped from below.

To their immediate front, Corrigan saw the squat outline of a sandbagged strongpoint beside two cottages – in the same moment that tracer started to hiss towards them.

'Sod this for a tale!' Sanders yelled angrily

and grabbed the turret machine gun. Hardly seeming to aim at all, he pressed the trigger.

Tracer streamed towards the Germans. They were bowled over in a mess of flailing arms, sprawling over the punctured sandbags like broken puppets, blood jetting in scarlet arcs from their wounds.

Sanders kept the trigger pressed down. He fired wildly to left and right, hosing the little cottages with bullets. Like angry red hornets the slugs stitched patterns on their walls. A German armed with a *panzerfaust* hiding to their right went down, releasing his rocket in his death throes to howl harmlessly into the sky. Another *panzerfaust* exploded to their left. Its rockets hissed through the air and struck the cottage opposite with an awesome crack. Metal ripped at the sides of their armoured car, gouging out great silver chunks of its plating. At the wheel Wolfers fought furiously to keep the vehicle from overturning, while Sanders crouched behind his machine gun and ripped the German with the second *panzerfaust* apart.

And then they were through, rattling northwards into the glowing darkness, leaving the angry firing behind them and the bright red stabs of gunfire. They were on their way again. The collision course was set.

BOOK FOUR

SHOWDOWN

ONE

Adolf Hitler stared dully at the dead body of his mistress. From outside and above came the steady muted thunder of Russian guns. Soon they would begin their final attack on this bunker in the heart of dying Berlin, which had been his last refuge and was now to be his burial place.

Eva lay sprawled over the armrest of the couch, dead by poison. Stiffly he bent down and smoothed her blue dress with white cuffs over her shapely knees. At heart, he told himself, he was still a bourgeois prude; he didn't want anyone to find her with all that leg revealed. Then he picked up the unfired Walther pistol which lay beside the couch on the red carpet. It was three thirty in the afternoon.

He sat down at little table. Beside him was a picture of his greatest hero, 'Old Fritz.'* Almost to the end he had expected to be saved from defeat in the eleventh hour, just as Old Fritz had been. But that hadn't been the case. Now there was no other way out. He looked at the pistol and then back at

*German nickname for Frederick the Great.

Eva, her long blonde hair hanging over her face, the dead body giving off a strong odour of cyanide, then back at the pistol again.

Slowly, very slowly, he placed its muzzle into his mouth, gagged a little at the taste of oily gun metal. His knuckles whitened. For one instant he hesitated; his knuckles grew even whiter. He took the last pressure and pulled the trigger. His head exploded.

Outside in the office they heard the shot and knew immediately what had happened. '*Los!*' Martin Bormann, Hitler's grey eminence, looking like a seedy run-down boxer, commanded urgently. Together with Hitler's chauffeur and manservant, he pushed open the door, pig-like little eyes quickly taking in the full impact of the scene, the strong bitter-almonds stink of cyanide making him wrinkle up his nostrils in disgust. The man who had once commanded the destinies of three hundred million Europeans, and who had ruled an empire stretching from the Channel to the Caucasus, was dead. The time had come to save what could be saved from the wreckage.

One hour later the bodies of Hitler and Eva Braun were burning brightly in the gasoline-soaked courtyard outside the Bunker, the Russian guns still pounding away furiously as Bormann sat down to draft the last cable he would ever send from Berlin.

In the last hour he had considered all the possibilities of how he could save his own skin, now that the vaunted 'Thousand Year Empire' was falling apart after twelve short years. Now again he would attempt to be the power behind the throne of 'the new Führer', Admiral Dönitz, the fanatical U-boat commander, whose headquarters were far away in Flensburg, right on the Danish border. Dönitz was no politician. He would need someone behind him, giving him constant advice, now that he would have to deal with the Anglo-American conquerors – and that someone would be Bormann.

As he bent over his desk to pen his message to the Grand Admiral, Bormann smiled evilly to himself. Surely, after the whole damned mess was settled, the Western Allies would be suitably appreciative of his efforts. He started to write quickly and confidently...

Grand Admiral Karl Dönitz, lean, hard-faced with steely bright blue eyes, who had once been a submarine commander himself in the Old War, received Bormann's message at six o'clock that same last day of April.

'In the place of former Reich-Marshal Goering,' it read, *'the Führer has designated you his successor. Written authorisation on the way. Immediately take all measures required by the present situation. Bormann.'*

Dönitz frowned. He hardly knew the man who was now selecting him to succeed the Führer. What did it all mean? Yet as he sat there at his desk, staring at the message blankly, he felt a certain sense of relief.

For weeks now he had contemplated suicide. His staff had daily been bringing him terrible reports of the sufferings of the hundreds of thousands of German civilian refugees from the East, struggling to reach the safety of the West beyond the River Elbe. They were undergoing dreadful miseries: rape, murder, pillage at the hands of the Red Army, indiscriminate sinking of their ships by submarines of the Red Fleet in the Baltic and widespread machine-gunning from the air. Their casualties were running into the thousands – and he, Karl Dönitz, whose submarines had once almost brought the perfidious English to their knees in the winters of 1941/1943, had been unable to do a thing about it.

Now, however, things had changed. At last he was in a position to stop the rot, to put an end to the misery of the refugees still streaming westwards and begin talks with the Anglo-Americans to bring about the end to the fighting in the West.

At midnight he had made up his mind and had soon roughed out his plans. 'This is what I am going to do, von Friedeburg,' he snapped in his usual clipped brisk manner to the plump, sallow-faced Admiral von Friedeburg, standing opposite him beside the big map of North-West Germany. 'This morning Montgomery attacked across the Elbe in strength. The situation below Hamburg – here,' he indicated a patch of red crayon marks on the map, 'is still unclear. But I think we can take it the English will start moving for the Baltic by morning. We have only one weak division defending the area. Now I shall order the soldiers to hold off the Russians between Lauenburg – *here* – and Wismar – *here* – as long as they can. That will give our sorely tried refugees from the East another day or so to get through what I call the open door to the West.'

The plump little Admiral who had worked with Dönitz for many years now, and who was the last commander of what was left of the German Navy, nodded his understanding. 'In essence then, *Grossadmiral,* it is a race between the Russians and the English to reach Wismar and the Baltic first?'

'Exactly,' Dönitz snapped. 'It would be a dream come true for us if the two of them, Russians and English, fell into open conflict.' He smiled a little sadly. 'But I am afraid we cannot allow ourselves the luxury of that kind of daydream. All we can hope and pray for, ironic as it may seem to you, is that the English will reach the Baltic first and seal off the Schleswig-Holstein peninsula to the Red Army.' He gave a hollow little laugh. 'Undoubtedly those same English will one day arrest me and hang me by the neck for war crimes, but at least they will give me a trial, however farcical.'

Von Friedeburg shared his bitter smile. 'I suppose that is something to be taken into consideration, *Grossadmiral*. The Ivans would probably just stand one up against the nearest wall and blow one into eternity.' His smile faded. 'And then what?'

'This,' Dönitz answered, as down in the port the sirens started to wail once again. The Tommies, he told himself, were coming back once more. It would be another night without any damn sleep. 'As soon as the English force their way to the Baltic and we no longer have my, er ... my open door, I'm going to send you to Montgomery.'

'*Montgomery?*'

'Yes.' Dönitz looked at him directly with those hard, piercing blue eyes of his. 'I am sending you to discuss with him the surrender of the Greater German *Wehrmacht*.'

Von Friedeburg gasped. 'So that is the way it is going to be? The end...'

'The very end,' Dönitz echoed solemnly. Down in the port the first hollow detonations of the flak cannon indicated that the RAF raid had commenced. 'Now all we can

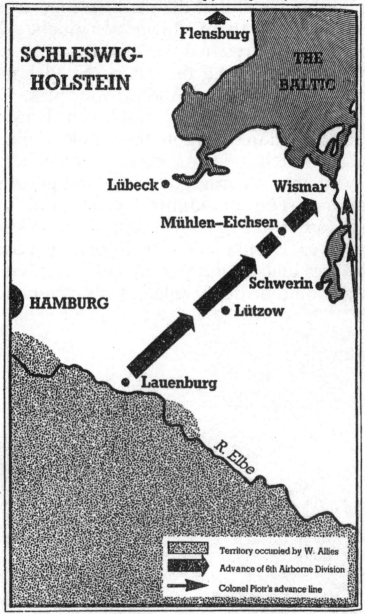

North-West Germany, May 1st, 1945

SCHLESWIG-HOLSTEIN

Flensburg

THE BALTIC

Lübeck

Wismar

Mühlen–Eichsen

Schwerin

HAMBURG

Lützow

Lauenburg

R. Elbe

Territory occupied by W. Allies

Advance of 6th Airborne Division

Colonel Piotr's advance line

hope for is that the British move a little quicker than they are accustomed to – it is undoubtedly all that damned tea they drink which slows them down so much. No matter.' He stretched out his hand. 'Stand by the phone at all times, von Friedeburg, and await my orders. And do your best.'

'*Jawohl Herr Grossadmiral.*' Von Friedeburg clicked to attention, then took Dönitz's hand and felt the firm pressure. 'I will, sir.'

With that he was gone into the glowing darkness. The two admirals would never see each other again. Before this terrible May was over. Dönitz would be imprisoned as a war criminal, awaiting trial; and von Friedeburg would be dead, killed by his own hand.

TWO

The speaker was obviously drunk and perhaps exhausted too. As they grouped around the armoured car's radio, taking their first break of the morning, they could tell that all right; even Sanders, who was not the most sensitive of individuals, could tell the man was drunk – not that it interested him as he counted the gold rings he had taken off the bodies of Germans they had killed that morning. All the same, the famous traitor ended his last broadcast from Radio Hamburg with slow obstinate dignity, spitting out the last phrases in that nasal voice of his, which for years had sent shivers of rage and fear down the spines of his English listeners.

'Britain's victories are barren,' intoned that well-known voice, which almost was as famous now as that of Churchill himself. *'They leave her poor and they leave her people hungry. They leave her bereft of markets and the wealth she possessed six years ago. But above all they leave her with an immensely greater problem than she had then.'*

Corrigan frowned as he balanced there on the edge of the turret, enjoying the warm sunshine of the first day of May. The arch traitor, William Joyce – 'Lord Haw-Haw' as the British radio public had nicknamed him – was right. Britain might have won the war, but she had also lost it in a way. The Americans and Russians were now the top dogs, and Britain's own future was uncertain and of little concern for these new superpowers who had emerged over the last few years. How long would they tolerate a British Empire and all that it meant?

'*We are nearing the end of one phase in Europe's history,*' Lord Haw-Haw continued slowly and deliberately, '*but the next will be no happier. It will be grimmer, harder and perhaps bloodier. And now I ask you earnestly: Can Britain survive? I am profoundly convinced that without German help she cannot–*'

Abruptly the radio went dead, as if someone over there in Hamburg had thrown a switch and cut the renegade Englishman off for good. Still the men squatting in the turret did not move, each absorbed with his own thoughts, wrapped in a personal cocoon of meditation.

'Penny for them, Sarge?' Wolfers broke the heavy silence suddenly, reaching for a slice of thick black German Army bread spread with ersatz treacle.

Hawkins shook his head like a man coming out of a heavy sleep. 'I was just thinking about what yon Lord Haw-Haw said.'

252

'Frigging traitor!' Sanders snarled. 'Hope they string him up from the nearest lamppost when they catch him.' Carefully he deposited the rings with the rest of his 'swag' – gold teeth, silver spoons and the like.

'Ay,' Hawkins agreed, brow furrowed as if he were finding it difficult to put his thoughts into words. 'All the same, I hope the treacherous bugger ain't right. I mean, he didn't exactly paint a rosy picture of the future, did he? I mean to say, we ain't been fighting for six years for *that* have we, sir?' he appealed to Corrigan.

Corrigan was staring at the far horizon. It was empty save for the usual column of pathetic refugees from the East, outlined a stark black against the sun as they plodded along the country road. 'I don't know, Hawkins,' he said a little wearily. 'I *hope* it hasn't all been for nothing. I know the Yanks don't think much of us any more. We're too slow and old-fashioned.'

'They're too bleeding full of themselves,' Sanders said. 'Bleeding Yanks. All bloody piss and vinegar! But when it comes to real fighting...' He shrugged his shoulders and left the rest of his sentence unfinished.

'As for the Russians,' Corrigan continued as if Sanders had not interrupted, 'I think they'll be out for number one, out to grab what they can.'

'But how did it happen, sir?' Hawkins asked plaintively. 'I mean, with the kind of army we've got now and all the victories. How come we're gonna get the shitty end of the stick?'

Corrigan forced a grin. 'The historians'll tell us how, in another forty years' time – if we're alive then, which I doubt. It'll be something about lack of inner confidence and willpower. We will be a jaded, war-weary people who hadn't the energy to take up the new challenge. So,' he shrugged cynically, 'the new boys will come along and nick the silver trophy right from under our noses! That's the sort of thing the historians will say.' He swung his legs over the side of the turret and dropped to the ground. 'But for the time being we've simply got to soldier on and win the war for an ungrateful nation. Give the men five more minutes... Then I want a word with you, Sergeant.'

Hawkins cupped his hands to his mouth and cried to the Assault Troopers lazing on their vehicles: 'Five more minutes, you lot! So get yer digits outa yer orifices and start packing up... Five more minutes now!' Next moment he too had dropped over the side and strode over to where Corrigan was staring at his map.

For the last thirty-six hours, they had been to the right flank well ahead of their old comrades of the Rhine, Colonel Jones's paras of the Sixty Airborne Division, pushing steadily for the Baltic. How the Red Devils had been able to move with such speed was beyond the comprehension of Corrigan and his men. The paras had suffered forty per cent casualties on the Rhine, had no heavy weapons to speak of and barely any transport, yet they were moving with the speed of an armoured division.

Once, Corrigan had queried their means of transportation over the radio which now linked him directly with Jones. The para commander had replied airily, 'Oh, we've collected a bit of transport from Old Jerry, naturally. A couple of butchers' vans, some of those wood-burning trucks of theirs – one of my chaps has even organised a steam roller.'

'A bloody fast steam roller, no doubt!' Corrigan had burst out. 'If you'll forgive my French, sir.'

Whatever the truth of the matter, Jones's Battalion was now within one day's march of Wismar. And, as far as they had been able to discover, there was nothing to stop the paras from marching into Wismar without firing a shot. The Germans were laying down their arms everywhere, even waving to the men of the Assault Troop as they rolled through their lines, scouting ever closer to the Baltic.

'On the face of it, Hawkins,' Corrigan

said, raising his head from the map, 'it looks like roses, roses all the way for the Airborne,' he consulted the map momentarily, 'with only about seven miles to go between us here, just beyond Gadebusch, and their forward positions north of Lützow. Then it's on to the last place between here and Wismar itself – the small town of Mühlen-Eichsen.' He sucked his teeth and stared at the horizon. It was still bare, save for the refugees, plodding steadily westwards, crossing the road that led north-east and heading for Schleswig-Holstein. 'All the same–'

'It looks almost too easy, sir?' Hawkins prompted.

'Exactly, Hawkins. And then there is the matter of the Russians. We know they are out there somewhere. Those poor buggers running away from them are ample proof of that – and look!' Corrigan indicated a sudden pink flickering on the horizon to the east.

'Gunfire,' Hawkins nodded his agreement. 'Somebody's copping a packet over there ... but it's a long way off. Can't hear no sound of guns.'

'Yes, it's a sign that the Russians are out there and that the Jerries are putting up some sort of resistance.' Corrigan gave a hollow laugh. 'Here they toss down their weapons at the first sight of a British soldier.

There they fight on. You might think that the buggers want us to win the race to the sea.'

'Ay, yer might at that, sir. But say the Jerries over there *do* pack up today and the Russkis *do* start bashing on for Wismar this very afternoon, before the airborne lads manage to get cracking from Lützow, what can we do about it, like?'

'That's the big question, Sergeant Hawkins.' Corrigan's face was grim as he tapped the map. 'You see, if they do break through, there are basically two ways they could push westwards and interdict the Sixth Airborne's route to Wismar. Either north or south of this lake here – Lake Schwerin.'

Hawkins looked at the map for a moment, eyes narrowed thoughtfully. 'I don't know, sir, but I think you're wrong.'

'Wrong?'

'Yes... You see, sir, assuming the Jerries are still intent on holding the Russkis, they're gonna stop 'em fairly easily along that estuary line or whatever it is that leads from Wismar to the lake. They'll need bridging equipment to cross it, and my guess is that their leading outfit won't have that equipment.'

'Yes, agreed – but go on, Hawkins,' Corrigan urged. 'Tell me more.'

'Well, sir, they're only likely to get through by going *south* of that lake, here at Schwerin and Gadebusch. Once we're in position and the lads of the Airborne have caught up, there'll be no stopping us. I think it all depends upon who gets to Gadebusch first,' he ended, looking at his CO a little triumphantly, a broad grin on his wizened face.

Corrigan returned it. 'I think you're right, Hawkins, I really do. My God, we're almost there!' he exclaimed in sudden exultation, as he remembered how long they had been trying to achieve this moment. 'Christ, do you realise we've been on the road over a month, Hawkins!'

'That long, sir? Well, all I can say then, sir, is that we get cracking to Gadebusch and get the bloody thing over with, once and for frigging all!'

Corrigan beamed at his little over-aged sergeant, the grey showing quite clearly through his dyed hair now. 'Sergeant Hawkins, I think you are frigging well right! *Mount up!*'

Hawkins needed no urging. He swung round at the troopers, lazily putting away their kit or checking the armoured cars prior to moving out. 'All right, don't just stand there like a frigging spare penis at a frigging wedding! *MOUNT UP!* We're moving out – Gadebusch is the next stop! And after that, nice old Sergeant Hawkins is going to take yer to the seaside for the day!'

Laughing like a bunch of schoolboys

released from their dreary class routine, they clambered onto the armoured cars. The motors bust into noisy life. One by one the long ponderous convoy of vehicles started to move out. They were on their way to that final confrontation...

Standing on the balcony of the looted bur-gomaster's office at Gadebusch, *der Dicke* looked in disgust at the rowdy, drunken mob of *Ostarbeiter** below. He too was plan-ning his final confrontation. He knew he was fated to die soon. His *Jagdkommando* had vanished this spring, some dead, a few prisoners, most simply gone, deserted dur-ing the night while he was asleep, throwing in the towel now that Third Reich was almost destroyed. 'Rats deserting a sinking ship,' he muttered bitterly to himself as he watched the antics of the mob with con-tempt.

They had just finished kicking to death the wounded SS man they had found hiding in a garage, and one of them was crying out in Polish, 'Tear his eyes out ... for my tortured father!... Tear his eyes out!' But already the others were turning their attention to the Burgomaster and his daughters and wife. They had ripped the women's clothes off and were using them to tie the fat-bellied

*'East Workers' (i.e. forced labour from the East).

official to a tombstone. Now the drunken Poles were beginning to rip open their flies. Forgetting her nakedness, the wife threw herself on the ground and kissed the men's feet in a vain attempt to stop them assaulting her three daughters. The Poles just kicked her out of the way. Women and men cheered their comrades on as they raped the hysterical girls. The Burgomaster struggled to free himself, his face purple, his eyes bulging. Suddenly he gave a mighty wrench, just as a giant of a Pole thrust himself into the youngest of his daughters, who was barely ten years old. The Burgomaster had torn the tombstone out of the earth – and dropped dead beneath it. The raping continued.

Moodily *der Dicke* walked back into the room and took a drink from the bottle of schnapps which somehow had survived the looting. He knew from talking to the Poles – they took him for one of their own, now that he wore the tattered jacket with an *'OST*⋆ patch on the back – that the Russians were just outside Gadebusch now. They were expected to enter within the hour. One man, riding a looted motorbike to the east of the little Mecklenburg township, had spotted them in the distance and had driven back

⋆'East' (the badge that all the forced workers from the eastern countries had to wear).

260

hell-for-leather to report he news. Now the Poles celebrated, taking their revenge on their former masters, before the new masters, the hated Russians, came and put an end to their wild, rapacious pleasures.

The Fat One suddenly flung the bottle angrily at his image in the mirror. It shattered in a thousand pieces and his ashen, moonlike face vanished. 'What am I going to do?' he asked himself, speaking aloud in the empty room. 'How am I going to teach the pigs a lesson before I go? *How?*'

'That Ukrainian whore has just stolen my loaf of bread!' an angry cry went up from outside.

'Typical Ukrainian!' another voice shouted. 'They were always letting the Fritz farmers fuck them in the barns while we did all the hard work in the fields.'

'Yes, yes, those Ukrainian son-of-bitches are all the same!' More angry shouts were joining in.

The Fat One waddled to the balcony once more. In the window of a looted department store opposite, two drunken Poles, one of them entangled in a shredded bridal veil, were kissing each other on the mouth and tenderly stroking each other's hair. But it wasn't the two men who caught *der Dicke's* attention. It was the lone girl surrounded by the mob, who had finished with the Burgomaster's daughters now. She was small and ugly, with a big head that looked like a turnip stuck on top of a pole, but she was defiant.

'Go on, you Polish pigs, hit me if you dare!... Go on!' She spat the words at the surrounding Poles. 'Remember that *our* Army will soon be here.' She threw her head back proudly. 'And then they will take their revenge.' She tore open the front of her flowered looted dress to expose immature breasts with fat purple nipples like plums. 'Strike there, Polish swine! Strike there – *if you dare!*'

In spite of their drunkenness the Poles hesitated, a sudden hang-dog look appearing on their flushed faces; and the gross youth watching the scene from above on the balcony knew why. They were afraid; they were afraid of the ugly Slavic bitch who stood there defiantly exposing herself to them! Why? Because she represented the power, the lethal threat of those Popov pigs who would soon advance and take Gadebusch.

Slowly, contemptuously, the Ukrainian girl closed the neck of her dress, then, head held up high, she made her way through the suddenly silent mob, which parted to let her stumble through in her clumsy wooden clogs, as if she were some queen paying a state visit. Just before she turned the corner, she flung a bitter glance over her shoulder and in the same moment threw up her skirt to reveal her skinny naked bottom. 'Kiss my arse, *Polacks!*' she sneered. Next minute she was gone, leaving the crowd staring sullenly in her wake, or looking down at their feet, as if they were embarrassed. Slowly they began to drift apart, talking softly among themselves, their excitement vanished now, their pleasure spoilt by the ugly Ukrainian girl and the thought of the new oppression to come.

Der Dicke watched them go, heading back for the squalid camp that had been their home ever since the German police had dragged them from their homes in Poland and forced them onto the trucks which would bear them to the Reich and a life of virtual slavery. Slowly, very slowly, an idea was beginning to unfold in his mind in the way that some deadly serpent might uncoil itself, fangs glistening as it prepared to strike.

'Holy strawsack,' he whispered to himself, his piglike eyes gleaming with barely suppressed excitement as he realised the full implication of his idea, 'that's got to be it! *It's got to be...*'

Outside, a German priest who had gone mad was wandering naked through the littered square carrying a cross, his arm muscles rippling as he held it aloft, eyes fixed on some distant horizon known only to himself as he stumbled over the dead bodies. 'Alleluia!' he called dementedly. 'The Lord is victorious, and the spirit of unrighteousness has been reduced to dust and ashes! Alleluia!... The chains that fettered the hands of the righteous have been removed and the smoke of sacrifices is rising to heaven!' He cackled madly. *'Alleluia!...'*

'Alleluia!' the Fat One shouted, and the big room echoed and re-echoed with the crazy cry of triumph. *'ALLE-FUCKING-LUIA!'* And then he was off, waddling hastily to the door to carry out his last plan.

THREE

They finished off the Cossacks that same midday. The younger ones had fled west with the rest of the defeated *Wehrmacht* in front of Piotr's triumphant Gulag Rats. Perhaps they thought they would find safety in the camp of the Western Allies, though Piotr doubted it. Stalin would have them back eventually; Old Leather Face never left a score unpaid. But the old ones had stayed behind to fight one last time. Perhaps, Piotr reasoned, as he led his men into the attack on the Cossack position that barred the way to Gadebusch, they had grown sick of running and were now resigned to dying here in this hated foreign soil so far from the Don.

It was all over in a matter of minutes. His Rats stormed the hill with an elan they had not possessed for months. Perhaps they knew this would be the last attack of the war, and after all, the place *was* defended by a handful of tired old men.

The old Cossacks had not had a chance. They were swamped by that savage attack as Piotr's Rats slammed into them, hacking and gouging, cutting them down where they crouched, slaughtering them without thought or mercy.

Piotr watched how one of his Rats aimed a tremendous kick at a wizened-faced old man with his heavy nailed boot. The old man reeled back, gurgling throatily, choking on his own blood, nose smashed to a pulp, spitting out his ancient yellow fangs.

'*Swine!*' Piotr cursed and lowered his sabre. The old man had sunk to his knees, eyes already glazed with the unseeing look of death. With his free hand, Piotr touched that bag of earth around his neck with fingers that trembled violently. Why did Russians have to do this to their fellow Russians?

'*Red pig!*' The cry rang out above the shouts and pleas that filled the air.

Piotr swung round.

A deeply wrinkled Cossack face was glaring at him. But if he were old, there was a distinct authority about this Cossack, who was standing there now in his ill-fitting uniform, holding a sabre that looked too heavy for him.

Piotr's mouth dropped open stupidly. For a long moment he was too awed by this ancient apparition to move. But as the aged Cossack raised his sabre, he realised his danger. He stepped back, his own weapon half-raised. 'Don't, old man,' he called desperately. 'Don't make me kill you!... Drop it!' he pleaded.

'Die, Bolshevik!' the old man quavered, swinging his sabre down.

Desperately Piotr parried the blow, steel clashing with steel. He could see the look of pain on the old Cossack's face at the impact. Again he cried, 'Leave it!... Don't fight, man! Nothing will–'

He reeled back as the old man thrust home the point of his blade, using the old fencer's trick of aiming at the pit of Piotr's upraised arm.

At the very last moment he dodged, twisting his wrist and forcing the old man's sabre to the right.

By now the old Cossack was gasping for breath, his raddled old cheeks flushed purple. With the last of his strength he raised his sabre once more. But Piotr did not give him a chance to use it. With a grunt he brought his own sabre down hard on the other's. There was the sharp ring of steel and Piotr could see the watery look of pain in the old man's eyes as he felt the shock of that blow. Then, before the Cossack could recover, he swept his sabre up, slashing at the man's wrist. The old man yelped with pain. His weapon had tumbled to the ground and he was backing off helplessly, knowing that his moment of truth had come.

Yet there was no fear in those faded watery old eyes as the two men faced each other, while all around them the Gulag Rats slaughtered the last of the Cossacks, gasping with the effort now, their cries and curses silenced. They were hacking and slashing at the Cossacks like weary butchers at the end of a long day in the slaughter-house; and the Cossacks accepted their fate just like dumb animals, in silence, with hardly a groan as that last fatal blow fell on their bent heads.

Slowly, very slowly, Piotr lowered his own sabre, the energy draining out of him as if a tap were open. The old man watched him carefully, backed up against the rocks so that he could go no further. His skinny old claw was clutching something under his shirt – and Piotr knew what it was. It was the old man's bag of native earth. He would die holding it, buried in his native earth as the Cossacks always vowed they would; and he would die at the hands of a fellow Cossack.

'Go, little brother,' Piotr said gently. 'Go away. I will not kill you... You are free.'

It seemed to take the old man a long time to digest Piotr's words and he still clutched his little bag. 'You are a Cossack?' he quavered.

Piotr nodded.

'Yet you fight for *them?*' The old man shook his head in disbelief. 'For those people who have destroyed our nation, have taken away our lands, driven us to the far corners of the world, have even made us

268

fight against Mother Russia?... You, a Cossack, fight for *them!*'

'I said *go*,' Piotr repeated, his mind in a turmoil, hardly daring to look the old Cossack in the face.

The old man laughed hollowly. '*Go*, you say, little brother! But go *where?* Who will have me? Who will take us, all us Cossacks? What can we do? Answer me that, eh!' His wrinkled face contorted contemptuously. 'Shall we become waiters in Paris again like after the old war? Or taxi-cab drivers? Perhaps even singers in a damned Don Cossack choir. Is that what you see as the future for the race of free warriors? Tell me that,' he spat out, naked contempt in his eyes now, '*Comrade Colonel!*'

Piotr flushed with shame at the use of the Soviet title. 'I don't know, old man, I don't know. All I say to you now is go – go where you please, do what you like... *BUT GO!*'

Suddenly the old man seemed to shrink as the anger fled his body. This tall renegade Cossack with the bold scarred face would not kill him, however much he taunted the man. His shoulders slumped in defeat. Wordlessly he picked up his sabre, laid the blade across his knee and with the last of his strength broke it into two pieces, tossing the pieces to the ground. Without another word he turned, back bent, and stumbled away to disappear into the fog of war.

For a long time Piotr watched him go, oblivious to the noises around him. Finally he too turned and began to walk slowly to the bottom of that body-littered hill, seeing or hearing nothing, totally engrossed in his own terrible thoughts. Behind him his Rats followed, silent and preoccupied too, staggering down through the bodies, unseeingly, like sleepwalkers possessed by some terrible, never-ending nightmare...

Piotr squatted on his haunches staring at the hillside, his broad face supported by both hands. Already the big fat blue flies, which looked like grapes on wings, were buzzing from corpse to corpse amid the shattered ground. The dead had begun to swell in the afternoon heat and occasionally they would groan and twitch as if they were still alive and angry at the importuning of the greedy flies. But Piotr knew that it was just the gases escaping from their swollen stomachs which gave off the noises and made them move. They were dead all right, and he was the one who had had them killed.

Standing to his right, squint-eyed and his face glistening with sweat, Igor cleared his throat noisily.

Colonel Piotr did not seem to hear. His gaze still remained fixed on the bloated corpses, though his eyes were blank, as though his mind was a thousand kilometres away.

Again the little Mongol officer cleared his throat, stepping into Piotr's line of vision so that the body-littered hillside was blocked from his view.

Slowly Piotr looked up. 'What is it?' he intoned numbly.

'Gadebusch, Comrade Commander,' Igor snapped, a new authority in his voice – and Piotr noticed that the strange un-Russian slur to his speech had suddenly vanished. 'The way is open at last. It is ours for the taking, Comrade Commander.'

But his words did not seem to have any effect on the big brooding officer.

Igor frowned. 'Comrade Commander...? Shall I give the men the order to move out?'

Piotr reacted slowly, finally taking his gaze off that war-torn lunar landscape to his front. 'What does it matter, Igor?' he asked lazily.

'What does it matter, Comrade!' Igor echoed, aghast; it was only later that Piotr recalled how Igor had omitted his rank, and by then it was too late. 'Why – the way to Wismar is open now! Already our ships of the Red Fleet are on their way from Danzig, ready to land troops in the Lübeck Bay for the push into Schleswig-Holstein and on into Denmark. Comrade, it is vital that we secure the coast before the English arrive so that our men can land safely!'

Piotr stared at the little yellow-faced officer with his bandy legs and slant eyes as if he were seeing him for the very first time. 'Suddenly you are very eager, Comrade Major,' he said formally. 'Why such haste to turn the rest of Europe into yet another Gulag for Old Leather Face? Tell me that, eh!'

Igor had flushed; his black Oriental eyes gleamed threateningly. 'Comrade,' he hissed, 'you go too far...'

Piotr flung back his head as if he were going to laugh out loud at the enraged Mongol, then he thought better of it. 'Come off it, Igor,' he said. 'You are a Gulag Rat like the rest of us. What is it to you whether we get there or not? The war is over now. It's all kiss-my-arse and play with yer salami now.'

Igor was not amused. 'For your information, *Comrade*–' he emphasised the word with the same contempt that the old Cossack had used earlier, albeit for a different reason. 'I am not one of your scum from the Gulag. And it matters a great deal to me personally that we *do* reach the Baltic before those capitalist English swine.'

Piotr's mouth had dropped open in sheer amazement. Like some stupid village yokel he stuttered, 'You're ... you're a Greencap – *a shitting NKVD Greencap!*'

'Yes,' Igor answered, stiffening proudly. 'Second-Lieutenant I.W. Timoshenko of the First Military District to be exact, Comrade!'

'Moscow!' Piotr breathed in awe. *You're a secret police cop from Moscow… But why?… What are you doing in my battalion?'*

'*Your* battalion will not be yours for much longer, if you are not very careful,' Igor answered haughtily, every inch the self-confident NKVD man now. 'Do you think our beloved Comrade Secretary J. Stalin–' he said the dictator's name as if it were in capital letters – 'would be fool enough to leave your bunch of Gulag Rats without supervision? Of course not! He knows your kind, what rats they really are. You have been under supervision from the day you took over the First Punishment Battalion.'

Piotr's head whirled, disbelief and shock written all over his broad honest face. 'Did Marshal Rokossovsky know about this?' he stammered.

'Of course not! We of the NKVD take few into our trust. Was he not a Gulag Rat himself once, before the Great Patriotic War? Once a Gulag Rat, always a Gulag rat, that is our motto. Now, Piotr, no more talk. You have your orders, carry them out. I am giving you a direct command to take Gadebusch before sundown tonight. By morning we must be in Wismar. It is imperative.' Igor spoke in the manner of a man long accustomed to giving orders – and having them obeyed.

Colonel Piotr rose to his feet, stretching himself out to his full height until he towered above the little yellow-faced NKVD man. 'And what, Comrade Second Lieutenant Timoshenko, if I say *fuck you – and your mother too?*'

The Greencap flushed at that grossest of all Russian insults, and Piotr saw a nerve in his cheek beginning to twitch. He clenched his fists as if to prevent himself from striking Piotr there and then. 'If by that,' he answered through gritted teeth, 'you mean that you are refusing to obey my direct order, I shall tell you what will happen.'

'Pray do so,' Piotr taunted, enjoying himself in spite of the harsh little voice at the back of his mind that hissed a warning: *You're digging your own grave, man...*

'I shall order your immediate arrest by the senior officers of the Battalion. You will be tried and sentenced forthwith – and there is only one sentence,' Igor rasped, visibly trying to keep calm. '*Death!*... Thereupon I shall take over the command of the Battalion myself. I am not as good a soldier as you; it is not my task. But I shall succeed in capturing Gadebusch and pushing on to Wismar... Now Piotr, what is it to be? *The attack on Gadebusch immediately – or death?*'

But before Colonel Piotr could answer him, there was that old familiar obscene howl of a mortar bomb, hissing down from the sky. With a sudden sinking feeling, Piotr knew the decision had been made for him, as the hilltop exploded in flame and the air was abruptly alive with deadly whizzing lumps of red hot steel...

FOUR

Der Dicke had found his victims without difficulty. In Gadebusch on the first crazy day of May 1945, it had been easy. Their delighted giggles and the squeaking of rusty bedsprings had alerted his attention as he prowled the littered back streets, gasping for breath in the heat, looking for someone suitable. Bending double with difficulty, he had approached the broken window through which the sounds were coming – and had realised immediately that they were the ones, the sight of their naked bodies making his loins stir pleasurably.

There were two of them. Poles. Slim and naked as they writhed back and forth on the big German bed, with a dead SS man lying forgotten on the floor beside them, kissing each other, running fingers into each other's secret places. Completely drunk. It would be as easy as falling off a log.

He crossed the room on tiptoe like a grotesque ballet-dancer, almost noiselessly. But they were too preoccupied with their own perverted pleasure to hear him anyway. He seized the bigger of the two by her long blonde hair, pulled it back hard to expose the throat and, even before she could scream, slashed through her jugular. The blood jetted from the severed vein, spraying the breasts of the other girl, who now began to scream like a maniac.

Drooling with pleasurable anticipation, *der Dicke* took his time, knowing that none of the drunken Polack swine would pay any attention to the noise. Grunting with delight, he thrust the knife home, deep into that plump right breast. Her spine arched with the exquisite agony of it and she thrust up her loins like a woman in the throes of sexual passion. A moment later she collapsed on the bed – dead.

The Polacks fell for his story afterwards, hook, line and sinker. *'Russians!'* he panted, wringing his pudgy hands and making a great scene of it – he even managed to force out a few tears. 'I saw them! A patrol it was … and I wasn't armed! So what could I do to stop them? But something must have disturbed them. Otherwise they would have raped the poor dear girls.' He shook his monstrous head and paused to look numbly at the two corpses on the bed as if he were too overcome to go on. 'Instead,' he choked, 'they did – *this!'*

There were cries of rage and despair from the assembled crowd as they stared down at the savagely slaughtered girls. Just then an old Cossack came wandering down the street, his face set in a look of misery and bewilderment. He couldn't have come at a more opportune time for *der Dicke*.

'Look,' he cried, seizing the opportunity, 'there's one of them murdering bastards – and he's a Cossack, too!'

'The Cossacks!... The Cossacks did it!... The Cossack murderers did it!' The angry cries rose on all sides, reviving old memories of the cruelty of the Cossacks to the Polish people in the days when Poland was still ruled by the Czars. Suddenly they were streaming forward to surround the old man, who simply stood there too bewildered even to defend himself as the mob systematically beat him to death, trampling him underfoot, until in the end he had been flattened into a gory mess, every bone in his body crushed.

Standing back at the edge of the excited, panting, shouting crowd *der Dicke* now made his suggestion. It worked like a charm. 'You realise,' he said slowly, as the crowd fell back from the man they had just trampled and kicked to death, 'that they will take their revenge when they find the dead pig? Russians never forget an old score, the swine!' And he spat contemptuously to the ground.

There was a hushed murmur of agreement; suddenly they were deflated, faces abruptly sombre and worried as they considered the full implications of the fat youth's words.

'But what can we do?' one man asked, a big scar-faced fellow who had the look of a one-time soldier about him. 'We can't flee. We have no transport to do so.'

Der Dicke swung round on him, panting and sweating as always, but in a hurry to get the thing started before it was too late. 'Think, my friend, think! Most of us have had military training. We know how to use weapons and there are weapons enough left by the Fritzes in the barracks. We could arm ourselves and fight the bastards off.'

'Yes! Yes!' shouted some, but others were not so certain, including the scar-faced Pole. 'But we couldn't hold them off for long...' he said uncertainly. 'I mean, I'm as much for fighting the Red bastards as the next man. I come from East Poland, seized by the communist swine back in thirty-nine. But you have to be realistic. They are trained soldiers after all.'

Der Dicke had had his answer ready. 'But don't worry, my friend. You won't have to hold the bastards more than an hour or so. You see, the Anglo-Americans are approaching the town in force. Just hold the Bolsheviks at bay till they arrive and we are saved! The Anglo-Americans won't let the Russians do anything to us, believe me!'...

And they had.

Now, as the first mortar bombs howled towards the Russian positions, *der Dicke* knew the time had come to implement the last stage of his plan. My God, he told himself excitedly as he mounted his looted bicycle, dwarfing it with his enormous bulk, if only he could pull this off he might save something from débâcle after all. With a grunt he lurched forward. Now he would speak to the Anglo-Americans...

They had been driving two hours now. The road had seemed an endless burning white in the hard afternoon sunshine. Their faces were caked with dust, their eyes red-rimmed with the glare as they stared to their front. The endless fields of potatoes were giving way to tight little gardens ringed with sunflower plants, and they knew they must be getting very close to Gadebusch. Now and then they passed tumbledown, half-timbered red brick farmhouses, which looked as if they hadn't seen a lick of paint for a century. As Sanders sneered, 'Christ, they look as if they don't have a pot to piss in even!'

At two that afternoon they started to meet the first of the German refugees from Gadebusch: bent old men, their faces contorted with fear, clutching at their women, many of the younger ones with torn clothes and hanging stockings, sobbing and cowering as they saw the soldiers in the vehicles, as if they half expected the beatings and the rapes would start all over again.

It was about now that they first became aware of the faint sound of firing coming from Gadebusch, mostly the snap-and-crackle of small-arms but interspersed with the occasional throaty crump of mortar fire.

Hawkins looked at Corrigan and asked, 'What do you think, sir?'

Corrigan sniffed. 'I would have thought the Jerries would have hoofed it by now,' he answered. 'One thing is clear though. The Russians are pretty damned close to Gadebusch.'

'Is there no way we can swing round and avoid the place and keep going north to the sea, sir?'

Corrigan shook his head. 'We'd lose too much time that way. We've just got to keep praying that the Jerries – if that's who it is up there – can hold the Russians back until we're through. Always providing,' he added with a lop-sided grin, 'the defenders let us through!'

'Cor, stone the crows,' Hawkins exclaimed, scratching his head. 'It's a right old bleeding Fred Karno's, ain't it? *Jerries fighting Russians, who's our allies, to let us get through, who are their enemies!*' He shook his head in wonder. 'Who'd've thought that World War Two would bleeding end like this!'

'Who indeed, Sergeant Hawkins,' Corrigan agreed, gaze fixed on the smoke of war drifting across the little town to their front.

'But let's concentrate on finishing it before we start discussing it… Wolfers!' He raised his voice to reach the big youth crouched below at the controls of the German armoured car. 'Give her all you've got! Time is running out…'

Time was running out for *der Dicke,* too, as he puffed and panted down the road on the bicycle, his face purple and streaming with sweat. He would dearly have loved to forget about the whole damn thing and just collapse in the shade of the big trees bordering the dusty road. It was only his burning desire to involve the English swine in the fight now taking place in Gadebusch that kept him going.

He remembered what Goebbels, the 'Poison Dwarf' himself, had said.* Speaking on the radio, he had predicted more than once that it would take only one small incident to involve the Anglo-Americans in a new war with their erstwhile Allies, the Russians. A handful of soldiers killed by error and their whole great armies would be firing at each other. And then the West would need the Germans once again.

He could visualise it already. Whole divisions of German troops, supplied by the Allies, finally bringing the Popov pigs down

*Doctor Goebbels, Nazi Minister of Propaganda.

to their knees – thus finishing off the task that the Führer had given them back in 1941. And his own part in causing this dramatic change in the course of events wouldn't be forgotten either; of that he was sure. He felt a surge of pride as he pictured himself receiving all the honours that would be bestowed upon him when his role was made public. Then the authorities would forgive him his little peculiarities; of course they would! Who could object to his taste for teenage girls? No one. He smiled pleasurably, in spite of the strain, at the thought of ripping open yet another virginal young body with the monstrous thing that hung between his legs, just as he had done to kids of the vanished *Jagdkommando*. They always screamed and writhed at first, but in the end they always liked it. However much they protested and denied their pleasure afterwards, he knew they'd liked it and wanted more.

Thus preoccupied with his thoughts, *der Dicke* did not see the girl until it was almost too late. He hit the brakes and the bike slithered to a crazy stop. For a moment he stared at her breathlessly. She must be about twelve or thirteen, he thought. She wore the black and white uniform of the *Jungvolk*,* but her swelling breasts were

*Junior members of the Hitler Youth.

quite clearly outlined beneath the white blouse. He licked his fat sensual red lips. She'd be a ripe little plum for the plucking if only he had time, he told himself. She'd be a virgin, he was sure of it; you could tell just by looking at her – and he liked virgins best; they wriggled and screamed more.

'Hey you! Polack!' the girl barked at him, still standing in the road. 'Where did you get that bicycle from? Stolen probably, eh, Polack!'

Der Dicke did not know whether to be angry or amused. Imagine the little slit talking to him like that, and thinking him a dirty Slav to boot. 'I'm not a Polack, you little arse with ears,' he declared. 'Now be off with you. Get out of my way – or I'll rip the knickers off you here and now, I swear I will!'

The girl did not move. Her face was set and hard. 'Don't you dare be familiar with me, Polack!' she snapped. 'We don't like you filthy Slav trash around here, especially when you're looting from honest German folk. Now, let me have that bicycle and be on your way back to Gadebusch, before you land yourself in trouble, *Polack!*' She emphasised the word maliciously.

He flushed angrily. To be called a 'Polack' by the kid was almost as bad as being called a 'Yid'. He was not going to tolerate it. He moved forward, pushing the bike towards

284

her and gasping as if he might have a heart attack at any moment.

'Move it, cunt!' he wheezed. 'I'm as much a German as you–' He stopped short, startled. The girl had whipped up the patrol leader's whistle that hung from her black jacket and blown a shrill blast on it. 'Hey, what is this?' he cried. 'What d'you think you're playing at, you little–'

The brick caught him squarely at the back of his shaven head. Caught off guard, he went down on his knees with a grunt of pain, the bike wobbling out of control into the ditch.

The next moment he was submerged in lithe young bodies. The other girls who'd been hiding in the trees were swarming forward now and beating him with sticks and staves, shrieking excitedly in high-pitched voices, and already, even as they beat him, tearing off his clothes to reveal his mountainous, hairless, pudgy white body.

FIVE

'Why – they're not even Fritzes,' Piotr exclaimed as guards shoved the two prisoners down on their knees in front of him, their unshaven faces ugly with unreasoning fear, 'they're Poles! Polish civilians!' He gently pushed away the bigger of the two prisoners, who was crying for mercy and trying to kiss his feet at the same time.

Igor shrugged and looked down at the two prisoners contemptuously. 'What do I care? Fritz or Polack, the only thing that matters is to take that damned town, whoever is defending it, and then move on to the sea before the English get there.'

Piotr ignored him. He was touching the bigger man's shoulder and trying to make him raise his head. Then, in slow careful Russian so that the Pole could understand, he asked: 'Why do you fight us, little brother? Poles and Russians, we are both Slavs. We fight on the same side, for the same cause.'

For a few moments the terrified prisoner continued to babble hysterically in his own tongue, but gradually it dawned on him that the giant Russian Colonel looking down at him did not intend him any harm. Sobbing and stuttering in heavily accented Russian, mixing in Polish words, he began to talk: 'We were afraid. We thought you would kill us all, so we decided to fight... Forgive us, *Gospodin* Colonel!'

Igor sniggered at the use of the old pre-Soviet title and spat in the dust. 'Typical Polack swine. Polite to your faces but waiting to stick a knife in you as soon as you turn your back on him.'

But Piotr continued to ignore the Green-cap. He stared down at the Pole, whose shabby clothes barely covered his emaciated frame. He could almost have been one of Piotr's fellow inmates from the Gulag, back in the days when he too had been a walking skeleton, dressed in rags. 'Are you so afraid of us Russians?' he asked gently.

The Pole nodded, biting his lips as if trying not to speak, but in the end unable to resist the urge to do so. *'Da, da, Gospodin,'* he quavered, his dark eyes flickering wildly from Piotr to Igor, as if he somehow knew that his life depended on the outcome of some strange battle of willpower between these two men. 'Poles, Lithuanians, Letts, Balts, Germans – we are all afraid of you!' He held up his hands in the classic pose of supplication. 'But I beg you not to kill us – we were simply trying to defend ourselves!'

Piotr laughed sadly. 'So you are all afraid

of us, eh?' he said, almost as if he were talking to himself.

'And a damned good job, too!' Igor snapped. '*Horoscho,* you guards – take these Polish pigs away and shoot them. At the double now! *Davai!*'

'Stop!' Piotr commanded and held up his hand. By now his Rats all knew who was the real power in the Punishment Battalion, the NKVD man Igor, but the old habit of command still worked. The guards stopped in mid-stride, lowering their rifles. On the ground the two Poles had begun to sob again and one of them was gabbling what sounded to Piotr like a prayer.

Igor let his hand drop significantly to his holster. 'I am not going to waste any more time on you, Comrade,' he told Piotr icily. 'You have already refused to obey me once. I overlooked that act of disobedience, but I shall not be so forgiving next time. I am now going to give you one order and one order only. And I shall want it complied with immediately. Understood?'

Colonel Piotr was watching him calmly, no sign of fear in his eyes. The only indication that he had reached a momentous decision was that one hand fiddled nervously with the bag of earth dangling from his neck. 'I have come to a decision,' he announced quietly.

'A decision!' Igor cried, while the Poles

288

looked on, frightened and bewildered. 'What in the devil's name are you talking about, man? *I* am the one who makes the decisions here now.'

Piotr remained relaxed and calm, even detached, like a man who has come to terms with himself at the end of his life. 'Probably, but not on the matters which concern me, Igor. My decision is this. I shall help to enslave no more innocent people, whatever their nationality, for that monster in the Kremlin. In short, Igor, I herewith cease to fight for the Soviet system.'

At first the NKVD officer was too shocked to be able to react. He just gaped at Piotr, mouth hanging open stupidly. At last he found his tongue. 'You ... you...' he stuttered, head twisted to one side like a man who was being strangled, 'you will no longer ... fight?'

'Exactly.' Almost casually, Piotr unbuckled his belt and allowed it and the pistol attached to it to drop to the ground.

While the Poles crossed themselves one of their guards breathed, *'Boshe moi,* the Colonel's gone mad!' Then he crossed himself, too.

Piotr smiled at him, a strange sad sort of smile. He knew exactly what he was doing and what was going to happen to him now, for he would receive no support from his men; they were too frightened of the NKVD to help him. 'No, little brother,' he smiled. 'The Colonel *was* mad, mad these many years to keep on fighting for Stalin. Now the Colonel is sane at last.' He looked at Igor, who was already fumbling for his pistol. 'There will be others, you know, Igor,' he said softly, no trace of fear in his voice. 'You cannot shoot us all...' Slowly he folded his arms across his broad chest, the faint smile still on his face, one hand resting on that precious sack of his native earth, and waited.

'Bitte, bitte... No – please let me go!' the Fat One screamed, his voice high and hysterical like that of the teenage girls he had raped so mercilessly. He was writhing back and forth, trying vainly to free himself. The ropes that bound him, naked and spread-eagled on the ground in the middle of a little glade, were stoutly tied to the trunks of nearby trees.

'We're going to have some fun with you, Polack!' cried the girl who had first stopped him on the road, while the others clapped their hands with delight, some of them jumping up and down like the over-excited schoolgirls that they were.

'But I'm *not* a Polack!... Please, let me explain! I'm a German like you–' His screams were suddenly cut off.

One of them, a big strapping country girl with heavy full breasts, had gagged him, stuffing a bundle of leaves and twigs into his gaping mouth.

Piglike eyes bursting from his crimson face with humiliation and fear, *der Dicke* could only stare up at his tormentors, utterly helpless now.

The first girl flicked at his slack penis with a twig, inviting the others to laugh at it. 'Look at the Polack pig's dirty thing! And do you know what he said he would do to me with it?' She cupped her hand to her mouth, as if she were shy and didn't want to be overheard, and whispered what he had threatened to do to her on the road.

Amid excited gasps of outrage someone cried, 'Imagine – a Slavic swine saying that to one of *us!* Why, he ought to be severely punished for that kind of piggery!'

'Yes! Yes! *Punish him severely!*' The cry was taken up enthusiastically on all sides.

Trussed and gagged, *der Dicke* wrestled ever more frantically against the chafing ropes. He knew something terrible was going to happen to him. These perverted schoolgirls would stop at nothing. Suddenly he caught the glint of steel. They had drawn out their knives, those short, stubby, black-handled *Jungvolk* knives that they wore in sheaths on their uniform belts, and now they were circling round him, nervous and excited, waiting for the word to begin.

The girl with the twig bent over him again

– only now she had thrown away the twig in favour of her knife. He watched with horror as she gently lifted his organ and pressed the blade against its underside. Her face was a study in concentration: brow furrowed, the tip of her tongue showing between her lips, a bead of sweat trickling its way down between her eyebrows.

'With pigs,' she said thickly, almost as if her speech were slurred with drink, eyes gleaming feverishly as she stared down at the flaccid flesh, 'they cut them off, if they want the boars to stop rutting and grow fat. You know what I mean, girls?'

The others nodded, too excited to speak now, each one of them gazing down as though mesmerised by the organ and the knife.

'They say it doesn't hurt the boar,' she continued, her voice strange and distorted. 'What does it matter? As long as it stops...' She didn't end her sentence. Instead she drew the point of the blade down the length of his penis.

His fat body arched with almost unbearable pain, eyes popping from his terrified face, blood spurting all over his groin. *'No!'* he tried to scream, but the makeshift gag prevented him. *'No ... no ... please no...'* And then he was actually praying. *Oh please God, have mercy on me ... please!*

But there was no mercy to be expected

from God this afternoon, nor from these deranged schoolgirls, brought up under the sick, sadistic regime of Adolf Hitler. Nothing was going to save the Fat One now. His life would end in the same perverted fashion in which it had been lived.

For one long moment the girl stared, eyes glittering crazily, at the long line of red that still oozed out of the wounded organ, her lips slack and wet, her breath coming in short, hectic gasps. Suddenly she acted. The knife flashed. The Fat One screamed, finally bursting through the twigs and leaves that gagged him, as that horrific pain seared his loins. Then the knife flashed again. The pain exploded within him. He couldn't stand it any longer. He had to die.

Suddenly he was zooming out over a dark heaving sea, in the same instant that a salvo of bullets sent the girls screaming and running for safety, leaving him there to die in agony, alone in a woodland clearing with only the bullets zinging overhead for company.

Wolfers gagged, then turning his back hurriedly was sick in the ditch. Next to him Sergeant Hawkins placed a reassuring hand on the big youth's heaving shoulder. 'Spit it out, lad,' he said in a broken voice, 'spit it out.'

Sanders swallowed hard. 'Christ Almighty,

what the hell did those little girls want to … to do that to the poor bugger for?'

Corrigan shrugged. 'God only knows, Sanders. The day of freedom arrives and the poor devil has to die like that.' He picked up one of the black jackets the girls had left behind in their flight and draped it over the dead man's mutilated loins. He shook his head like someone trying to wake up from a nightmare and finding it hard to escape the dark horrors of the night. 'Come on,' he ordered. 'Back to the vehicles. Nothing we can do here – not now… And the paras are on their way. Look!'

Hawkins, beside the still retching Wolfers, turned and stared in the direction that Corrigan was pointing.

Clouds of dust were rising over the burning white road, but he could just make out a motley collection of looted German vehicles – there was even an old cart pulled by a weary, bent-backed nag – trundling towards them. And on either side of the ragged procession were soldiers wearing the red beret of the Airborne Division.

'It's Colonel Jones's boys all right, sir!' he chortled, the horror of the mutilated youth pushed to the back of his mind again. 'By gum, sir, how have they managed to keep up with that kind of MT?* Christ, it's ripe for a

*Motor Transport.

museum, most of it!'

'I don't know, Hawkins. All I know is that we've got to get our finger out. Listen to that racket over there on the edge of Gade-busch. They've started firing again. It sounds to me as if the Russians are going in for a last attack.' He cocked his head to one side and could just catch the faint cheers of attacking infantry. 'Come on, Hawkins – it's now or never!'

As Jones's paras behind them started to fire green recognition flares to indicate that they had spotted Corrigan and his men, the tall Recce Captain sprang aboard the lead armoured car and bellowed, *'Roll 'em, boys, roll 'em! It's neck and neck now!'*

SIX

All was chaos, noise and horror. Scarlet flame stabbed the grey drifting fog of battle. Mortars belched obscenely. Heavy machine guns chattered. Tracer, white, green and red, zipped angrily back and forth between the ruined houses. On all sides, panicky voices cried out in Polish or Russian or German.

As Corrigan's armoured car nosed its way round a bend, a tall apartment block to the right was struck by a HE shell. It exploded in a vicious ball of flame. A great hole appeared and the shattered brickwork and masonry slithered down in an avalanche of stone and dust. To the left the static water tank for use by firemen in air-raids hissed and bubbled as debris settled into it. Somewhere further ahead church bells were tolling, their din mingling with the shrill wail of air-raid sirens.

Corrigan ducked as a burst of slugs ripped the length of the turret. Next to him, Sanders reacted angrily. He pressed the trigger of his machine gun and hosed the face of the building opposite with bullets. There was a shrill scream as a man hurtled from an upper window to hit the pavement like a bag of wet cement.

A stick grenade whipped through the air. Wolfers, face lathered in sweat, swung the wheel to the right. Just in time! The grenade exploded only feet away. Crouching behind the cover of the turret, Corrigan heard the shrapnel howl off the outer plating, while the stink of burnt cordite filled his nostrils.

Now his little force of armoured cars was packed together tightly in the ruined street, and the rubble forced the frantic drivers to slow down to a snail's pace. It was a dangerous moment; they made an ideal target like this.

Corrigan pressed the button of his throat mike. '*Sunray to all*,' he yelled above the murderous racket punctuated by the screams and yells of men involved in the confused fighting out there, 'tell your gunners to fire all out! Take alternative sides of the street ... and let's get the hell out of this death trap! Out!' He dropped the R/T lead and thrust his head above the turret, rifle at the ready. Behind him the machine-gunners were already in action, blasting away furiously, spraying the houses on either side with a hail of bullets.

Here and there, through the thick rolling waves of smoke from the burning buildings Corrigan could glimpse running figures, but whether they were German or Russian he could not make out; the smoke was too dense.

Next to him Hawkins raised his Sten gun anxiously. 'What do you make of it, sir?' he yelled, clutching the turret sides to steady himself as Wolfers sent the vehicle lurching forward, dodging shell-holes in the road.

'Don't know. All I know is it's a mess–'

'A frigging mess of a mess!' Sanders yelled angrily, letting loose another vicious burst of tracer.

'Right. And we're taking no chances,' Corrigan continued grimly. 'It's outlaw country here and everybody out there has got to be treated as an enemy.' He snapped off a quick shot to his immediate front as a bearded man suddenly popped up from a shell-hole, grenade poised ready to throw. The man fell back with a shrill scream of agony. Next moment his grenade exploded on top of him. His body flew out of the hole again – but this time it was in two halves. Seconds later the armoured car's heavy weight had rolled over the severed torso and finally squashed it out of all recognition.

A rickety girder bridge loomed up out of the fog of war, a group of dead bodies lying huddled at its entrance like lovers in a final lethal embrace. Instinctively Wolfers took his foot off the accelerator.

'Keep going!' Corrigan shrieked.

'But sir – the stiffs!' Wolfers yelled back in

horror. 'There's no way round them.'

Corrigan kicked him savagely in the small of the back. *'Go over them!'* he bellowed.

Momentarily Wolfers closed his eyes and then the vehicle was bumping and climbing up the pile of dead bodies, crushing them to a bloody pulp. Behind them one of the armoured cars came to an abrupt stop, its front axle buckled and sagging, thick white smoke streaming from its shattered engine. No one got out.

Hawkins moaned out loud. 'My God ... oh my God, my poor lads ... my poor lads!'

'Shut up!' Corrigan cried at him, eyes narrowed to slits as he searched the gloom. If he made a wrong decision now, they would be finished. Once they were stationary – even for a moment – they'd be slaughtered.

A figure was racing across the bridge towards them with a grenade in his hand. Corrigan loosed off a wild shot, without even aiming. The man staggered, dropping the grenade into the stream below as he lurched towards the parapet. Then, with dramatic slowness, like a high diver going into a double somersault, he toppled over the side. As he fell, Corrigan had one quick glimpse of the double-eagle badge on his arm. God almighty, he cursed to himself, he had just shot an ally! The man had been a Pole!

At last Wolfers managed to get them over the bridge. Behind them the next vehicle nudged the wrecked one aside, and the others gathered speed as they followed Corrigan's armoured car. They seemed to be leaving the worst of the fighting behind now. There were occasional bursts of machine-gun fire, but they were no longer so intense as before. Corrigan started to believe that they might get through without any further casualties.

A black and yellow road sign flashed by. He saw the arrow and the name: *'Wismar';* and then the distance: *'vierzehn kilometer'.*

'We're going in the right direction!' he cried happily. 'Take the next branch to the left, Wolfers. That's the way to Wis–'

The words froze on his lips.

There, immediately to their front, as Wolfers hit the brakes and the armoured car skidded to a halt, was a 75mm anti-tank gun, the long lethal barrel pointing directly at them. And there was no mistaking that blood-red flag with its golden hammer-and-sickle fluttering over the makeshift barricade which housed the gun. It was the flag of their allies. *They had met the Russians at last!*

Piotr groaned. He opened his eyelids with difficulty; it felt as if they were laden with heavy weights. For a moment all was blurred and confused, save the tremendous agonising pain at the back of his head. Slowly, gradually, things came into focus once more and he remembered where he was and what had happened.

Igor, the red swine, had not had the courage in the end to shoot Piotr himself. Instead he had ordered two of the Gulag Rats to do it for him. Piotr had enjoyed the farce in malicious pleasure: those two ruffians with their bearded faces and hang-dog looks, killing him in order to preserve a system that sooner or later would kill them, too. *'Davai!'* Piotr had bellowed at them. 'Aim true and do the job properly!' He had laughed uproariously. 'Come on, you running dogs, *fire!'*

That had done it. They had blazed away at him with their round-barrelled tommy guns, ripping his guts apart, filling him with such an intensity of pain, pain of a kind he had never experienced before, that he had screamed aloud, screaming, screaming... Then he had slammed back to the ground with such force that he had even let go of that precious bag around his neck. But, of course, they hadn't been able to do it correctly.

'Typical Russian,' he gasped to himself, his ashen face contorted into a horrible caricature of a smile, 'never can do anything right. Never...'

He placed one hand on the ground, ears taking in the noise of battle now, and tried to raise himself. A dreadful hot wave of pain swept through his body and for a moment he blacked out, sobbing with the agony of it. *'Boshe moi!...* My God!' he panted, struggling to overcome the racking torture in his guts. Then he tried again, and succeeded in raising himself on one elbow.

The scene to his front swung into focus. Igor stood at a barricade, back to him, but hands on hips and legs spread apart, as if he were proud of himself for some reason or other. Typical NKVD pose, Piotr thought. How often had he seen the Greencap swine standing like that in the camps, lording over the human scarecrows with their fat, well-fed bodies?

Next to Igor, a bunch of Gulag Rats were crouched over a 75mm anti-tank gun, which was pointed at a little convoy of armoured cars, manned by men in an unfamiliar khaki uniform. For a moment Piotr thought they might be German allies – Rumanians perhaps. Then he dismissed the idea. They were Anglo-Americans all right – and instinctively he knew why they were there. *They, too, were racing for the sea.*

'Of course,' he whispered to himself, as for a moment everything wavered and shook in front of his eyes, as if he were viewing the scene from a wildly rocking boat. 'Igor is trying to stop them ... so that he can extend the Gulag right across Western ... Europe.'

In front of him Igor was slowly raising his right arm. When he let it drop, Piotr knew, the anti-tank crew would open fire on the Anglo-Americans. And at that range wouldn't miss.

'*No,*' Piotr groaned aloud, like a man moaning in his sleep. 'They must get through...' Painfully he reached out one arm to feel around in the rubble for his pistol belt. He must stop the Greencap swine before it was too late. *He must!*

Suddenly his fumbling fingers found his pistol belt. He grasped it clumsily and pulled it towards him, opened it with an effort and clicked off the safety catch. Then, silently cursing his trembling hand, he raised the pistol and aimed it.

Igor's narrow back swung into view. The iron bar on the pistol sight dissected it neatly. Now he could see Igor's shoulder muscles tensing and rippling as he prepared to bring his arm down in the signal to fire.

Piotr fought to control his hectic breathing. He must not miss now; he daren't. If he did, millions of innocent people would suffer the same kind of fate as so many of his fellow countrymen. '*No,*' he cried out, keeping his hand steady with a last desperate bust of willpower. '*Never!*'

He pulled the trigger, then collapsed back

onto the rubble, dead...

Corrigan was watching the odd little figure who stood with one arm raised, wondering curiously about those almost Oriental features – and even more curiously about that raised arm. It looked like the gesture a gunner watches for when he's expecting to fire. No, it couldn't be–

There was a sudden shot. The man stiffened. Abruptly those dark slanting eyes were filled with unspeakable agony, and a bright red stain began to seep across his earth-coloured blouse. Then, while the crew of the gun stared in open-mouth bewilderment, the man slowly toppled forward.

For a moment Corrigan was too petrified to react. It was all so like the final scene in some Hollywood B movie; too melodramatic for words. A burst of machine-gun fire close by brought him back to reality. He sprang into action. 'Wolfers!' he yelled. '*ADVANCE!*'

The big trooper at the wheel needed no urging. He slammed home first gear and let out the clutch. 'Hold tight, everybody!' he cried, and sent the big car rolling forward.

At first the crew of the gun held their positions. But as Igor finally crumpled to the ground and with one last sigh let his yellow shaven head drop to one side, they fled, fighting and clawing at each other in their panic-stricken haste.

The armoured car slammed through the barricade. It rocked violently as Wolfers fought the controls, cursing, sweat streaming down his ugly flushed face – and then they were back on an even keel once more.

'Bash on Recce!... That's the stuff to give the troops!'

Corrigan flashed a look behind him as they raced on. It was Colonel Jones of the Paras, perched with some of his Red Berets on the top of a great lumbering German steamroller, its driver pulling the steam whistle joyously. They had linked up. The Paras were there. Gadebusch was theirs and nothing could stop them now.

'Wolfers!' he yelled exuberantly, as they shot forward down the dead straight road that led to the Baltic. *'Full steam ahead!'*

'Ay, ay, skipper,' Wolfers joined in the joke happily. 'Full steam ahead it is, sir!' Laughing crazily, he slammed his big foot down on the accelerator.

Behind them the confused, smoke-shrouded mess of Gadebusch disappeared, and with it the body of a dead Russian Colonel, already stiffening, the blood-stained fingers clawing that precious bag of native earth at last...

Wismar was in chaos as darkness finally settled on the newly captured town that May day. The gutters ran with wine, looted by the thousands of refugees and broken in a frenzy of destruction. A column of gypsies had appeared from nowhere, their horse-drawn caravans blocking whole streets as they joined in the looting. Newly freed British prisoners, as drunk as the refugees, were heading to the rear on any conveyance they could find, some even swaying alarmingly on ponderous stolen carthorses. And in the midst of the chaotic carnival, the beaten Germans sat slumped in glum bewilderment at the roadside, waiting for orders.

Standing on the balcony of the house that the Assault Troop had commandeered, listening to the troopers fulfilling their promise to themselves by getting blind drunk, Corrigan and Hawkins smoked in moody silence.

'Funny isn't it, sir?' Hawkins said finally, as down below the men broke into a drunken chorus relating the exploits of the 'woman who couldn't be satisfied' and the celebrated 'prick of steel'.

'What's funny?' Corrigan asked tonelessly, gaze fixed on the bonfires to the east, which marked the Russian positions: flickering cones slightly blurred by smoke or by the mist that was beginning to creep in from the sea.

'Funny that it's almost over ... and I can't feel nothing – save for the lads who copped it on the way here.' The sergeant's rheumy old eyes flooded with sudden tears. 'Funny!'

Corrigan couldn't say anything. He was aware of an inner caving-in, followed by a sort of sore-throat feeling, at the thought of all those who had died for this moment and the hollowness of their victory. For a moment he stared at the Russian bonfires and fancied that they were ghost fires, the fires of other 'historic triumphs' which had led to yet another war. He shook his head almost angrily.

'Now this is number one ... an' he's got her on the run, roll me over, lay me down and do it again!' they were singing drunkenly below. *'Roll me over in the clover; roll me over, lay me down and do it again...'*

'The men have done well by us, Hawkins.' Corrigan reached for his helmet; then thought better of it. He wouldn't need its protection now. He took up his cap and placed it on his head.

'That they have, sir,' Hawkins agreed loyally. 'A real good set of boys.'

'Come on, Hawkins...'

'Where are we going, sir?'

Corrigan grinned at him, though his eyes still held a dark, grim, unfathomable anger. 'Where do you think, Hawkins, you old rogue? To join the lads and get pissed as that proverbial newt. Come on!'

They went inside again, the racket hitting

them in the face almost physically. To the east the bonfires continued to burn, to illuminate the new Gulag Archipelago being set up over there... It had all been in vain.

ENVOI

They came in a Mercedes. In front of them there was a British armoured car, carrying Montgomery's representative, who had escorted these senior German officers from Hamburg that morning. As they stepped out of the car they presented perfect caricatures of Nazi officers, complete with jackboots, long belted coats that reached to their ankles, and a general air of pent-up defiance.

At eleven thirty precisely they strode over the wet heather to where Montgomery's staff officers waited for them outside 'the Master's' caravan. All four of them were doomed men, one way or another. Only one of them would survive the end of this May victory. There they lined up on the white mark that had been prepared for them, while 'the Master' himself surveyed them silently from the steps of his caravan, dressed as always in that careless, half-civilian manner of his.

Suddenly Montgomery turned to the interpreter, although perfectly well aware of who the Germans were, and barked: 'Who are these men?'

Standing on the sidelines, Corrigan grinned. Monty was living up to form.

The interpreter duly told him the men's names, ranks and positions.

'What do they want?' Montgomery demanded next.

Admiral von Friedeburg explained. 'We have come,' he told the interpreter, 'to ask you to accept the surrender of three German armies now withdrawing in front of the Russians in Mecklenburg.'

There was an excited murmur from the duffle-coated correspondents all around Corrigan. This might well be the big surrender, they told themselves.

Montgomery shook his head. 'No, certainly not,' he snapped. 'The armies concerned are fighting the Russians. If they surrender to anybody, it must be to the Russians. Nothing to do with me.' He half turned, as if he were about to go back into his caravan. Von Friedeburg's face fell. Corrigan thought he looked as if he might break down in a moment and cry. Suddenly, however, Monty started to speak again in that hard, clipped, precise manner of his. 'Will you surrender to me all German forces on my western and northern flanks – including all forces in Holland, Friesland with the Fresian Islands and Heligoland, Schleswig-Holstein and Denmark? If you will do this, I will accept it as a tactical battlefield surrender of the enemy forces immediately opposing me.'

Next to Corrigan one of the correspondents whistled softly. 'Well!' he exclaimed. 'The old bugger! He's gonna collar the lot and give the Yanks a real nice juicy one in the eye. Ike'll hit the ceiling when he hears.'

'*Nein!*' von Friedeburg cried, now that Montgomery's bold demand was translated to him; but his voice was no longer so confident. He's weakening, Corrigan thought.

'I wonder whether any of you,' Montgomery persisted, sensing blood now, 'know the battle situation on the Western Front?'

The Germans shook their heads.

Montgomery clapped his hands. As if by magic, a staff officer appeared, unrolling a huge map of the front in Germany.

Corrigan's grin broadened. Monty wasn't missing a trick.

Swiftly, with the aid of a pointer, Montgomery took them over the battlefront, covered with a rash of red crayon marks indicating the progress of his armies. They were everywhere.

Von Friedeburg broke down completely. He began to weep openly.

Corrigan's grin faded. Why didn't they get the damned thing over with? But the correspondents thought it was great fun. They smiled and held up their thumbs to one another, as if they personally had achieved some kind of triumph. Yet Corrigan knew that Montgomery was gambling for high odds. Without Eisenhower's permission, he was attempting to get the whole of the German Army to surrender to him. If he succeeded, it would be a great personal triumph for Field Marshal Montgomery – over-shadowing the fact that his army had been relegated to a side-show since the crossing of the Rhine. He would have the kudos of the final great victory after all, even though it had not taken him to the glittering prize of Berlin. It might well be the British Army's last victory…

Now it was six o'clock and growing dark. A thin drizzle was falling and the air was distinctly cold for May. Above the little tented camp on that remote heath, the Allied fighter planes circled and wheeled. But this evening they need not have feared for the little commander. The enemy's will to resist had broken; there would be no danger now. The Germans were coming to surrender.

Montgomery emerged from his caravan, dressed as informally as before in a brown duffle coat. One hand was thrust deep into his pocket, which contained a single sheet of buff Army paper. On that paper depended the fate of many millions of people this evening. It was the document of surrender.

He nodded to the silent spectators and disappeared into the big tent where the surrender would be signed.

Then the Germans came, making their way awkwardly across the damp turf of the little hillside, with von Friedeburg, still sobbing softly, leading the way. They halted on the white line outside the tent and waited.

'Bullshit reigns supreme,' one of the correspondents whispered cynically. Someone sniggered.

Corrigan frowned. What did they know?

The Germans were ushered through the open door of the tent. They seated themselves opposite Montgomery at a trestle table covered in a grey army blanket. One of them tried to cover his nervousness by fumbling for a cigarette. Montgomery, the non-smoker, frowned – and he decided against it.

Then Montgomery read out the surrender document, ending with: 'All hostilities to cease eight hundred hours, British Double Summer Time, Fifth May, 1945... The German delegation will now sign, General-Admiral von Friedeburg first,' he commanded, voice hard and inflexible.

Von Friedeburg, face suffused with grief, rose and signed rapidly, as if he wanted to get the business over and done with.

One by one the others did the same, while

Montgomery watched over them like some severe headmaster supervising the work of reluctant schoolboys. Finally it was over. Montgomery raised his voice above the whir of the newsreel cameras: *'Now I will sign,'* he announced, *'on behalf of the Supreme Allied Commander General Eisenhower.'* Rapidly he scratched his name on the document with his army issue wooden pen and sat back with a faint sigh. It was done. The war in the West was over.

A few moments later he emerged from the tent. He beckoned to the Army cameraman, who had been filming the German group arriving to surrender. 'Did you get that picture under the Union Jack?' He indicated the flag flapping above his head in the night breeze.

'Yessir!' the cameraman told him.

'Good, good.' Montgomery beamed at him and then round at the crowd standing there in the cold drizzle. 'An historic picture,' he asserted. For a moment he stared up at the flag, as if it were an object of great significance; then he turned to the correspondents once more, and crooked a bony finger at Corrigan. 'Captain Corrigan,' he snapped, 'come here, please.'

The correspondents parted ranks to let him through, the tall lean officer in a tattered dirty uniform, an ordinary infantryman's rifle slung over his shoulder.

Awkwardly Corrigan clicked to attention in front of the little Field Marshal and slapped his hand to the butt of his rifle in salute.

Field Marshal Montgomery beamed up at him, then suddenly turned him round with both hands so that Corrigan was now facing the puzzled correspondents. 'This kind of officer, gentlemen, made my victory possible,' Montgomery proclaimed. 'The Captain Corrigans of this world will never go very far in the British Army. They are not disciplined enough. They take unkindly to accepting orders – as I admit I do myself. They are bold and brave, however. They will let nothing stop them until they have achieved their goal ... save perhaps death.' Montgomery sighed and bent his head for a moment, as if he were thinking of all those Corrigans who *had* died so that he could achieve his great victory here this evening. 'So remember the Corrigans in your reports, gentlemen,' he continued, 'remember them well, for they are the men who have made the British Army great.' He patted Corrigan on the arm of his ragged, burn-scorched tunic. 'Now, gentlemen, it looks as if the British Empire's part in the German War in Western Europe is over... I shall now eat my dinner and undoubtedly be persuaded by my staff to drink half a glass of champagne to celebrate.' He laughed and turned, going back into his caravan still smiling – and leaving Corrigan standing there alone and awkward...

'What did His Nibs say, sir?' Hawkins asked as Corrigan rejoined the survivors of the Assault Troop's dash to the Baltic, sober at last: a handful of shabby-uniformed young men, who looked older than their years, each man wrapped in his own thoughts.

'*His Nibs!* Tut-tut, you old rogue, what a way to talk of your commander-in-chief! What did he say? He said the Corrigans of this world won't get much promotion, but they do make the British Army great. Something like that.' Corrigan smiled a little wearily and allowed Hawkins to haul him up into the half-track, where Wolfers sat behind the wheel, eating stolidly as usual, while Sanders rummaged in his swag bag, counting his pieces of loot no doubt.

'So that's about it, sir?' Hawkins said.

'Yes, that's about it,' Corrigan agreed and slumped down in the hard armoured seat. 'All right, Wolfers stop feeding your face. Start up!'

'Sir.' Hurriedly the big Yorkshireman bolted down the rest of his sandwich and started up.

Sanders put away his swag bag reluctantly. 'I'll miss the frigging war,' he announced. 'There won't be this kind of loot in frigging peacetime!'

Corrigan smothered a smile as he gave the old command: 'All right, driver – *advance!*'

Wolfers thrust home first gear and let out the clutch. The half-track started to move. Five minutes later they had disappeared into the night – and into history...

The publishers hope that this book has given you enjoyable reading. Large Print Books are especially designed to be as easy to see and hold as possible. If you wish a complete list of our books please ask at your local library or write directly to:

Magna Large Print Books
Magna House, Long Preston,
Skipton, North Yorkshire.
BD23 4ND

This Large Print Book, for people
who cannot read normal print,
is published under the auspices of

THE ULVERSCROFT FOUNDATION

... we hope you have enjoyed this book.
Please think for a moment about those
who have worse eyesight than you ...
and are unable to even read or enjoy
Large Print without great difficulty.

You can help them by sending a
donation, large or small, to:

**The Ulverscroft Foundation,
1, The Green, Bradgate Road,
Anstey, Leicestershire, LE7 7FU,
England.**
or request a copy of our brochure for
more details.

The Foundation will use all donations
to assist those people who are visually
impaired and need special attention
with medical research, diagnosis
and treatment.

Thank you very much for your help.